BREAKING GIANTS

L.M. HALLORAN

COPYRIGHT

for Amanda

&

for Lacee,

my real-life Aunt K

1

THAT KIND OF DAY

Outside the cozy interior of Tullamore Café, the rain comes down in heavy, rippling sheets. Water coats the windows like vaseline, morphing street traffic into pulsing ribbons of light. It's only five o'clock in the afternoon but so dark it might as well be midnight. If there's a world beyond the windows, I can't make sense of it.

Beneath the mellow jazz filtering through speakers, there's a low rumble of thunder that makes me shiver in delight.

"Earth to Rose."

I'm stuck to the storm like an insect to flypaper, lured by the violence of nature, by my base craving for inspiration. *Fill me up then let me fall, water through your hands.* Lyrics float through my mind, a melody teasing up from the depths. *Take me back to the deep, I have no skin, no defense.*

"She'll be right with you."

The voice is hollow, a distant foghorn.

"Rose!"

Much closer this time, my name spoken with a mixture of humor and aggravation.

The door to the music in my mind slams shut. The present roars into the vacuum, bringing all the varied sounds of life: murmured words, clanking of knives and forks, pings of ceramic mugs on saucers, and the sweet rustling of newspapers and books.

Owen, my cousin and co-owner with me of Tullamore, shakes his head as I offer a rueful smile.

"Sorry," I say with a shrug.

"Daydreamer," he chides, then nods to the heavy binder braced on his forearms. "I'll watch the front if you want to do inventory."

"Hell no," I say, punching him lightly on the shoulder. "It's your turn."

I scoot past Owen, making my way across the café and around the ordering counter. On the other side of the registers stands a solitary man, currently gazing down at our trifold menu. When I reach him, he glances up with a distracted smile. I only see his face for a second before he refocuses on the menu—but a second is enough.

Holy shit.

A wave of tingling shock electrifies my scalp and zings down my spine.

Julian Ashburn. In the flesh.

Despite the black beanie pulled low over his ears and forehead, despite a week's worth of stubble on his jaw and the rain jacket obscuring his physique, I instantly recognize the frontman of Breaking Giants.

If I were still a teenager, his band's poster would be on my wall. Being twenty-seven and relatively mature, however, my obsession is limited to purchasing every album and single—digital, CD, and vinyl—that the band releases.

I knew they lived in Seattle but never imagined I'd see any of them in person. Least of all Julian. He's notoriously reclusive, rarely grants interviews, and generally avoids press like the plague. He didn't even show up at the Grammys last year despite Breaking Giants being nominated for Album of the Year and Song of the Year. Not shockingly, they'd won both. The three other members of the band had accepted the awards without their frontman.

By the furtive glances I'm receiving from warm brown eyes, he *really* doesn't want me to expose him. And as much as I might want to, I won't. Not only would it be rude to ignore the prompt, it would also be bad for business. Seattle is ripe with big-name athletes, actors, and musicians. If we alerted the press every time a celebrity walked in we'd lose our integrity.

Tullamore is a retreat for those who crave the funky, noisy vibe of a non-corporate establishment. Our customers come to blend in and relax. They like that we're family owned and operated, tucked on a narrow side street in the Seattle neighborhood of Fremont. They like our organic menu and copious vegan options, and the way we showcase local artists on exposed brick walls instead of mass-produced prints and marketing slogans.

On any given day I'm not wowed by celebrity, having grown up with a music producer father and singer-song-writer mother. Elton John was at my tenth birthday party. But this man…

This man is a different story.

My armpits prickle with fangirl sweat as I imagine the sound of his voice. I want—no, *need*—to hear his voice.

I clear my throat. "The BLT is a huge hit. If you like bacon. Do you? Or are you a vegetarian? We make a mean SLTA." I clamp my lips shut to halt the nervous outpour.

"SLTA?" he echoes, a little frown appearing between sloping black brows.

Yep. His voice in person surpasses my wildest dreams. Smoke with a touch of honey. There's a light ringing in my ears—I'm pretty sure several million of my braincells just spontaneously combusted.

"Sprouts—" My throat constricts, squeezing me silent, as Julian finally gives me the attention of his stare.

Brown, I immediately decide, is a tawdry adjective to describe the color of his eyes. They're aged whiskey and tobacco. Sunset in the desert. Gold on brown. Leonine.

Words clog my circuits. *Predatory eyes track me, unbutton my thoughts and expose my underbelly.* I instinctively reach for my pocket journal, then see it sitting on the counter ten feet away. Tortured, I huff out a breath, clenching and unclenching my fingers.

"Are you all right?"

Heat rushes to my cheeks. "Yes, absolutely. Sorry. Um, what was I saying?"

Those phenomenal eyes fly over my face, and I finally understand what romance novels refer to as a piercing gaze. I feel pierced. In a fuzzy, roll over and pant sort of way.

Julian's lips quirk, displaying a dimple like a playful afterthought to his finely formed lips and strong, tapering jawline. The sight of it is shocking, transforming him into a more approachable version of his abnormally attractive thirty-two-year-old self.

"You were going to tell me what an SLTA is, but I think I've got it. Sprouts, lettuce, tomato, and avocado, right?"

Put a fork in me, I can die happy.

"Y-yes," I stammer, then blush some more. I'm a lightweight blusher on a good day, and clearly this is the Best Day Ever. "But it's really good. We do it on home-made rye bread, all organic, heirloom tomatoes, with a little balsamic—"

His sudden grin slaps the air from my lungs. In the rare photos I've seen of him, he's never smiling.

He should smile all the goddamn time.

"Sounds great but I'm a certified carnivore. I'll take the BLT. Can you add avocado?"

At this point, there's so much extra blood in my face that I can't feel my toes.

"Absolutely. Good choice." I scribble down his order. "Anything to drink?"

His gaze lifts over my head to the row of blackboards listing beverage options. Momentarily surrendering propriety, I stare at the strong column of his throat, feast on the broad shoulders beneath his jacket, worship the slight indent beside his mouth where I saw the dimple. He's taller than I expected. Around six-three. Until this moment, I've only ever seen him onstage and always from at least fifty feet away.

At length, he murmurs, "So many options."

Descending from memories of his electrifying stage presence, I find his gaze roaming my chest. It takes a second or two for me to realize he's looking for a name tag. Unfortunately, my nipples don't get the memo. My white t-shirt, soft and thin, barely puts up a fight. I cross my arms quickly over my chest, vowing to never again forego an apron.

For a moment I think I'm in the clear—then his whiskey eyes snap up and narrow on my face. His jaw clenches, and he looks up again, pointedly staring at a blackboard. Some emotion I can't name flashes across his chiseled features. It's not quite revulsion but definitely not lust. Annoyance maybe, or disappointment.

Whatever it is, it stiffens my spine.

Does he think I have a hidden remote control for my nipples? That I use them like other women use cleavage and perfume?

Rabid fan I may be, but groupie I am not.

"My name is Rose." My voice is on the edge of snappish. "I recommend an Italian Soda with the BLT. Raspberry and cream is my favorite. Or if you want something caffeinated, a cappuccino with a side of ice water. And by the way, although I love your music, I have absolutely no desire for your autograph." I wait for him to look down at me, then glance significantly below his belt. "Or anything else, for that matter."

His eyes widen; I hear a startled inhale. Ignoring the mouthwatering sight of a chagrined flush on his cheekbones, I lift my brows, press my lips into a thin line, and wait.

Finally, with a self-effacing shrug, he smiles crookedly. I translate the gesture to mean, *What can I say? Women throw themselves at me all the time.*

"I'll take the cappuccino, please." Almost as an afterthought, he adds, "Rose."

A few minutes ago my name in his mouth might have produced a different, more salacious result. Now, however, it makes my teeth clench in resentment for my traitorous body and stubborn mouth. I actually *do* want an autograph.

Oh well.

I quickly ring up his order, take his money, and hand him a laminated card for the miniature easel on his table. I'm turning to escape when his voice stops me.

"Is this hand painted?" he asks, holding up the card.

My head-to-mouth filter stops me from asking why he's still talking to me. It's not his fault he has a voice like sex. Besides, Owen and I need happy customers more than I need to cling to the shreds of my hero worship for Julian Ashburn.

Making an effort to sound pleasant, I reply, "Yes. An owner's mother painted them."

Julian flips the card up between his fingers, showing me the image. "The Prince of Swords, huh?" The dimple makes an appearance. "Tarot is an interesting choice."

I shrug and point at the little placard in front of the register where Aunt Katherine posted a succinct rundown of card meanings. I love the woman to death, but she's a bit of an oddball. If it were up to her, we'd have Fortune Telling and Astral Journeying on the menu.

Julian bends forward to read the placard. "Prince of Swords. Creative. Master of words. Idealistic. Argumentative. Dangerous." He looks up, eyes molten with humor. "Huh. Well, let's hope the first two prove true."

Does that mean you're writing new songs?

I bite back the question. "Your food will be out shortly, Mr. Ashburn."

"Just Julian, please."

I nod, smile hard, then book it for the kitchen window to place his order. As I turn, I see our part-time associate Christy walking out of the back, returning from her meal break. *Thank God.*

"Christy, can you fix a cappuccino for, uh…" I glance across the chaotic sea of tables and eclectic furniture and finally spot Julian sitting in a stuffed armchair near the front windows. I nod in his direction. "Black beanie. An ice water, too."

"Sure thing, boss," she chirps and sidles past me.

Freed from my counter-watching duties, I make a beeline for my journal and pen. Leaning against the back of a bakery case, I scribble down a series of disjointed thoughts. Some will become lyrics. Others, such as *pompous introverted artist ego,* make no sense and will fade along with their ink.

I'm dimly aware of Christy delivering the cappuccino. The sounds of the coffeehouse fade as the current of words takes me under.

> *His fingers scrape me raw,*
> *Sandpaper on my lips.*
> *Tumbling rocks, whispered thoughts,*
> *Why has it come to this?*
> *Lost before I'm found.*
> *Why has it come to—*

The voice of my current muse asks, "Do you have a second?"

I release an undignified squeak and look up. Julian, wearing a slight smile, glances from my journal to my burning face. I slap the notebook closed.

"Of course. How can I help?"

"By any chance, is a manager or, uh, the owner here today?"

No convenient lie comes to mind. "You're looking at one of the owners."

"Truly?" His brows lift in surprise. At my frown, he adds quickly, "I didn't mean… What I mean to say is, that's great. You're—well, you're young. Under thirty, right? Owning a business is a big accomplishment. I've heard a lot of solid feedback about this place."

He shuts his mouth, exhaling through his nose. That

soft flush is back on his cheeks, and he's looking everywhere but at me.

He babbles. My God, Julian Ashburn babbles.

My recent embarrassment is forgotten. Like I just tossed back a shot of liquor, my belly feels warm and wiggly. I grin helplessly, bowled over by the unexpected, charming vision of a songwriting prodigy stammering like a preteen.

He's human just like me.

"Nice save," I tell him.

He chuckles softly—*honey over tumbling rocks*—and glances up. "Yeah, sorry about that. I'm a little rusty at, uh, talking to people."

"You don't say," I deadpan.

"You're really enjoying this, aren't you?" he mutters, but he's smiling at the floor.

"Yes, very much," I admit, then take mercy on him. "What's the question?"

He looks up, pointing vaguely over his shoulder. "I saw a flyer for open mic nights on Fridays. Is that a seasonal thing or is it happening tonight?"

The warm feeling in my stomach turns queasy. "Every Friday, tonight included." I glance out the windows, inordinately pleased to see the continued downpour. "Not sure what kind of crowd we'll pull tonight. Might not be worth staying for."

Don't stay. Please don't stay.

Julian rubs a palm over his jaw and winces. He's back to avoiding my eyes. "Uh, this is a little awkward for me, but is there any chance I can get on the list?"

My stomach nosedives and I gasp, then choke horribly on my next breath. Coughing and wheezing, I bend in half, one hand braced on the bakery case. The only coherent thought in my head runs on a loop. *This is not happening, this is not happening…*

Christy's small hand pounds unnecessarily on my back. "Rose! Are you okay? Do you need something?"

"No," I croak, straightening with effort.

Slow breath in. Slow breath out. I wipe my watering eyes, grateful I passed on mascara this morning. When I can take a breath without pain, I finally risk looking up. Julian's expression is tight with concern and uncertainty.

"Are you sure I can't get you some water?" asks Christy.

I shake my head. With a curious glance at Julian, she retreats back to the ordering counter.

"Are you all right?" asks Julian softly.

I rub a hand over my aching chest. "I'm sorry, you just took me by surprise. Did I hallucinate you saying you wanted to perform at our open mic night?"

He blinks in bemusement, shaking his head slowly.

I laugh with an edge of hysteria. "Are you fucking kidding? Why?"

His lips tighten, and he looks down. "If you don't want me to, that's fine. Just thought I'd ask."

"No!"

Too loud, Rose.

I look nervously at the several customers who are now staring in our direction. Christy's eyes narrow speculatively.

Lowering my voice, I hiss, "Of course you can perform." Grabbing the clipboard hanging on the wall behind me, I use the attached pen to cross out my name and add another. "Is eight to eight-thirty okay?"

His smile is warmer than sunshine. "Great." He turns to leave, then hesitates. His gaze hits my face. *Piercing.* "Thanks, Rose."

He's halfway across the room before I realize he never answered my question.

Why?

2

INCOGNITO

*A*round six-thirty, the draw of impending live music ramps up our customer traffic. Two more associates, Allison and Gerard, clock in for the closing shift. It's still raining pretty hard, but in Seattle rain is like traffic—annoying, but an unavoidable fact of life. There's no point letting either one mess up your day.

Since Owen and I started hosting open mic night last year, the event has steadily gained in popularity, drawing crowds between thirty and fifty each week. There's a six-week waiting list for performing, mainly because of my last name.

My parents are dead, but Grace and Patrick Cunningham remain powerful names in the industry. It makes people think my name has significance too. Like I keep producers and talent scouts in my back pocket or something. For the record, I don't. But at least the prospect of discovery draws us continuous, strong talent.

Gerard and Owen handle the task of pulling tables away from the small stage in the back corner of the café. They fill the newly opened floorspace with folding chairs, each one claimed the second they touch down.

At a quarter till seven, anticipation rises and with it the level of noise. A wide range of ages and personal styles crowd the couches, remaining tables, and chairs. We don't serve alcohol on the premises, but there are more than a few flasks being emptied into cups.

"Hey, gorgeous."

I look up from tweaking the microphone stand and smile. "Hey, Greg, how's it going?"

"Good, good." He sets down his guitar case and sits on the stage. "Did you reconsider my offer?"

I chuckle. "Nope."

His eyes round with exaggerated affront. "Is it the dreadlocks? I'll shave them off!"

I tug on one of the faded blue strands. "You can't. These are essential to your image. Without them you might look like a normal person."

He holds up his hands, all but the last knuckles of which are tattooed. "Pretty sure that ship sailed," he says with a wink.

Across the café, the front door opens and closes,

another stream of customers coming in from the cold. Greg looks around, whistling under his breath.

"Big crowd tonight. Nervous?"

"Actually, I'm not going on tonight."

His head whips around, dreadlocks flying. "What? Why not? Are you sick?"

"No, just gave up my slot." After a two-second internal debate, I lean closer to him. "Swear to me you'll keep this to yourself."

Blue eyes sparkle at my nearness and focus on my mouth. I slap his shoulder until he dutifully looks up.

"Anything for you, Rose," he says with an unapologetic grin.

After a surreptitious glance to gauge our privacy, I lean a little closer and whisper, "Julian Ashburn is taking my slot."

Greg jerks back, eyes blown wide and mouth open. "Are you fucking kidding?"

I lift my brows. "That's exactly what I said!"

He scans my face to see if I'm joking, only I'm dead serious. After a few stunned moments, he blows out a noisy breath.

"You want my slot? I'm suddenly not feeling well."

"Not a chance."

He rubs palms over his stomach. "I think I'm going to puke."

I laugh and squeeze his shoulder, then return to the mic. "You'll be great. You always are."

He nods, but I can tell he's having a panic attack. I don't blame him. I've been fielding my own spikes of breath-stealing anxiety for the last hour, since Julian left after finishing his sandwich and cappuccino. He didn't say anything, just slipped out stealthily. For someone of his height, he moves like a freaking jungle cat.

My emotions volley between hope that he blows it off and desire to see him again. Hear him. *Holy shit he's going to sing at Tullamore.*

"What about crowd control?" murmurs Greg worriedly. "This shit is going to blow up once he takes the stage."

I frown. "I don't see anyone trying to tackle him or anything." Greg looks at me like I've grown another head. "I think he's going incognito anyway."

Owen's voice lifts above the din. "Five minutes, Rose!"

"Gotcha!" I look at Greg. "Get your ass up here, champ. Stage is yours."

He groans in dismay, then abruptly brightens. "If he's taking your slot maybe he won't show up until after my set. Do you see him?"

I stand up and shade my eyes against the stage lights. *Jesus, it's packed.* I scan the sea of people, a number of whom are staring at me. My name is called a few times, and I give distracted waves. I don't see Julian, but as I turn to tell Greg, the front door opens and four men walk inside.

My heart thuds hard against my ribs. It's Julian, along with Matt Sullivan, Jackson Everett, and Nick Henderson. The whole ever-loving band.

They're not alone. In true rockstar fashion, four waifish, beautiful women are with them. Julian himself has a stunning blonde tucked into his side. She's smiling up at him like he's sugar-free icing on her favorite nonfat cupcake, but his focus is elsewhere, gaze pinging around the space until it lands on me. I feel the impact like a sucker punch, but retain enough wits to wave weakly.

His lips quirk, and he gives a short nod.

Greg moves up behind me, his hands clasping tight on my shoulders. "Fuck me, is that Breaking Giants?" he whispers.

I realize it's a damn good thing the mic is off.

"Yeah," I whisper back.

He grunts. "Well, except for the bimbo parade, they're definitely incognito."

Julian's wearing a baseball hat, jeans, and a dark grey hoodie. Black-framed glasses sit on his nose, but he has one of those faces that makes nerdy sexy. I briefly wonder if they're a prop or actual prescription. The other band members are similarly attired minus glasses. Long sleeves and hats pulled low.

To me, it's obvious who they are, but as I watch them move toward the ordering counter, I realize that despite glances of appreciation from nearby ladyfolk the men aren't being recognized.

Owen appears before the stage, frowning. "Why are you two standing there with stupid looks on your faces?"

Greg and I share a pointed glance. I lift my brows. *Should I tell him?* He shakes his head and grins. I laugh and hop off the stage, winding my arm around Owen's waist.

"Come on, coz, let's let Greg do his thing."

Greg grumbles, "Fucking hell," and settles on the stool to unpack his guitar.

Owen and I weave through the crowd toward the counter. Behind us, the mic clicks on.

"Check, check. Hey Rose, will you go out with me?"

The crowd cheers. He starts his set with the same question every week. I'm so used to the ritual I don't even blush.

"Just say yes!" someone yells.

Owen laughs, stepping aside as I turn toward the stage. And like I do every week, I call out, "Not a chance, Greg!"

The crowd laughs and boos and whistles.

As I catch up with Owen, Greg tells the audience,

"She breaks my heart, guys. Those big doe eyes, all that curly hair."

I roll my eyes and step up to the second register to help the next customers in line, who happen to be Julian and his date.

Swell.

"Hey, Rose," he says, dimpling.

Thankfully my nipples behave themselves, but I still feel unstoppable heat in my cheeks.

"Hey." I make sure to smile harmlessly at his date. The blonde blinks at me, unimpressed, then resumes rubbing herself on Julian. My smile goes a little rigid but holds. "What would you two like?"

Over the sound of guitar tuning, Greg's amplified voice continues, "You know what else breaks my heart? Rose won't be singing for us tonight."

A few regulars throw out groans and *whys* and *no!*

I freeze.

Julian's stare hits my face, heavy and searching. "You gave me your slot, didn't you? The name you crossed off was yours."

I shrug. "It's no biggie. I'm up there every week."

"Your own material?"

"Julian," whines the blonde, "let's order and find somewhere to sit."

He watches me another few moments, then looks down at his date. "Sure, Jess. What do you want?"

In all my fantasies of sharing oxygen with Julian Ashburn, none involved a life-sized Barbie. Or him finding out I write songs. Feeling strangely deflated, I take their orders and move on to the next customer.

When the line dwindles, I join Owen at the end of the bakery case. It's the best view in the house, the space between us and the stage a necessary walkway to the bathrooms and patio in back.

Greg's set is flawless as usual, a blend of surf and alt-rock. He's talented, easy on the eyes, and funny as hell.

"Why don't you go out with him?" murmurs Owen between songs. I don't answer. "Please don't tell me you're still hung up on that bullshit about art and love."

I shake my head. "Not talking about this."

Greenish hazel eyes the exact shade of mine scan my face. We also share the same pale skin and dark curls, the Welsh blood on our mothers' side having trumped all paternal efforts. Most people mistake us for siblings.

"Just because your parents—"

"Seriously, stop."

His arm comes around my shoulders, dragging me in for a kiss on my head. "Okay, I'm sorry. I just love you, and I worry."

The tension in my chest abruptly unravels. I sigh and rest my head on his chest. "I know. But I'm fine being single. I'm happy."

Greg's set wraps up, and loud applause erupts. He

sketches a cheeky bow before stepping off the stage in our direction. His face is flushed, blue eyes shining as he approaches Owen and me. His attention, though, is on my face.

"Rose—"

Owen shoves his hand out. "Solid set, man."

Greg sighs and takes the hint, shaking Owen's hand. My stomach clenches with guilt, but I can't help feeling grateful for the diversion. I've known Greg for years. I consider him a friend. Maybe even a close one. I really don't want to hurt him, but I'm not dense.

The moment of truth in our relationship is coming. It's a distant freight train, small and wavering now, but eventually it will roar right over us. I only hope our friendship is strong enough to survive it.

As Owen and Greg chat, bubbly folksinger Kelly West takes her place on the stage. I skirt around the edge of the crowd and head toward the front door.

I'm outside before my brain catches up to remind me it's freezing and I'm not wearing a coat. The cold feels amazing on my flushed skin, though, and the rain has let up. I gulp in the dewy air, my breath emerging in a visible waterfall.

A small group approaches Tullamore from the street. I step away from the door, walking past the front windows and beyond the spill of light. Cold seeps through my jeans and t-shirt, lowering my core temperature. I breathe deeply and evenly to stave off the urge to shiver.

Just another minute, then I'll go inside.

Cars whiz past, tires turning up water in a fine mist. Streetlights paint the wet ground with streaks of color.

> *Flashing lights and caution signs,*
> *Not enough to stop this train.*

"Aren't you freezing?"

My bare arms erupt in goosebumps at the sound of his voice. *My God, his voice.* My heartbeat pounds in my throat as Julian walks toward me, unzipping his sweatshirt. Before I can process what he's doing, he pulls it off and wraps it around my shoulders.

The tattoos on his forearms tickle my vision as I'm flooded with his warmth and scent. He smells deliciously of faint citrus and sandalwood, with an unmistakable undercurrent of clean male. It's too much for my already raw nerves—I start pulling the sweatshirt off.

"I'm okay, really."

He tugs the halves closer, folding them over my chest and virtually entrapping me. When I stop struggling, he nods approval and takes a step back.

"Want a cigarette?"

I blink in surprise, trying to read his features in the shadows. "You smoke?"

"No, actually. I'm just looking for an excuse to keep you out here for a minute."

My thoughts scatter. "Wh-what?"

"You heard me."

There's something in his tone that turns my knees to jelly. A firmness, a power so out of odds with our previous conversations that I feel unhinged.

I suddenly have no idea who the real Julian is—the awkward introvert or this man whose gaze is no longer restless but fixed intently on my face.

Then it clicks: *this* is the frontman of Breaking Giants.

"Are you hitting on me?" I blurt, my tone thick with disbelief.

His head tilts, eyes dropping briefly to my mouth. "I haven't decided yet."

I shake my head helplessly, caught between rising arousal and sinking fear. "Don't you have a girlfriend, that blonde inside?"

"Not my girlfriend. Just a date."

"You… I don't…Uh…"

Nice, Rose.

He laughs—a deep, genuine sound that strokes down my body, lifting more goosebumps. *His voice is a fucking weapon.*

"You never answered my question," he says, a smile lingering. "Is your material original?"

"Yes," I say weakly.

"I overhead someone inside—are you really Grace Cunningham's daughter?"

"Yes."

Julian leans a shoulder against the wall beside me, unbothered by its wetness. With less than a foot between us, I abruptly realize how big he is. I'm no shrimp at five-nine, but I honestly can't remember the last time a man made me feel small, even delicate.

"She was a visionary," he continues, crossing his arms over his chest. I stare at the corded muscles of his fore-arms. "Way before her time."

I swallow and force my gaze to the street. "Yeah, she was amazing."

As a songwriter, if not a mother.

"I'm sorry you lost your parents so young. What were you, thirteen or fourteen?"

My chest squeezes. "Not big on small talk, are you?"

From the corner of my eye, I see his lips curve. "This is small talk."

I shake my head. "Too personal."

"Sorry." But I can tell he doesn't mean it. "So, who are your main influences?"

"God, so many."

"Pick a few."

"Belle and Sebastian. Tom Waits. Nick Cave. Neko Case. Pulp." I glance at him and decide to throw the gauntlet. *What the hell, it's not like this is going anywhere.* "Breaking Giants."

"Flatterer."

I shake my head. "I think *Crest* is one of the greatest albums ever written. And in case you don't read magazines or music journals, a lot of critics agree. Oh, and two gold gramophones and millions of fans."

He's silent for so long, I wonder if I've made some grievous error. *Can he really not take a compliment?*

Finally, he asks, "Why aren't you pursuing a music career?"

I raise a brow. "Maybe I'm not talented enough."

"Maybe you're afraid."

The door to Tullamore opens with a screech of wet metal. Owen steps outside. "Rose? Are you out here?"

I step quickly forward, away from Julian and into my cousin's line of sight. "Yeah. Sorry, I'm coming in now."

Flustered, I try to yank off the sweatshirt and end up getting my arm caught in a sleeve.

"Hold still," murmurs Julian, and gently extricates my arm.

The touch of his fingers on my bare bicep sizzles like a brand. *How are his fingers warm?* My breath catches. For a moment I imagine what it would feel like to have that strong, elegant hand wrap around my arm. Then his touch is gone.

I shiver in the cold.

"Our eight o'clock is a no-show," says Owen, walking toward us. He glances at Julian curiously before addressing me. "You're on in five."

Cue freefall.

"No," I gasp.

Owen frowns. "Huh? What do you mean?"

Julian's interest is a tangible pressure on the side of my face.

"I don't feel well," I blurt.

"Would it help if I go first?" asks Julian.

Owen, never slow on the uptake, offers a hand. "Nice to meet you...?"

"Julian."

"You're who she gave up her slot for?"

How does he not recognize him!

"Yes," I answer first. "Because he's Julian *Ashburn*."

Julian's sigh glances over my cheek as Owen's eyes widen. "Holy shit, man. It's great to have you here." He turns a wicked grin on me. "No wonder you don't want to perform. He's like your fucking idol."

I laugh weakly. "Hate you, Owen. Really, really hate you."

He gives an unaffected shrug, still smiling. "Whatever. Get over it. You've sung a duet with Elton John for Christ's sake."

"You have?" asks Julian with surprise.

"When I was ten," I grind out. "Let's just move the setlist up."

"Don't be a coward," murmurs Julian.

Owen guffaws. "Oh no, he went there!"

I turn slowly to Julian, my face frozen, eyes narrowed and glaring. He blinks, then smiles.

"Got you with that, didn't I?"

"I'm not a coward," I growl.

His smile vanishes, eyes darkening with intensity. "Prove it."

"Done," I snap, and storm past Owen.

3

FORBIDDEN FRUIT

Oh fuck, what have I done?

I shift on the stool, tuning my mother's Martin acoustic and staring at the floor before the stage. Anxiety thrums in my veins, prickles the soles of my feet. It's the real reason I'll never pursue a career as a musician. I'm just not cut out for the spotlight. Nor do I crave it.

Fame and all that comes with it destroyed my parents' relationship. It drove them to explosive conflicts, icy indifference, and eventually to death.

If I could turn off the switch inside me, the *need* to write songs, I would.

"Rose, play *Breathe!*"

"No, *Excess!*"

Greg's distinctive voice calls, "*How to Catch a Storm!*"

I glance into the crowd, but look down before—God

forbid—I see the members of Breaking Giants. Angling my face to the mic, I say, "Eeny, meeny, miny, moe. Catch a storm by the toe."

Greg whoops as my fingers pluck the opening chords. Noise from the crowd dims as the tempo increases, notes spilling over, twinkling and light. The song rises, filling me to the brim.

Everything fades… the people, the lights. Even Julian is gone. It's just me, overflowing.

Take what you want,
Steal what you need;
I don't have your answers
But I happen to believe
I can feed on your sorrows
Until we're both freed.

Just catch me—
I'll wait till you're mine.
I'm here on your time.
Every time.

And when the tide takes us back,
We'll be spared all regret,
Cause we walked on the waters
And we laughed at Death.

> *We swam in the skies and*
> *Caught storms with our breath.*
> *Because you've got me.*
> *You caught me.*
> *Every time.*

Another chorus, then the bridge and two more choruses. And finally, the melody lifts from darkness back to light. The last chords fade. Applause erupts, shattering the soft world of my creation.

I smile and duck my head. "Thanks, guys. How about we lighten it up?"

I transition smoothly into a silly number, the already requested *Excess*. I wrote it in college after witnessing the ridiculous and often humorous behavior of co-eds. As I sing, I let my gaze wander over the crowd, smirking when I see Barbie on Julian's lap.

> *She's got lust in her eyes,*
> *The manufactured kind.*
> *As false as her eyelashes*
> *And as deep as her mind.*
>
> *There's a boy on her hook but*
> *He doesn't know what's coming.*
> *He can't see it coming.*
> *Poor boy, he's blind…*

I try not to look at Julian's face but can't resist. As soon as our gazes connect, I'm sucked in, as helpless as the boy in my song. And I know, suddenly and with unnerving clarity, that I could pull an entire catalog of songs from him. From his eyes, his voice, the overwhelming sense of depth he exudes, the gears turning in his brilliant mind.

He's forbidden fruit. A dark dream. And the look in his eyes strips me bare. I can't take it—I wrench my gaze away, staring instead out the dark windows.

By the end of the song, my spine is so stiff it's aching. When the applause dies down, I say, "I'm going to cut it short tonight. One more and then we'll be moving on."

Before they can complain, I launch into a cover of *Another Sunny Day* by Belle and Sebastian. It's a house favorite, a bluesy version of the original. The crowd isn't disappointed. I'm off the stage before the applause dies.

Owen squeezes my shoulder as he passes, heading for the mic. After consulting the clipboard, he clears his throat.

"Next up… uh… John Doe?"

Laughter sounds from the back, where the men of Breaking Giants sit. They, at least, get the joke. Julian stands and makes his way around the clusters of tables and people. His path leads him directly to me, which I realize too late to escape.

He stops before me, head cocked, gaze roaming my

face. After a pregnant silence—wherein I feel the weight of fifty set of eyes on us—he asks, "Can I borrow your guitar?"

My ears ring. *There go more brain cells.* But I shake my head. "Sorry, it belonged to my mother. There are three other guitars up there."

"I'll be good to her, I promise."

Owen says lightly, "John Doe, any day…"

I look down at the guitar in my hand, then up at Julian's face. "Who am I kidding, you're Julian Ashburn," I mutter, and hand him the instrument.

He dimples. "You have an incredible voice, Ms. Cunningham."

Then he's gone, striding toward the stage with a guitar I never let anyone touch. And I stand frozen, a mannequin with a painted face of surprise, red-cheeked as a virgin.

I've barely relearned to breathe properly when Owen joins me. Julian makes himself comfortable on the stool, completely at ease in the spotlight. The hat and glasses stay on, and his sleeves are pulled down to cover his tattoos. I study the crowd for signs of recognition. There are a few speculative ripples, but nothing overt.

I lean toward Owen. "How does no one recognize him? Or the other band members? Are we really that clueless in Fremont?"

Owen chuckles and shrugs. "Not everyone is as

obsessed as you are. They look like regular people, especially with the hats and long sleeves."

The first notes drift from the guitar, pulling my attention to the stage. To Julian's fingers on the strings. *My strings.*

I can barely hear the melody over the blood rushing in my ears. All I know is that it's distinctively Julian Ashburn. There's no one who writes like he does.

Then he opens his mouth.

> *Your face is a sea a thousand miles deep.*
> *If I knew how to swim,*
> *I'd let go, I'd dive in.*
> *Fuck safety.*
> *Fuck life rafts.*
> *I'll do it—I'll drown in you.*
> *Laughing and spinning,*
> *I'll drown in you…*

"Holy shit," I breathe.

"This is… different," whispers Owen.

> *Remember that time I got lost in a library?*
> *I tried calling—No answer.*
> *So I ran through the rain*
> *and collapsed on your doorstep.*
> *You answered—*

You didn't answer.
He answered…

As I listen, I know it's not an acoustic song. Or rather, it won't be. I can almost hear the drum line, the bass guitar, the two electrics. It's different than anything I've heard from him before. His voice is rougher. Harder.

I watch his profile, his moving lips, and wonder what happened to him in the year and a half since the band's last album. Something happened. Someone hurt him.

Now I'm back in that library,
And I'm looking for whys,
But every page I find
Is as blank as your eyes.
I'm sick of my voice
But you don't say a word.
You won't say a word—don't even try.

In the garden we made, the flowers are dying.
Too much water, too much love—
You stopped trying.
Your face is a sea a thousand miles deep.
I did it.
I'm drowning.
I drowned in you…

When the song wraps and the final notes fade away, Julian shakes his head a little to come back to himself. The audience is dead quiet, paused on the precipice of an explosion. There's no mistaking him now. Not with a voice like his, with fingers like his.

I don't see who claps first, but the wave suddenly breaks. Chairs screech as the front rows stand. Owen grunts at a particularly shrill whistle. I glance across the room to the members of Breaking Giants. Matt, Jackson, and Nick wear expressions varying from pride to smugness.

My question is now answered: Julian is experimenting and wanted a pulse check on how fans would respond.

Like there was any doubt.

Julian laughs softly. "Thank you. Okay, settle down. By the way, my name is John Doe."

He glances at me and winks. But I see through the smile—I see what it cost him to expose his broken heart.

I tell Owen, "I'm going to head home if that's all right."

"Are you serious? Why? Isn't this your dream come true?"

I scramble for an excuse and decide on my dead parents. They owe me that much.

"The anniversary is coming up. Fourteen years."

His eyes instantly melt with concern. "On Sunday, right?"

I nod and give him a quick hug. "I'm in at three tomorrow, see you then. Just put my guitar in my office, will you?" He nods.

I allow myself another eyeful of Julian, knowing I'll probably never see him in person again. And it's just as well.

My mother always told me that love and art can't coexist, that eventually you were forced to choose between them. I believe it. I saw the truth for myself, up close and personal, played out in my parents' relationship.

I don't love Julian Ashburn. Hell, I don't even know him. But he's dangerous. A pool of kerosene to my pyromaniac.

I have a weakness for broken men.

I slip down the hallway, through the silent kitchen, and stop in my office for my coat and purse. The backdoor yields at my touch. I steal into the night as Julian's fingers begin plucking the strings of my mother's guitar.

♫

FOR HOURS, I sit hunched over the piano in my spare bedroom as rain patters on the roof and mist swirls around the windows. My muse pushes hard, her fingers talon-like on the back of my head.

I play with melodies and lyrics. Build a song, then tear it down. Build it again. Tear it down.

By four o'clock in the morning, I can no longer see straight, and my diaphragm hurts from hours of irregular breathing. I stumble into my bedroom and crawl into bed, still wearing clothes from yesterday. The gentle tapping of rain lulls me first into quiet stasis, then finally into sleep.

I dream of drowning in an ocean of whiskey. Of reading blank books with red bindings. And a voice.

Julian's voice.

The ringing of my phone wakes me, though it takes several groggy moments to separate the sound from a fire alarm in my dream. Opening heavy eyelids, I squint into the strangely bright room.

Oh, that's what sunshine looks like.

I swipe my phone off the nightstand and answer, knowing the caller from the obnoxious ringtone.

"Owen, what time is it?" I croak, rubbing my eyes. "Am I late for work?"

"No, it's only ten. Did you write all night again?"

I yawn hugely and shiver under the blankets. "Yeah. What's up?"

"Don't hate me."

My eyes drift closed, sedated by the knowledge I don't actually have to get up. "Huh? I don't hate—"

"Julian Ashburn asked me for your phone number."

"Fuck off," I murmur.

"I'm serious."

Between one second and the next, my brain comes fully online. I shoot upright in bed.

"W-what? You're joking, right?"

"Nope. When his set was over, he came straight up and asked me where you were. I was going to tell him it was none of his damned business, but then I remembered... he's Julian Ashburn."

To rule out the possibility I'm still dreaming, I pinch my arm hard, then wince.

"Rose, are you still there?"

"You gave him my number, didn't you?"

"Of course I did. What if he wants to ask you out?"

"I don't date musicians, Owen!"

"Stupidest rule ever," he says blithely. "Anyway, I don't know if that's why he wanted your number or not. He did mention wanting to thank you for letting him borrow the guitar."

Relief has me sagging back to the pillows. "He was just being polite, then. Thank God. My head was two seconds from popping off."

"You're the weirdest woman on the planet. You

worship this guy. Why don't you want him to ask you out?"

"You just answered your own question. Maybe I don't want to ruin the fantasy with reality. What if he's a total dick and I can never listen to Breaking Giants again?"

I'm not lying, but neither am I being totally honest. The real reason I feel like puking right now is the song he played last night. And his broken heart and crooked smile and piercing, whiskey eyes.

I'm terrified of Julian Ashburn. The kind of terrified that should be reserved for dark alleys and strangers with knives.

"Whatever you say, Rosie. I know I can't win this one. Oh, Greta wants you to call her. She's out shopping with her mom right now, but she'll answer."

I latch onto the shift in topic. "I bet she's pissed she missed seeing the Breaking Giants boys, huh?"

"Totally. She'd drop me in a hot second for a chance with any one of them."

I laugh; though she'd never leave Owen, it's true that Greta's almost as fanatical about them as I am.

"By the way, have you two figured out how I'm going to pull off being both the best man and the maid of honor?"

"No. Don't remind me. We still have eight months. Maybe Greta will find a new best friend by then."

"Not happening," I quip.

"Whatever, we were family way before you two were bffs."

"That's negotiable."

He snorts. "So rude. Hey, I gotta run. Do you hate me?"

I make him sweat for a few seconds. "Nah. He won't call."

"I wouldn't count on that."

He hangs up before I can reply. I stare at the phone in my hand like it might rear up and bite me. Then it does, buzzing with a new text message. I almost throw it across the room but clench my fingers at the last second.

I read the message, and the tips of my fingers go numb.

Hi Rose, it's Julian. Are you working today?

Heart pounding, I type out,

Yes. Why?

What time?

Chills break out on my skin.

Why?

I want to ask you something

I blink at the ceiling, looking for guidance on the smooth white landscape. Instead, I hear my mother's voice, the memory of which is most potent around the anniversary of her death.

You can't fight it, Rose. It's inside you. You're going to be just like me.

Whether in response to her or Julian, I don't know, but I type my response.

No

No?

Resolve flows through me.

The answer is no

I wait five long minutes, but a reply doesn't come. Eventually the screen blurs, and the surprisingly sharp edge of disappointment fades.

4

SUN IN MY EYES

The brilliant, gemlike blue of the sky is a trojan horse, distracting intelligent people from the fact it's still February and cold. Even born and raised in Seattle, I'm not immune. The desire for spring is primal and overwhelming, suckering me into wearing a tank top and light cardigan in winter.

As I drive the ten minutes to work—with the heater on full blast—I'm relieved to see I'm not the only one to have fallen for the ruse. Passing a street corner crowded with pedestrians, I even see a few sets of bare legs. I'm instantly grateful that some part of me was sane enough to wear jeans.

I park in the private lot behind Tullamore, bypass our small outdoor patio that stays closed until *actual* spring, and let myself in the back door. Before it fully shuts, I'm flooded with music to my business-owner ears. The café is packed.

Picking up my pace, I follow the sound of Owen's voice to the kitchen. He's standing over the grill while our day cook, Antonio, is dashing between the industrial fridge and a countertop strewn with vegetables.

"Where's Henry?" I ask, referring to our weekend busboy and assistant cook.

"Rose!" The relief in Owen's voice is thick. "Henry's out sick." He glances at his watch, then frowns. "It's one o'clock. Why are you two hours early?"

I smirk and reach for an apron. "Tell Aunt Katherine to alert the authorities. My psychic powers have finally revealed themselves."

Owen groans at my joke but snaps a hand out when I move into the kitchen. "They need you more out front. We can handle it back here. Right, Antonio?"

Antonio grins and winks at me. "Piece of pie. Sì, bella?"

I grin, while Owen shakes his head. "Close, Tony. It's piece of cake."

A plate breaks in the café. I hurriedly tie on the apron and leave the kitchen as behind me, Owen asks Antonio how to say *take off your clothes* in Italian. Laughing under my breath, I veer to a closet for a broom and dustpan, then hightail it into the café.

I come to a skidding halt beside the bakery case.

Despite being somewhat prepared based on the noise level, I'm still stunned by the chaos before me. Every table, couch, and chair is occupied. Sunlight streams boldly through the windows, highlighting laughing faces that haven't felt UV in weeks.

There's an almost frenetic energy to conversations and gestures. Behind the register, two part-timers are ringing orders for a line that reaches almost to the door.

As I stand there grinning like the village idiot, Christy hustles toward me with another broom and full dustpan.

"Rose, thank God! I got the plate. Need your help making drinks, though." She dumps the trash and washes her hands as I rush past the registers to the espresso station. Catching up with me, she asks, "Is it a holiday or something?"

I recall that she's a California transplant, a freshman at the nearby UW. Smiling, I answer, "Nope. Random sunny days always bring the circus to town." I glance down at her impractical, wedged sandals. "See? Spring fever got you, too."

Two hours later, I'm as grateful for my tank top as Christy is for her sandals. We're sweating like beasts. She has chopsticks holding her blonde hair up. My curls, unfortunately, eat chopsticks for breakfast. I resort to using an extra thick rubber band to fix a messy knot on the top of my head, but only after Christy promises to cut it out for me later.

The lunch rush finally tapers off around three. As Christy takes a much-deserved break, I lean against the counter near our loose tea selection and guzzle raspberry Italian soda like water. When the bell on the door chimes, I glance over quickly. Just like I've done every fucking time I hear it.

But it's not him.

It's irrational to look for Julian. I know this. But emotional decisions have emotional hangovers and mine makes me wonder, makes me want… something.

A cynical part of me toys with the idea that I rejected him to test him. To push and play hard to get. The thought makes me faintly ill.

You're just like me, Rose.

I screw my eyes shut to block the memory.

"Rose?"

I open my eyes at Gerard's voice, coming from behind a register.

"Someone's here to see you."

My heart catapults into my ribs, my gaze swinging fast. It's the man who just walked in, and as he turns to look at me, I recognize him.

Not Julian, but almost as scary.

Matt Sullivan, lead guitarist for Breaking Giants, grins and lifts a blonde brow at my befuddled expression. I don't think he's as heart-stoppingly gorgeous as his frontman, but plenty of women disagree with me.

Julian is brooding, dark, and a little wild—Matt is light to his darkness, the charming, public face of Breaking Giants. And it's easy to see why the public gobbles him up. He looks like a Swedish underwear model, tall and muscled and vaguely icy. Add to the mix a panty melting grin, incredibly talented hands, and a *catch and release* reputation with the ladies, and Matt Sullivan exudes the unmistakable charge of a Grade-A heartbreaker.

When Matt realizes I'm not going to walk over, his grin gets even bigger. He strolls toward me with purpose. I'm suddenly glad to be behind a counter.

Stopping opposite me, his gaze dips lazily to my cleavage and back up. Smokey blue eyes smolder with appreciation, but the look strikes me as rehearsed.

"Hi Rose, I'm Matt."

I clear my throat, half-annoyed and half-amused. "I know who you are, Matt," I say flatly. I'm not sure, but I think I see surprise flicker in his eyes. It teases a smile from me. "I'm sorry, were you expecting me to flash my tits or something?"

Both brows go up, and he barks out a rusty laugh. "Julian did warn me you wouldn't be impressed." He shrugs, his smile softening and becoming genuine. "Can't blame me for trying."

I ignore the flutter caused by the mention of Julian.

"Why are you here?"

His eyes narrow, unnervingly intense, likes he's trying to read between my lines. "We have a business proposition for you."

"I'm sorry?" I ask, after filtering the words for a few seconds.

"Your voice is perfect for our needs."

I shift against the counter. "What are you talking about?"

"The new album...."

My vision goes dark around the edges, then slowly brightens. I realize Matt's still talking.

"...three, possibly four tracks. We've been looking for a voice for months. Julian had basically given up after—" He clears his throat. "Well, let's just say the previous singer isn't around anymore. Then we heard you. We all agreed the job is yours if you want it. No audition. You're classically trained, right?"

I lift a shaking hand to stall him. "I'm sorry, hold up."

He grins wickedly. "I just blew your mind, didn't I? I've been known to have that effect on women."

I scowl to hide the truth: *yes, my mind is officially blown.*

"Slow your roll, Romeo."

He shakes his head affably. "Sorry, this is my only

speed. So, can you come over to Julian's tomorrow night?"

Panic bursts through me and I sag against the counter, lightheaded and unable to catch my breath. Words ping in my fuzzy head, monosyllabic and sharp.

Yes! No! What! Wait!

"No," I whisper, then shake my head and repeat more loudly, "No, I can't. You'll have to keep looking. I'm sorry. I already told Julian I don't do industry work."

Instead of the disbelief I expect from him, Matt frowns concernedly. "Hey, are you okay? You look really freaked out. Super pale." He glances toward Gerard, who's ringing another customer. "Can I get you something?"

I suck in air past my thundering heart. *No big deal, just having a Titanic-sized panic attack.*

"I'm fine," I croak. "Sorry your time was wasted, but I can't do it."

His handsome features scrunch with disappointment. "Really? There's nothing I can say to change your mind?"

For some reason, the words take the edge off my anxiety. "No offense, Matt, but I'm surprised you're being so nice about this. About me declining. For some reason, I don't think Julian would have taken it so well."

Matt laughs, loud and unfettered, drawing even more

attention than he already has—at least ten people are panting in his direction.

"Seems you've got a pretty good handle on our top dog. Yeah, Julian's gonna blow a gasket. He's kind of a control freak. Once he makes up his mind about something…" He shrugs.

My palms tingle. "He's not going to, uh, push this, is he?"

"Nah. Not his style." He must see the regret I can't quite smother, because his gaze clears, searching my face. "Are you sure you want to pass this up? I think we both know it's the opportunity of a lifetime for an unknown."

I smile sadly. "That's the thing. I prefer to stay unknown."

He shakes his head. "You're a weird cat, aren't you?"

You have no idea.

"Certifiable, probably. Um, tell Julian I'm sorry, okay?"

Matt nods, still looking at me oddly. I don't blame him. I just turned down what would probably be a shit-ton of money, not to mention a potential platform for success that any normal struggling artist would kill for.

For a moment, I entertain the fantasy. Minus, of course, everything it means and the chaos it would create in my life and heart. *Singing with Julian Ashburn.* Then the moment passes, the vision too delicate to withstand reality.

I step away from the counter, turning toward the espresso bar. "Do you want a latte?" I ask Matt as I prep shots of espresso. "On the house."

"Yeah, that'd be—hey Julian, I was just coming out."

"She said no, didn't she?"

A muscle in my neck spasms as my head jerks up.

Jesus, he's a fucking ninja.

"Where the hell did you come from?" I blurt shrilly.

His eyes narrow—in the sunlight, they shine darkly gold. "Are you really that terrified of the public hearing your voice?"

Angry heat unfurls in my cheeks. "You don't know me," I snarl back.

He stalks past a wide-eyed Matt and faces me, the espresso bar between us. A muscle ticks in his jaw.

Multiple personality disorder, much?

I don't have any idea what expression I'm wearing, but suddenly his tension evaporates. He sighs, dragging a hand through his tousled dark hair. For a few seconds, he stares at the ceiling, his throat working as he swallows.

"For what it's worth, I appreciate the offer," I say weakly. "It's a huge opportunity you're offering me. But it's just not a good idea. I haven't sung harmonies with anyone in years, or had any voice coaching for at least a decade."

Julian studies my face. "You have perfect pitch, Rose. Give me a better reason."

Flustered, I say, "I don't need to give you a reason."

His eyes gleam with challenge. "Use a pseudonym. I'll have the lawyers write up a contract ensuring your privacy. No press. No pictures. Complete anonymity."

Irrepressible excitement erupts in my chest. *If I can be anonymous...*

Julian sees my resolve faltering and pounces. "I'll even let you do it for free."

Matt gapes. "What the fuck, man? How does that sweeten the deal?"

Julian keeps staring at me. "Rose?"

I'm sinking, weakening. He knows it—I know it. I gaze around wildly, looking for relief. An escape. But the music inside me gurgles up, the need for it. Like oxygen.

Singing with Julian Ashburn.

"Are you for real?" I whisper.

He smiles broadly. His beauty hits me hard in the gut, feeling like heartbreak and falling in love.

This is a mistake.

I don't realize I've spoken aloud until Julian shakes his head. "It's not a mistake to try. To step outside your comfort zone. Besides, there's always a chance we'll sound horrible together."

Matt snorts in disbelief. I, too, know it's unlikely. I'm actually very skilled at harmonizing—my mother made sure of it. My throaty alto will perfectly complement his tenor. It already does every day in the car, in the shower…

Straightening my shoulders, I take a slow breath and walk straight off the ledge.

"Okay."

"Whoa," murmurs Matt. "I *never* would have thought to tell her she could work for free."

Julian shoots Matt a grin, then turns back to me. "Can you come to my place tomorrow?"

My lips go tingly. "W-what? Why? Don't I just go into a studio after you guys record? Wait—have you already laid tracks for a new album?" I say the last in a whisper, leaning forward while spying for eaves-droppers.

Eyes twinkling, Julian bends to put our faces level. "Yes," he whispers back, then stands with a small chuckle.

Matt laughs. "Look at those red cheeks! I almost forgot real women blush."

"As opposed to fake women?" I ask, then blush deeper as the lightbulb in my head belatedly turns on. "Oh. Groupies. Ha Ha. Yeah, I'm not that. Back to busi-ness—I'm busy tomorrow, actually. I'm busy a lot. So, maybe you can just pass along a studio time, and I can go in? By myself?"

Julian rubs the bridge of his nose. "No, Rose. You're

not going to do some sterile singalong with my recorded voice."

Oh.

I clear my throat nervously.

"Come over tomorrow," Matt urges. "It's just a small get together. Bring a friend. Meet Jackson and Nick." With an abrupt laugh, he mutters to Julian, "It's kind of fun having to work for it."

I roll my eyes. "It's nothing personal, but I really can't. I have a family commitment."

I glance across the café and spy Owen coming out of the kitchen. I immediately think of Greta, who nearly screamed at me for not telling her Breaking Giants was here last night. Not that she would have left her restaurant—she's the executive chef at a downtown hotspot—but according to her, it was the *principle* of the matter.

She'll never forgive me if she finds out I turned down bringing her to meet Breaking Giants.

I look at Julian, then blink when I find him already staring at me. "Text me the address. I won't be there until close to ten, though."

He smiles slightly and nods. "That's fine. Good. Great."

"You're kind of a bully, you know that?"

He shrugs. "Going after what I want doesn't make me a bully. It makes me determined."

Matt clears his throat. "Uhh, Julian…"

We both turn to see the source of Matt's low warning. Outside Tullamore, a crowd has gathered, faces pressed close to the windows. As soon as they see Julian's attention shift, they begin pounding on the glass.

Julian freezes in place, muscles locking and gaze fixed on the scene. Keeping the men from being mobbed is an enormous man in a black suit standing just outside the front door.

Our paying customers, maybe fifteen or so scattered across the café, watch the unfolding drama with camera phones out.

"What the hell is going on!" yells Owen, jogging across the café to us. He looks at Julian and Matt, and his expression clears. "Back so soon?"

"Not the time for small talk," I grumble, and swing myself up and over the countertop, landing beside Julian.

Grabbing his forearm, I tug him toward the kitchen. He comes, but stiffly, his movements lacking their customary grace. The muscles under my fingers are rock hard. I can hear his breathing, short and uneven.

Panic attacks and I go way back—I know the signs.

"Matt," I say over my shoulder, "I assume you know how to handle this?"

He nods quickly, gaze flickering to Julian. "I'll send a car around back."

"Thanks," grunts Julian.

I glance up at him, feeling a pang of sympathy when I see his clenched jaw and bloodless face. Giving his arm a squeeze, I murmur, "Reason number two I want nothing to do with fame."

He snorts in humor and gently extricates his arm from my grip. I miss the heat of him instantly, then blanch at the thought.

"This way," I say quickly, taking the lead past the kitchen and down a short, private hallway.

I veer into my office and crouch beside my desk to rummage through our Lost and Found bin. When I rise and turn, hat and sunglasses in hand, I nearly collide with Julian.

"You're like a ninja," I blurt, flushing at the almost-contact of our chests.

His brows lift, lips quirking. "Sorry. I thought I was following you."

Where? Out the window in my office? Biting my tongue on the quip, I hand him the camouflage.

"Put these on."

He tugs on the baseball hat, his hair sticking out in silky tufts. My gaze snags on the curve of his cheekbone, the contrast of hair and skin. A low buzz makes me jerk, but thankfully Julian doesn't notice, already reaching for his cellphone.

"Two minutes," he tells me, sighing as he leans against the wall beside the door. *Between me and the exit.*

Suddenly claustrophobic, I push open the nearby window. The noise of the crowd is a distant, shrill din punctuated by screams.

"Thanks again, Rose."

"No problem," I say, wincing at the hoarseness in my voice.

"I've never been very good at handling crowds. It's why I tend to avoid situations like this. And why I'll probably never leave Seattle. Rain is the best camouflage."

"I get that," I say dryly, fixing my gaze on the dark computer screen. "Plus, I feel kind of responsible. You wouldn't have come if I hadn't been such a text-bitch."

He chuckles softly. "I told you, I'm determined." He shifts against the wall. "You thought I was going to ask you out, didn't you?"

"What? No! That's ridiculous." I force a laugh, which only lifts his brows. "Besides, I don't date musicians."

"Why not?" he asks, then shakes his head. "None of my business. That's good, actually. Better for this, uh, venture. Not that you're not… well, I did say last night I was considering hitting on you. But that was before I heard you sing. So, yeah."

As he talks, a stupid grin spreads on my face. He flushes under my scrutiny, ducking his head to stare at the floor.

"Exactly why I don't do interviews," he mutters.

I can't help it—I laugh. He looks up, eyes narrowing, and I lift a hand to ward off his glare.

"Sorry. I just find it incredibly endearing that you babble. It's so unexpected. I mean, you handle stadium crowds just fine, and last night you were… different."

He rubs his jaw. "It's easier when the band is around. To play the part."

I nod in understanding even though I don't really understand. My mother was the same volatile, larger-than-life personality offstage as she was onstage.

The silence stretches, tenuous and uncomfortable. Julian clears his throat and stares at his phone, probably waiting for it to buzz so he can get the hell out of here.

A question presses against my lips, driven there by a growing curiosity and another, more subtle feeling I don't care to examine.

What the hell, why not?

"Julian? That song you played last night… is it going on the new album?"

His expression shifts to careful neutrality as he looks up. "I don't think so."

"Oh, well, it was really great. Very… emotionally fresh."

Subtle, Rose.

He shrugs. "Not really. It's been almost nine months." I blink in surprise at his candor, and he adds quickly, "I only wrote it because the label was pressuring me, heartbreak being good for business and all that."

"Oh."

His phone buzzes. With evident relief, he says, "Car's out back. I'll get out of your hair."

I point at the disaster that is my hairdo. "Good idea. Save yourself while you can."

Mischief sparkles in his eyes as they track up to my messy knot. "That rubber band looks happy enough."

Matt appears in the doorway. "Ready, bro?"

Julian nods and pushes away from the wall. "See you tomorrow, Rose."

I swallow thickly. "So long."

"Bye, Rose!" yells Matt, already out of sight.

The back door slams and a moment later, Owen appears. "Why is your face red?" he asks, grinning.

Because while socially awkward Julian is adorable, and his frontman persona is magnetic, the playful, flirty Julian who just made an appearance?

Fucking lethal.

Shaking my head mutely, I go back to work.

5

GYPSIES AND PIXIES

*A*unt Katherine is perched on the porch swing, no doubt waiting for me, when I pull into her driveway at seven on Sunday. Biting back a sigh, I gather the two bottles of wine I hope to use as bribery for her silence.

With one look at her face, however, I know two bottles aren't enough. There isn't enough wine in the world to keep her quiet when she's in a mood. And she's definitely in a mood. Owen and Greta probably kicked her out of the kitchen.

A cigarette dangles from her ringed fingers, momentarily forgotten as I exit the car and approach. She's wearing a typically odd outfit. A sapphire muumuu belted around her narrow waist and rain boots even though it's not raining. Over her shoulders is an afghan faded with age and tailored into a shawl.

Necklaces dangle between her breasts, all supporting various arcane symbols. A pentagram. An ankh. Even a cross. She's an equal opportunity spiritualist. Her long, wild curls are even more schizophrenic than usual, and her lustrous eyes are on me with laser-like focus.

I'll never understand it—no matter how atrocious her fashion decisions, somehow she makes them work. She looks exotic and full of secrets. An ageless, mystical queen.

I eye her warily as I climb the steps. "Wine?" I offer halfheartedly, lifting the bottles.

"Sit with me, Rose," she says softly.

Damnit.

I deposit the bottles near the front door before settling beside her. As she takes slow, measured drags of her cigarette, I stare at the front yard of her Queen Anne house. Most of the trees are bare, but whereas her neighbors' yards look sodden and unkempt, hers appears lush and artful.

Aunt Katherine is an extremely kind, gentle, and generous woman. But I can't lie—there's a part of her that scares me. A few of her premonitions have been a little too close to the mark for outright dismissal. While alive, my father had called her his witch-in-law. It hadn't been a joke.

On the night of my parents' deaths, Katherine's incessant phone calls to the house had woken me. I still remember her screaming '*Find your mother!*' But both of them had been gone by then.

Later, I found out that she'd started calling minutes before my mother's time of death. Why my father hadn't answered the phone, I'll never know.

"A message came for you in the cards last night."

My stomach sinks. "Oh?" I ask noncommittally.

"Would you like to hear it?"

"No thanks."

We've had this exact conversation more times than I can count. My responses are always the same. Still, she keeps asking.

"Has she been speaking to you?"

Every goddamn year.

Careful to maintain a bland tone, I reply, "Mom is dead, Aunt K. She can't speak to me."

Several years ago, I'd made the mistake of telling her that around the anniversary I had vivid memories of my mother's voice.

Katherine stubs out her cigarette in an ashtray. I don't turn, but I can feel her stare on the side of my face.

"Whatever Grace is telling you, you shouldn't listen. Her messages are being distorted by the circumstances of her death."

I roll my eyes up to the white slats of the porch's roof. Though she knows the truth, Katherine has never been able to come out and say it. My mother, her twin sister,

OD'd on heroin. An accidental overdose according to the coroner's report, which only means there was no way to determine whether or not she'd committed suicide. There hadn't been anything as closure-related as a note.

Undisturbed by my recalcitrance, Katherine continues, "Did you visit their graves?"

I silently pray for Owen to come save me. "Not since the funeral, as you know."

Katherine reaches over to cover my hand with hers. "Maybe next year."

I nod, my throat clogged with too much emotion to speak. *I should have stayed home.* It's an empty thought, without force of motivation. I need to be here. I need to be reminded that my family loves me.

For all her eccentricities, Katherine is the closest to a mother I've ever known. After my parents' deaths, she adopted me and raised me alongside Owen.

When nightmares woke me screaming in the night, she stroked my damp forehead until I could sleep again. She came to every softball game, read every paper and book report, taught me how to pluck my eyebrows, and gave me my first beer. When Frankie Jensen broke my heart sophomore year of college, she'd been the one to hold me as I sobbed.

I love her. More, perhaps, than I ever did my own mother.

"Oh, honey, come here. I love you, too."

I sigh as her arms enfold me. Ducking my face into her neck, I breathe in her familiar soft musk.

"Owen tells me you've met someone." When I stiffen, she holds me tighter. "Be careful, Rosie. The Prince of Swords is volatile right now. The timing is inopportune."

Chills rush over my skin, and I jerk upright. Katherine watches me calmly, dark eyes fathomless.

"I haven't met anyone. Stop it. You are *not* talking to me about tarot. You know I don't believe in that stuff."

Katherine shrugs a narrow shoulder. "Truth isn't dependent on belief, honey. Any way you look at it, the truth is just the truth."

I don't know whether to laugh or yell.

The Prince of Swords, really?

I'm more disturbed than I'll admit. A memory of Julian rises, his amber eyes warm and laughing as he reads the description of the card in his hand. I wonder if Katherine knows she contradicted herself—if she's telling me to stay away from Julian, listening to my mother is exactly what I should do.

Heaving air into my lungs, I stare at the rapidly darkening sky. I consider texting Julian and calling everything off.

The front door creaks open, spilling light and warmth. I wilt with relief at the sight of Owen. "Dinner's ready—oh, hey Rose." He sees the strained expression on my face and immediately frowns at Katherine. "Mom, I thought I told you to go easy on her."

"I did!" she protests.

I stand quickly, squeezing her shoulder as I pass. "She did. Everything's fine."

I grab the wine, not meeting Owen's gaze as I slip past him, down the hall, and into the kitchen.

"Oh my God!" screeches Greta when she sees me. "How freaking excited are we!"

She bounds across the room, throwing her whopping, five-feet-three-inch body into my arms. I carefully deposit the wine on the kitchen island and hug her back.

"Sooo excited," I drawl.

She finally releases me, pretty features scrunched. "I know today's a tough one, Rosie. I'll try to tone it down."

I smile, feeling a loosening in my gut. It's hard to be sad with a blonde, green-eyed pixy around.

"Please don't."

She squeals and bounces. "Okay, I won't! Breaking Giants! Holy shit we're going to hang out with Breaking Giants! Are you seriously wearing jeans and a t-shirt? What's wrong with you?"

I glance down, frowning. "They're new jeans."

Owen strolls into the kitchen followed by Katherine. He veers around me to give Greta a peck on the cheek.

"Don't dump me for a rockstar, love."

Greta giggles and swats at his roaming hands. "That all depends on Matt Sullivan." Owen groans and staggers backward. Greta just laughs.

I watch them as they banter—Greta fussing with something on the stove, Owen pouring wine—and my heart is heavy and full at once. We all grew up together, the two of them dancing around what was obvious to everyone else until after college. To me, their love is magic. Unconditional, sometimes messy, but always full of warmth and respect.

From beside me, Aunt Katherine murmurs, "Yours will come, Rose."

I roll my eyes and snag a glass of wine.

♪

JULIAN LIVES IN EDMONDS, about a forty-minute drive north of Seattle. I can't say I'm surprised by his choice in real estate. The area is mostly residential, and his property backs right onto the Puget Sound. Private. Secure. And possessing what are sure to be breathtaking views of the water and mountains. A perfect musician's retreat.

As we pull up behind a row of cars stacked in the

driveway, Greta whistles. "I think it just hit me. What we're doing." She turns wide eyes to me. "Why are we doing this?"

I laugh, only partially forced. "Come on, cupcake, you hung out at my parents' house all the time when we were kids."

Greta gives a sober nod. "It's not the mansion," she says, pointing at the lit-up, rustic giant in front of us. "It's what's inside it."

I throw my trusty Subaru into park and turn off the engine. Glancing at my cellphone, I assure her, "It's already close to ten. We'll stay for an hour, then split."

"I think I just peed my pants."

Laughing for real this time, I step out of the car and wait for her to join me.

"If I can do this, so can you."

She snort-laughs and grabs my arm. "Deal."

We walk up the driveway to the front door. It opens as we near it, emitting music and laughter. In our direct line of sight are at least fifteen people. Men with tattoos and tight pants. Women in miniskirts or slinky dresses.

Greta, in leggings, boots, and a short dress, skates the line of fitting in. I'm completely underdressed.

"So much for a small get together," I mumble, and plaster a smile on my face.

Jackson Everett, Breaking Giants' bassist, stands near

the front door with a cellphone to his ear. He waves at me, quickly finishes his call, then lowers the phone and grins in welcome. He's blonde, stocky and handsome in an All American Boy way, and has killer dimples.

"Hi, I'm Jackson. You must be Rose."

We shake hands. "Yep. This is my friend Greta."

"Hi, Greta." He shakes her hand before turning back to me. "I've been ordered to bring you outside."

He doesn't wait for a response, turning and waving over his shoulder for us to follow. Radiohead croons through the house from discreet speakers. The lighting is recessed and mellow. That's about all I take in of my surroundings, as I'm mostly focused on not tripping and ignoring the odd looks cast in our direction.

Jackson leads us through the back of the house and onto a huge, two-story deck. Beyond the shadowed back-yard, a stretch of inky black signifies the Sound. Cool air bathes my face, and I breathe deeply, consciously, as we descend the stairs to ground level.

The breathing exercise brings my heart rate down from the danger zone, but my skin still prickles nervously. At least twenty people are standing or sitting on lawn furniture around a massive, sunken fire pit. I try not to scan the crowd for Julian's dark head. I fail repeatedly.

The second my feet hit flagstone, Matt's voice lifts above the din. "There she is!"

I don't see him until he leaps to his feet, jostling the woman sharing his chaise, and jogs through the crowd to me. He abolishes my personal space to give me a bone-cracking hug.

His whisper tickles my earlobe, "Can I chat with you for a minute?"

I step back, nodding and trying not to frown at the peculiar tone of his voice. I can't place it. Doubt? Disappointment?

"Sure, um…"

I glance uncertainly at Greta, who stares back at me with a *Don't you dare leave me* expression.

Jackson says quickly, "Greta, can I show you around? Get you a drink?"

There's something quintessentially kind about the bassist. A lack of conceit, maybe. Whatever it is, I see Greta's tension fade. She nods, smiling.

"See you in a few?" she hisses.

I nod firmly. "Definitely."

When Matt and I stand in relative private, I ask, "What's going on?"

He clears his throat, gesturing me further away from the fire.

> *Into the dark and down we go*
> *With frozen lips, on tiptoes.*

Somewhere in the back of my mind, I know that the reflex to write lyrics is a defensive one. I'm disconnecting my feelings from the present. Bracing for impact. Matt isn't bothering to hide that something's wrong.

He stops beside a tree and drags a hand through his pale hair. "So, er, I'm not sure how to say this…"

"I'm a smart girl," I say blandly. "The gig isn't going to work out. Right?"

He sighs noisily. "Right. I'm so sorry. Something changed today. The original artist who was going to sing is back in the picture."

I lift a hand, saving him from what looks like a seriously uncomfortable moment.

"Hey, it's all good."

Inside me, disappointment and relief share a slow dance. Then nostalgia butts in, which is weird. How can I long for something that hasn't happened, and now never will?

For less than a day, I'd been preparing to sing accompaniment to Julian Ashburn. It isn't the end of the world. It isn't the end of anything, because nothing started in the first place.

"Julian told me to tell you he's sorry," Matt continues. "He wanted to call and explain, but got wrapped up in some… things."

I nod absently, chewing my lips. "He's not here?" I finally ask.

Matt stares at the ground. "Nope. Caught a flight this evening to L.A."

The dots aren't hard to connect. Of course there's a woman in L.A. The woman he wrote that song about. *I only wrote it because the label was pressuring me, heartbreak being good for business.*

Funny, how my first impression was dead on the money. He's not over her. Not even remotely.

"Good for him," I say, a little less enthusiastically than I was aiming for.

Coughing to cover an odd sting of hurt in my chest, I glance around the backyard. Everywhere I look are attractive people laughing and chatting. It's a perfect, clichéd tableau of a rockstar's party. I spot another famous musician sitting near the fire pit with a bong in his lap. He's grinning down at a brunette who kneels beside his chair, her cleavage about three inches past modesty's border.

For a moment, I wonder if I could ever belong in this crowd, in the loud, passionate conversations, the devil-may-care attitudes. Then I let the thought go. It's an old, tired one.

Stranger in my rearview;
Once, I thought I knew you.

I turn my focus back to Matt. "Well, if you don't mind

I'll probably just head home."

"What?" he barks. "No way! You have to stay. Hang out."

Because he sounds so damn genuine, I smile. "Thanks, and thanks for being a cool person, but this isn't really my scene."

Matt grins at me. "I bet you like museums and art galleries and shit like that."

I laugh. "I do run a coffeehouse, you know."

He shakes his head, frowning a little. "Man, you're seriously the female version of Julian."

Ack.

My laugh this time is forced. "As far as I know my parents only had one kid."

Matt scrunches his face—a super adorable expression that no press has ever witnessed. "Ew. What if you *were* his sister? Julian would have to live with wanting to fuc—" He chokes, flushing bright red.

My eyes almost pop out of their sockets. I blink a few times. Matt doesn't say anything else, and the awkward moment stretches until we both wince.

"Okay," I wheeze finally. "Well, I'll see you around?"

He looks at me a few more seconds, a penetrating stare that makes me glad I'm not on the spectrum of women he goes after. Then he gives me another brief hug.

"If it's any consolation, we all think he's making a mistake."

I smile weakly, thinking of Aunt Katherine's unasked-for message about Julian: *The timing is inopportune.* As usual, she hit the nail on the head with her freaky fairy dust.

Or maybe she just reads the tabloids.

6

DON'T BLINK

FOUR MONTHS LATER

The song is everywhere. Radio. Television. Malls. Bookstores. Social Media. It even sneaks repeatedly onto my music streaming apps, earning an immediate finger swipe. Everyone loves it. It's edgy, darker than the band's previous work. A veritable anthem of passionate love. In short, an instant hit.

Entertainment journalists can't stop writing about the story behind the song—the relationship between Julian Ashburn and Missy McKenzie, bonafide country star. For a few weeks, their faces grace the cover of every gossip rag and trendy magazine.

Oh yeah, it's *that* song. The one he said wouldn't be

on the album. The one about how she cheated on him and dumped him, breaking his heart. Only the cheating bit vanished from the lyrics, replaced by something milder. Less incendiary. More... *I wasn't sure we were meant to be together, but now I am.*

For the first time in history, I don't buy the newest Breaking Giants single.

Also for the first time in history, I record songs. Part of the blame, I know, goes to Julian and his assertion that I'm too afraid to put myself out there. He's right. And I'm annoyed enough—about him bulldozing into my life, then disappearing like smoke—to want to rebel against him, to prove him wrong. Surprisingly, this motivation outweighs the deeply ingrained fear of becoming like my mother.

Greg helps me get the booth time and produces the six tracks for me, which luckily for me happens to be his day job. He owed me the favor, anyway, as he shares blame with Julian for why I broke my vow to never record.

One evening, about a month after the party at Julian's, Greg and I were fooling around with guitars at my place when I let slip that I'd written something new. After much egging on his part, I finally played it for him on piano, humming lyrics I was too afraid to voice.

Fast forward two and a half months and I now have twenty or so demo CDs that Greg insists on plugging every Friday at open mic. They sit beside his and a few others on a counter at Tullamore. And they've been selling, a handful a week.

We started with a hundred of them.

♪

IT'S an early Friday evening like any other, clanking dishes and rising excitement. The front door of Tullamore is open, emitting a warm June breeze and lingering daylight, soft and golden. Oversized ceiling fans crank steadily but don't do much more than churn hot air. As occasionally happens in Seattle, the weather is epic. Sunny and high seventies for the last week. There are more than a few people sporting tan lines and healing sunburns.

I'm relaxed. More relaxed than I've been in ages. Something inside me feels different. Looser and free.

On a psychological level that I'm sure a therapist would squee over, I get that recording songs was a huge step of growth. Overcoming the deep, irrational fear implanted in me by my parents' insane lives and realizing how irrational that fear is? Let's just say I'm no longer quite as neurotic.

Everyone close to me has noticed. Aunt Katherine says the presence of spirit guides is strong around me. Whatever that means. Owen and Greta don't have to hide worry when they look at me now. And Greg… Greg shaved his dreadlocks, revealing what the world already knew—he's pretty hot. We've grown closer, and though he's always respectful of our friendship's boundaries, he's been laying on the charm real thick. I'm still not dating him, but I'm not as repelled by the idea as I once was.

"Are you sure you don't want to go on tonight?"

I glance back at Owen, my arm submerged in the bakery case. Using tongs to retrieve the requested scone, I slap it on a plate and hand it to a cashier.

"Yep," I answer, closing the case and hanging the tongs on their hook. "My throat still feels scratchy from my cold last week."

"Maybe a cup of tea would help?" he suggests, shifting from foot to foot, gaze bouncing around but not staying on my face more than a second or two.

My eyes narrow. "What's wrong with you?"

He sighs, relaxing. "I suck at this."

I laugh. "Lying? Yes, you do. You always have."

He makes a valiant effort at keeping a straight face. "I just really think you should sing tonight."

I cast a suspicious look over the crowded café, scanning from the front door to the stage where Greg and two helpers are handling setup. Seeing nothing out of the ordinary—for example, men in suits—I turn my glare on Owen.

"Spit it out."

"Hi, Rose."

Julian's voice, coming from behind me, ricochets down my spine and electrifies the hair at the nape of my neck. My stomach does a five-second free fall, then slams down somewhere in the vicinity of my ankles. I have the absurd thought of crawling into the bakery case and sealing myself inside.

Owen winces and mouths, "Sorry."

Clearing my throat—*I'm a grown up, act like a grown up*—I turn around and smile at Julian. I'm so blindsided by his arrival, I don't really see him.

Tall, dark, and dangerous—Check.

"Hi, Julian. Great to see you again."

I sound like I'm sucking a lemon. Julian's lips twitch; he glances at Owen, then back to me. I can't meet his gaze. Not quite. He's wearing his glasses, which help. I stare at the black strip over his nose.

"Nice to see you, too." He coughs lightly. "Um, can we talk for a second? In private?"

I realize the café has quieted. Some patrons are oblivious, but most are listening to us while poorly pretending not to. I don't bother speaking as I turn and walk quickly down the hallway to my office.

Julian follows, entering as I'm tossing my apron onto a hook.

Oddly, after my initial response to his voice, I don't feel the visceral impact of his presence like I did four months ago. Almost, I wish I'd never met him. I could have kept on hero-worshipping him.

But now he's just a man, flawed like the rest of us. My biggest disappointment is that meeting him changed how I listen to his music. It's still great, but it doesn't transport me anymore.

Dropping into the chair behind my desk, I give Julian my best professional smile. "Congrats on the success of your new single. Do you have a release date for the album yet?"

"Rose," he said softly. "Don't be that way."

I blink. "Sorry?"

He sighs, lowering himself gracefully into the chair opposite mine. No beanie. Windblown hair. Caramel, piercing eyes. When he starts talking, it takes me a few seconds to restart my brain.

"...to see you and apologize personally for what happened. I haven't been in town much the last few months. I came as soon as I could."

He sounds so earnest, a flare of not-quite-healed hurt cracks my cheery shell. I patch it up and wave a hand.

"It's in the past. If we'd signed a contract, maybe I would have sued the shit out of you."

His dimple makes an appearance. "No, you wouldn't have."

Irked that he's right, I say, "Anyway, apology accepted."

I consider asking him to perform tonight to make it up to me but fall short on courage. And suddenly I really need to get away from him.

Voice like hot water on cold toes;
Secrets in your eyes nobody knows.

Smothering the urge to swipe my notebook off my desk, I stand and grab my apron.

"Sorry, but we're pretty busy out there." I scoot toward the door. "Is there anything else?"

He stands. There's abruptly not enough air in my small office. A hint of his cologne reaches me. Citrus and sandalwood. I have the unbidden memory of him wrapping his hoodie around my shoulders. His warm fingers on my forearm.

Julian takes an unnecessary step toward me, blocking my access to the door and crowding my personal space. I feel heat rising through my chest to my face, unstoppable. I shiver a little, and there's a betraying tingle in my breasts as my nipples tighten.

So much for being unaffected.

I toss my apron over my head, tying the straps behind me with jerky movements.

"Julian," I say, a tad breathless, "You're kinda in my space."

"Are you performing tonight?"

I immediately recognize the clarity and darkness of his voice. *Hello, rockstar frontman.*

"Nope," I squeak, then flush a deeper red. Steeling myself, I look up at him. "Getting over a cold. You probably shouldn't be standing this close to me. I don't think I'm contagious anymore, but I don't want to get you sick."

His gaze drops to my mouth, and his throat bobs as he swallows. His eyes darken.

What the hell is happening?

Tension sizzles between us, a palpable magnetism that feels reckless. And, if I'm honest, unbelievably good. He *wants* me.

But as heat spirals through me, my heart kicks harder, and my breath turns shallow, I realize it also feels unbelievably *wrong*. Julian Ashburn, according to the press and everyone else on the planet, is very, very taken.

"Julian, I—"

I don't get another word out. His mouth is on mine, hot and possessive. I gasp, then grunt as my back finds the wall. There's no thought—no consequences—just his hands under my thighs, jerking my legs around his hips.

His body presses hard against mine. Warm and solid and *real*.

He tastes like he looks, earthy and spicy and addictive. I hold on, my arms around his shoulders, and give as good as I get. Because this is *beyond*.

Minutes or centuries later, Julian finally surrenders my mouth. It's a damn good thing he's still holding my legs. Otherwise, I'd be a puddle on the floor.

I've never felt so possessed by a kiss in my life. I can't catch my breath.

My head drops against the wall with a thud. I'm drowning or dreaming; either way, reality is hurling toward me at a million miles per hour, and the aftermath isn't gonna be pretty.

Holyshitwhatjusthappened.

Skilled lips trail down my neck and back up, finding a sensitive spot beneath my ear. Drawing a deep breath, he whispers, "You smell like sunshine."

I lift my head, then let it drop again against the wall. One more time, a little harder, while Julian nibbles on my collarbone. I'm pretty sure he gets the memo, but he ignores it.

"Julian," I say softly but firmly.

He sighs, forehead meeting my shoulder as he lowers my legs. For a final, long moment, we stand as close as we can. I greedily press my face into his chest, breathing his scent, luxuriating in his heat, and *maybe* twitch my hips a little to feel the bulge in his pants.

From the hallway outside, I hear Greg's voice, "Rose? I saw you come back here—Oh."

We move, but not fast enough. Greg's wide eyes veer from Julian to me, and there's absolutely nothing to say. Julian's lips are swollen, his glasses slightly askew, and below the belt… *Ohmygod.*

My expression is probably a mix of horror and embarrassment. "Greg, uh—" I start.

"What the fuck, man?" snaps Greg, blue eyes blazing with anger at Julian. "Aren't you engaged? It was all over the radio this morning."

Shock punches me hard in the chest, stealing my breath. "What?" I whisper.

Julian's expression is granite—all the answer I require. Greg glances at me. There's sympathy in his eyes, but also hurt. A lot, lot of hurt.

"You can't say anything about this," Julian growls at Greg, "to anyone. If I hear even a whisper that you're talking to a reporter, I'll come after you."

Silly me, I thought it couldn't get any worse.

"I'm not going to tell anyone," Greg bites out. "It's your train-wreck of a marriage, and you'll fuck it up just fine on your own. But you're not going to use my friend to do it. She deserves better."

I close my eyes and press into the wall. My stomach turns, preparing to eject. I count my breaths until nausea passes.

"I know," murmurs Julian. "I'm sorry, Rose."

I hear Julian move but only open my eyes when I know he's gone. Greg watches me from just inside the door, his jaw clenched and head shaking slowly.

I want to apologize to him. But that would mean acknowledging that I know how he feels about me, and frankly, I'm selfish. I don't want our friendship to change.

We don't always get what we want.

"I'm done, Rose. I can't keep following you around like a schoolboy with a crush."

"Greg—"

He wards off my words with both hands. "You haven't led me on. This isn't your fault. I just… seeing you… You're never going to look at me the way you look at him."

I swallow hard, fighting flashbacks of the kiss. "You're one of my best friends, Greg," I say lamely. "I don't want our friendship to end over this."

He sighs. "Me, either. But I'm gonna need some time, okay?"

I say the only thing I can. "Okay."

7

THE WORST IS YET TO COME

I somehow survive the rest of my shift and drive home with the single-minded focus of someone who isn't sure they should be behind the wheel. I make it safely into the garage and go through my routine on autopilot. Car off. Collect keys and purse. Garage door down, house door open. Hallway light on. Turn deadbolt behind me.

I'm not the type of person to self-medicate, but once in the kitchen the first thing I do is grab a bottle from my small wine cabinet. As the daughter of an addict who was in and out of rehabs and twelve-step programs most of my childhood, I've always had a special awareness of my own consumption. I don't do drugs. Ever. I do drink, but only occasionally and never to excess.

Tonight, I'm making an exception. Julian-effing-

Ashburn kissed me to within an inch of my sanity, and Greg, one of my very best friends, dumped me right after. Oh, and Julian is apparently engaged. To be married. To his starlet country love.

I'm working on glass #4 when eleven p.m. rolls around. Knowing Greta will be off work by now, I call her.

She answers on the second ring. "Hey, I was about to call you."

"Did Owen ask you to check on me?" I ask, speaking slowly to avoid slurring.

She makes an affirmative sound. "He didn't tell me anything specific, only that you seemed off tonight. What are you doing right now?"

"I'm drunk alone at home."

There's a pause. "I'll be there in twenty minutes."

The line goes dead.

"Perfect." I squint at the bright screen of my phone. "Just enough time to do something stupid."

I pull up my contacts and scroll through the 'A' section. Selecting the desired number, I put the phone to my ear and listen to the ringing.

I'm not sure how many times it rings before he picks up. I might have blacked out for a second or ten. He doesn't say anything, and neither do I. Soft voices murmur in the background, then fall off. A door closes.

"Rose?"

Remorse aplenty. I think there's longing, too, but it might be the wine talking trash.

Speaking of talking…

"Oh hi, yeah, it's me. I just wanted to tell you something real quick. You *suck*, Julian Ashburn."

A slow exhale. "I know. I'm so sorry. Today shouldn't have happened. I completely lost my mind. There's so much craziness going on, and you've been in my thoughts the last few weeks, and today I suddenly had to see you. And then—"

"Whoa, cowboy!" I interject, refusing to be charmed by his babbling. "This isn't your confessional. This is me, a girl you know next to nothing about, telling you that you're an asshole for kissing me when you're marrying some other girl—who is smoking hot, by the way, and according to your latest single, really *swell*—and there's no excuse for your deplorap—deporal—

"Deplorable?" he offers.

"—bad behavior. You're a dirtbag. The end."

I hang up.

My phone vibrates with a call. I answer immediately with, "I'm not talking to you ever again!"

Aunt Katherine says, "You've been drinking. What's wrong?"

I slump back in my chair and stare blearily across my dark living room, waiting for my racing heart to slow. I don't feel better for having chewed out Julian. I feel worse. Now the sound of his voice is fresh, and yes, I'm still charmed by his damned babbling.

"Things were so good for a minute, Aunt K," I finally whisper. "I had my head on straight, I was moving in new directions, focusing on stuff."

She doesn't comment on my drunken vagueness. "Things are still good," she says in her equally vague, mystic-like way. "Every moment is a blessing, each challenge an opportunity for growth."

I peer into my wine glass, then take a sip. I can't even taste it anymore.

"I love you, Katherine, but I'm really not in the mood for one of your pep talks."

"Mmm. I did a reading for you." For the first time in memory, she doesn't bother asking if I want to hear it. "The Prince of Swords in a disadvantageous spread. Confusion, lust, dishonest living."

"Yeah, yeah, I know," I mumble, ignoring the goosebumps rising on my arms. "Why am I so sideways about him, then?"

What I'm really asking is, *Why did he kiss me?* but apparently the spirits can't read minds—or they don't exist!—because Katherine launches into mystic-babble.

"Because you are, and have always been, the Princess of Cups. Warm, compassionate, and creative, but you crave harmony and are easily overwhelmed by sorrow and conflict. The Prince of Swords in his bright aspect is a steady, capable, intelligent man, with a brilliant mind and creative passion to match yours. Together, the two of you are powerful, magnetic, and there is potential for lifelong love. But…" she pauses with uncharacteristic hesitance, "maybe not *this* Prince of Swords, hmm?"

I take a noisy gulp of wine. "Ugh. Stop."

"I'm receiving the answer to a question," she whispers, and I roll my eyes out of habit. "He kissed you because of… fear? Doubt? Hope? Hmm. I'm sorry, but I'm not getting a clear message."

Luckily my glass is already on the table, otherwise shattering would have been imminent. My skin is crawling, and when my phone vibrates with a new text message, I yelp.

"Hang on, Aunt K."

I stare at the three-word message until the letters blur.

Let me explain.

"Aunt K? I've gotta go. Don't you or your spirit guides worry 'bout me. Greta's coming to keep me company. Minor setback. Everything will be A-okay."

"Okay, honey," she says skeptically. "I love you."

There's a knock on my front door. "Greta's here! Love you, too."

I hang up, make it into the small foyer with only

minor injuries, and yank the door open. Greta blinks hugely, her mouth dropping open.

"You're wasted!" she says, pointing at me in case I'm too drunk to understand.

"Pshha," I agree, snagging her arm and hauling her inside. "Grab a glass. We're going to watch movies and have a sleepover like old times. Is that okay with Owen?"

I'm fiddling with my phone—*what's my damn passcode again?*—and run smack into a wall.

"Uhh," says my best friend, "I'm honestly not sure what to do right now. I haven't seen you like this in ages."

I laugh, rubbing my offended forehead. "I forgot to eat. That's the problem."

I finally unlock my phone and pull up Julian's text message. What I type isn't my best work, but it gets the point across.

> You explain not. Interested
>
> made album spite you
>
> don't know meeee

Greta grabs the phone, but I've already pressed the final Send. Her eyes scan downward, then lift and narrow.

"You're drunk texting Julian Ashburn. What the hell happened today?"

With her help, I make it to the couch. My head lolling against an armrest and my legs askew on the coffee table, I spill my guts about the most mind-blowing, toe-curling, dream-coming-true kiss of my life, which went so far sideways so fast I can't cope.

By the time I'm done dumping my emotional garbage, I've veered away from the cliff of blackout drunkenness and back into the realm of feeling-things-I-don't-want-to-feel.

Staring miserably at the chipped polish on my right big toe (I lost my shoes sometime recently), I mumble, "I guess I thought, just for a second… it was the way he held my face, maybe… that there was something, a chance he…"

Cue tears.

Greta wraps me in a hug that would make a bear proud, especially given her diminutive stature.

"Oh, Rosie, there's nothing wrong with feeling hurt and disappointed and even a little heartbroken. I know right now it feels super shitty but trust me, someday we're going to look back on this and laugh."

"I gave Julian Ashburn a giant erection," I say, testing the theory. "Nope, not funny yet."

Greta snorts into my hair. "It's kinda funny." She

leans back enough to see my mascara-streaked face. "Seriously, you made out with *Julian Ashburn*."

I take a mental step back and ponder her words.

After considerable thought, I manage a watery smile. "I guess that's pretty awesome, huh?"

She nods. "Something to tell the grandkids."

My emotional storm clears. I sigh with the beginnings of relief. "Seems I've been harboring a giant repressed crush on Julian the last few months. How pathetic am I? I only recorded songs because he dared me."

Greta says firmly, "Even if he's scum for kissing you while engaged to someone else, I could kiss him myself for that."

Greta knows—better than most—what a number my parents' deaths did on me. And the conditioning my sick, addict mother embedded in my young mind. If I ever drum up the courage to try therapy, I'll be stuck in a chair for the rest of my life.

Music is the only lover who will never leave you, Rose.

That little gem is the main reason I don't do relationships well and not at all with musicians. Even when I've dated good, honest, kind men, within a year or so all my demons have invariably reared their heads, and Good Honest Kind ran for the hills.

"Ungh," I say.

A series of beeps sounds from Greta's nearby purse. "It's probably Owen," she says, squeezing my shoulder before fishing out her phone and heading into the kitchen.

I catch, "She's okay…" before distance muffles the rest.

I snuggle deeper into the couch, the movement alerting me to a hard object wedged against my hip. Pulling out my cell phone, I check for new texts.

There's nothing.

8

IS THIS REAL LIFE?

*L*ate the following morning, I haul my hungover ass out of bed. Greta's in the kitchen, which is always an event worth witnessing, and I'm badly in need of coffee. Throwing on my fluffy purple robe and some slippers, I grab my dead cell phone—it hadn't plugged itself in when I told it to—and pad down the hallway.

"Morning, sleepyhead!"

"Bleh."

Greta laughs but doesn't turn from the stove where I'm hoping her signature crepes are happening. There are grocery bags on the counter. When I spy a half-used carton of blueberries, I almost do a dance. Almost.

Instead, I walk zombie-like to the coffee maker where —*God bless her*—there's a full pot waiting.

"That's it, Owen can't have you. You're marrying me."

She snorts. "You must have heard me come back in. I just started cooking. Eat some strawberries and relax."

"Take your time. Thank the Welsh gods, I don't feel that sick." Spying the two empty wine bottles by the side door, I wince and palm my stomach. "I take it back."

After pouring steaming coffee up to the brim of an oversized mug, I hop onto the counter beside an errant charge cable. I plug in my phone, then focus on what really matters. With every reviving sip, I pledge my undying love to caffeine.

Greta glances curiously over her shoulder. "What the hell is wrong with your phone?"

"Huh?" I look down. The slim device is buzzing a mile-a-minute, dancing all over the counter by my thigh. "That's weird."

I set down my coffee and pick up my phone. It continues vibrating in my hands like a live wire. Notifications fly down the screen, too fast for me to follow. Frowning, I unlock the phone.

"Uhh... I think my Facebook got hacked." Pressing the icon, I wait for the app to load. "Definitely. I have a hundred friend requests and a bajillion notifications. Ha! Hold on, lemme change my password and figure out what some jerkface posted on my profile."

"Rose?" asks Greta mutedly.

"Yeah?" I ask without looking up from my task.

"I'm looking at Facebook right now. You're tagged in a bunch of articles. E! Online, TMZ, Huff Post Entertainment, and a bunch of others I've never heard of. You… you're not going to like this."

Waves of cold radiate down my body.

"That makes no sense," I whisper, even as I see the articles for myself.

They all have varying titles of the same theme. All boast a damningly clear camera-phone picture of Julian and me beside the bakery case at Tullamore. We're standing about a foot apart. He's looking down at me, smiling, and the way my face is lifted toward his…

"It looks like we're going to kiss."

"Yes, it does," Greta confirms.

"One of my customers betrayed me!"

"*That's* what you're focusing on?" she asks with a little laugh, then blurts, "Shit, the crepes!"

I read the tagline of the first article again.

Recently engaged Julian Ashburn and Rose Cunningham, daughter of songwriting legend Grace Cunningham, share an intimate moment at her café, Tullamore.

A sudden pounding on the front door brings me off the counter and almost paints the floor with coffee.

"Good Lord," Greta gasps. "Who the hell is that?"

I set my mug down carefully. "I have a pretty good idea—cleanup crew."

Knotting my robe around my waist, I head into the foyer and peer through the peephole, then unlock and open the door.

"Hi, Matt. Where are the lawyers? And how did you find out where I live? Nevermind. I don't want to know."

Matt, looking like a Viking god on a mission to dominate Earth, storms past me without an invitation. He veers into the kitchen and jerks to a stop.

"Oh man, that smells good."

Greta, bright red in front of the stove, squeaks, "Would you like a crepe?"

"How about some coffee?" I ask, moving past him to grab a new mug.

"Yes, thank you. Black."

He plops down at my kitchen table like he's been here a hundred times. After serving his coffee, I sit opposite him and cradle my mug between my hands. As I take measured sips and stare out the kitchen window, I can feel him studying my face.

Finally, Matt sighs and sinks back into his chair. "You look like hell."

I lift my brows, angling bloodshot eyes his way. "I'm probably still a little drunk, which is why I'm not kicking you out right now." I wiggle my fingers. "Where's the non-disclosure agreement?"

He frowns. "It's not that simple. Our publicist is working on retractions, but that's not the only photo that surfaced. We have twenty-four hours to spin this before the other photos destroy Julian's reputation."

"You mean his farcical engagement," snaps Greta.

I blink in surprise as she drops plates of steaming crepes on the table, then slams down syrup and butter.

Despite her obvious awe, she glares at Matt. "You should tell Julian to clean up his own messes."

Yeah, go Greta!

Aloud, I attempt maturity. "How bad can the other photos be? It's not like we—"

Matt holds up his phone, presenting me with an image of Julian standing in the private lot behind Tullamore. His t-shirt is rumpled, hair mussed, and... well... he looks freshly fucked.

With a purposeful swipe, the next image appears. I'm standing behind a register, staring blankly, my hair chaotic and... yep, that's a hickey on my neck.

My fingers cup the spot on my throat.

"Our publicist came up with a solution," Matt says, lowering the phone. "A win-win."

Staring at my plate, I mutter, "I'm banning cellphones in the café. Forever."

Fingers snap in front of my nose. "Focus, Rose!"

I do, and see that Matt's extremely upset.

"We need to fix this!" he pleads.

I sigh, rubbing the bridge of my nose. "I don't see how. Besides, it will blow over." I narrow my eyes. "You know I'm not really interested in helping Julian, right?"

"And isn't all publicity good publicity?" asks Greta.

"Not this kind," says Matt matter-of-factly. "Not mere months before an album launch. Not when sixty-percent of our fanbase is female between the ages of fifteen and forty."

"Can't have Julian looking like a cheater," I mumble while drowning a crepe in maple syrup.

Matt is silent a few seconds, then asks quietly, "Is that what you want? Female revenge stuff? I didn't think you were the type."

I wave a fork at him. "Quit with the reverse psychology, Mattie. I'll write a statement saying Julian and I are just friends. I'm not talking to the press though. Happy?"

"Not exactly. I want you to be my girlfriend."

A spoon clatters in the kitchen. I freeze with a forkful of crepe halfway to my mouth. "Say what?"

The look Matt gives me is the polar opposite of romantic interest. "We're going to a charity function downtown tonight. I want you to come with me as my date. I'm going to lie to the press and tell them we've been dating in secret. That Julian was a decoy so I could get you alone in your office. And that it backfired when someone snapped photos of you two."

"Are you kidding?" Anxiety travels down my arms

in flashes. "No way. Not a chance on this blue planet am I going to some celebrity event with you!"

Matt doesn't react to my words, just watches me calmly. "This could ruin his career. It could ruin Breaking Giants."

The words filter in slowly, settling with a harsh scrape of conscience and consequence.

"Goddamnit," I hiss, breaking eye-contact to stare at my cooling breakfast. "This is *so* unfair."

"I know," murmurs Matt. "I don't like putting you in this position, but the band comes first for me. It's everything to me. Please."

I squeeze my eyes shut until the burn in my chest fades, then blink at Matt. "Let me guess, we have to kiss in front of the cameras."

Relief breaks like sunshine on his handsome features. "So much kissing," he agrees with a wicked smile. "Can I touch a boob?"

Greta snort-laughs from beside the coffeemaker. "This is so funny. Messed up, but funny."

I glare at her. "Maybe someday I'll laugh with you."

She grins. "Trust me, you will."

"One more thing," says my new boyfriend. "Please, please don't call me… whatever you called me."

I blow him a kiss. "Sure thing, *Mattie*."

♩

THE PARTY LINE is that Matt—whose image is largely based on being a certifiable lady's man—was pressured into keeping his relationship with me a secret.

The band's label isn't a fan of the implication that they were the ones doing the pressuring, but allowing the secondary, more damaging photos to surface is less of an option. I don't ask how much money will be flung at the wannabe paparazzo who captured the shots. It's no doubt exorbitant.

Owen, after being filled in on the details, excuses me from work, ending our conversation with an explosion of maniacal laughter.

I'm still not laughing.

At two o'clock, a team of stylists shows up at my house with suitcases and garment bags and begins turning a pumpkin into a coach. Or a mouse into a horse? Whatever the transformation, I'm definitely not feeling the role of a pauper to a princess.

The preparation required for a public appearance of this caliber isn't as enjoyable as people think. You basically don't exist except as a body and face with a million flaws that have to be squeezed, compressed, plucked, and powdered into the semblance of perfection.

The team—three women and a man—are nice to me in a distant, professional way. They don't know who I am beyond the chick in the gossip blogs this morning and are no doubt contractually bound to not ask questions.

Around five p.m., as the stylists pack up their various instruments of torture, I stand in front of the full-length mirror in my bedroom and feel… indifferent.

Sure, the dress I'm stuffed into is gorgeous. Tight as a glove, some dreamy color between rust and gold. I'm sure I look like a million bucks. But all I see is a taller, curvier, less beautiful version of the iconic Grace Cunningham.

I hear the front door close behind the stylists. Moments later, Greta knocks on my bedroom door.

"Come in," I say, turning from the mirror. The smile blooming on her lips falters as she sees me. "Yeah, I know. I look like mom."

"It's the eye makeup," she says, coming forward. She trails fingers along my bare shoulder, grazing one of the diaphanous straps pretending to hold the dress up. "This gown. Crap. It probably costs more than my car."

"Yeah, mine too."

Greta fixes a concerned stare on my face. "I gotta say, I'm a little surprised you're not more, um…"

"Freaked out?" I ask, and she nods. "I'm nervous as hell, but honestly I'm mostly just hungry, tired, and hungover. The faster this is over with, the faster I can shove a spoon in some ice cream."

She doesn't look convinced but smiles anyway. "Well, you look stunning. Like a bohemian goddess." The doorbell rings, and she peeks out the nearby curtain. "Limo's here."

I grab the tiny clutch with enough room for my ID, house key, and a half-empty tube of lipgloss, and give Greta careful hug.

"I'll let you know how it goes."

She grins. "Have fun kissing Matt Sullivan, you bitch."

I laugh because the only other option is crying hysterically. I don't want to kiss Matt. I don't want to leave my house. I don't want to.

It could ruin his career.

And as jacked up as it is, I care.

So I go.

Matt waits on the curb for me, looking exactly as expected—a wet dream in a tuxedo. His pale hair is swept back, blue eyes electric and dancing with mirth. He grins rakishly, gives me a kiss on the cheek, and gestures me into the limo before him.

I maneuver carefully onto the backseat and scoot over. Matt slides inside and slams the door, then turns and pounces, caging me with his arms.

His face is very close. "Darling," he purrs, in a tone

that—even knowing its feigned—makes me blush. Before I can form a coherent thought, his soft lips graze mine. "You look edible."

I can't help it—I laugh, leaning back to catch the surprise on his face.

"Does that shit work for you?"

Matt gasps in exaggerated affront, falling against the opposite door with a hand over his heart. I laugh harder.

"Actually," says a light female voice, "it usually does work for him."

In my efforts to get inside the limo without tearing my dress or falling on my face, I'd completely over-looked the potential for company.

Idiot, it's a limo.

My gaze snaps to the two people seated on the bench behind the driver. My heart catapults into my throat.

Julian and Missy.

Because life.

I really, really want to jab my elbow into Matt in punishment for not warning me. *Seriously—what the hell?* Instead, I smile brightly at the siren in a blue evening gown.

"Hi, you must be Missy. Great to meet you."

She really is beautiful. Blonde, but not a canned beauty. Fresh and natural, with lush, straight hair brushing her shoulders and pale eyes. A young Margot Hemingway.

"Nice to meet you," she says mildly.

I hear only a trace of twang and wonder if she pumps it up in public. I also wonder how much she knows—then register the calculating gleam in her eyes.

She knows, all right. And for whatever reason, she doesn't seem the least bit bothered by the fact I swapped spit with her man.

I feel like I'm missing something. A big, ugly something.

My shoulders knot with tension.

Matt, sensing my distress, threads his fingers through mine. I'm so grateful for the support that I clutch him like a lifeline, scooting closer until I'm leaning against his hard shoulder.

Julian stirs, his gaze flickering briefly in our direction before returning to the passing scenery. In fact, small movement aside, he could pass as a wax statue of himself. Sharp and elegant. A rockstar James Bond.

Then he tells the window, "Thanks for doing this, Rose."

"Sure," I squeak.

Aaaand kill me.

Missy gives me a cool smile. "Julian tells me you're a songwriter like your mother."

Annoyed that he felt compelled to tell her a single fact about me, I say rigidly, "It's a hobby."

"Ahh," she says knowingly.

The implied insult, of course, is that it's a hobby because I lack the talent to succeed professionally.

Matt and Julian both stiffen, no doubt anticipating a cat fight. But it takes two, and I've never been much of a hothead. At least, not when I'm sober. As Matt opens his mouth to defend me, I squeeze his hand.

"It's fine," I tell him, then look at Missy. "I write songs because I love to, not because I want to be famous and sell out stadiums. I know it's hard to understand, but all the things you have? I don't want them."

Her eyes narrow with feeling. "I think we all know there's at least one thing I have that you want."

Touché.

Julian frowns out the window. Matt gets a text and eagerly occupies himself with his phone. Missy, after glaring at me for a few more seconds, guzzles down a plastic glass of champagne.

By the time we reach our destination I've inspected the fingernails of both hands twice, and it's a damned miracle their polish survives the trip.

9

FRAUD AND FORTITUDE

The night passes in a blur of reporters, flashing cameras, fantastic food, and benefit performances to raise money for breast cancer research. By the tenth time Matt and I offer a staged kiss to a camera, two things are certain: we have zero chemistry, and we're damn-fine actors.

At one point, he whispers, "If you want, we can give it a go backstage somewhere. You know, for posterity."

"You're just annoyed you've finally met a woman you can't get—" His hand covers my mouth. I bite his fingers. Cameras flash as we laugh at each other.

I'm not exactly ignoring Julian—we're supposed to be friends, after all, and he and Missy are seated across from us—but call me evil, I rather like the anger I catch simmering in his eyes on the rare occasions he's not clapping, eating, or making out with his fiancée. He's a good actor, too, and Missy's even better.

Nothing seems amiss with the power couple; in fact, they leave Matt and me in the dust in the PDA department over the course of the night.

I try not to feel anything, I really do.

Why is he with her?

Despite the PDA, I can't shake the weird feeling that they don't like each other much. Missy's adoring smiles ring false, her eyes on him full of calculation. And even while whispering in her ear, Julian's shoulders stay high and tense.

Whatever their deal is, their relationship is seriously fucked up.

"Stop staring," whispers Matt in my ear.

I wrench my gaze away and speak through my teeth, "I'm past done. Do I get my merit badge?"

Matt nods, sliding his palm over my shoulder. I fight the urge to throw his hand off by reminding myself he's trying to soothe me. After checking his watch, he meets my gaze.

"Ready for the finale?"

I nod and push back my chair. The performances are over, and around the massive ballroom people are beginning to mingle in earnest. There are intrigued glances being cast in my direction, some belonging to artists of my mother's generation who've been waiting until now to single me out.

I need to escape before the onslaught of well-meaning, decades-late condolences and walks down memory lane.

There's already been a handful of shocked, "You look just like Grace Cunningham!" exclamations, followed by my bland responses of, "She's my mother," and "Excuse me, I need to use the lady's room."

Matt and I stand.

"Goodnight all," he says jauntily, grabbing me suggestively by the waist. A chorus of goodbyes lifts from the ten-person table. I met them all but can't remember a single name. "Julian, can we send the limo back for you?"

I don't want to look at him—*don't look at him*—but I do.

Leonine eyes meet mine. "No problem," he says, smiling easily while his gaze sears through me. Marks me and dissects me. It's not a comfortable feeling.

"Great," says Matt, and then we're moving toward the exit.

Arm in arm, we walk fast to illustrate our impatience to tear each other's clothes off. Three unavoidable stops later—a camera, a famous producer, and a Grace Cunningham fan—we step into the warm night. Minutes later, we're in the limo heading to my house.

Sprawled opposite me, Matt groans. "You're fun and I like you a lot, Rose, but no offense, I don't want to kiss you ever again."

I snort and throw one of my treacherous high heels at him. I miss by four feet. "You're welcome."

Laughing, he sits up to loosen his bow tie. "Thank you. And I have to say, I think we pulled it off. Hopefully no one caught Julian glaring daggers at me all night."

I wince. "You're fun and I like you a lot, Matt, but no offense, when are we breaking up?"

"In a few months. Can you keep it in your pants that long?"

"Har har," I retort.

He grins. "Our publicist already has the statement written. Amicable parting, yadda yadda." Seeing my dismayed expression, he grins. "Don't worry, we only have to do this a few more times. Nothing as stressful as tonight. A few lunch dates, maybe a movie. Cool? We're already going with the slant that you're a private person and don't like media attention."

I do feel a little relieved. "Yeah, that's fine. I suppose I can put up with you a while longer."

Matt throws an empty plastic cup at me. "I'm charming, sexy, and funny! You should be grateful!"

I throw the cup back. "And fishing in the wrong pond if you want ego-stroking."

To the sound of Matt's laughter, I yawn and knuckle

my eyes. Eventually I remember the fake lashes, heaps of mascara, and dark eyeshadow.

"Damnit, I just racooned myself, didn't I?"

Matt mimics sealing his lips, eyes shining with suppressed laughter.

I arrive home without further incident. Matt offers to walk me to the door, but I decline (after we make sure no paparazzi have followed us). I wave from the curb as the limo pulls away, then let myself into the house and sink down against the closed door.

And there I sit, in the dark, until everything catches up and sinks in, sweeping aside the tattered remains of my acting skills. My fake smiles. My politeness. My big girl attitude and *Everything's fine, really,* and I can't fucking believe all he said to me tonight was *Thanks for doing this, Rose.*

Asshole.

A burst of primal *angermiseryfatigue* has me throwing one high heel, then the other, as hard as I can at the opposite wall. Then I sink back again, the dress sliding on wood until I'm sprawled in my foyer with my gown bunched around my waist, raccoon eyes, and a head full of Julian Ashburn.

The emotions boiling inside me aren't refined enough for lyrics. They're images of fantasy, chaotic and compulsive. Him abandoning Missy and hailing a cab. Racing to my house and finding me just as I am. There'd be apologies and melting, days-long kisses and *I don't love her I can't marry her*. Clothes would rip, and he'd take me against the wall because he can't wait and the bedroom's too far.

By the time the images run their course and fade away, I'm aching with need and near tears. And that's when the music comes, tickling the edges of my perception.

Love is good for music, Rose, but heartbreak is good for art.

"Shut up, mom," I tell her memory and push myself from the floor. I head into the kitchen, flipping on all the lights in further effort to banish her.

After pouring myself a glass of water, I grab my phone from the counter where it's been plugged in all day. The first notification I see isn't for the newest hundred Facebook notifications. It's a text from Julian, whose name I'd drunkenly altered last night to *J. Asshole*.

I need to see you

I laugh, not only because the message echoes my x-rated fantasy, but because reality can't possibly compete. Mostly, though, I laugh because *how dare he think I'm that kind of girl?*

Besides, I have other things to do. The music is rising in my veins, and like the brilliant Grace Cunningham once said, *Love kills art*. Or in this case, something more corporeal and sticky than love. I know a booty call when I see one.

No

I don't linger to see if he replies, but turn on the coffee maker to reheat this afternoon's pot, then head to my bedroom to get out of this fucking dress.

♪

By morning I have a new song. It's raw and unfinished, and chances are even when it's complete I'll never perform it. But I feel purged, which is all I really wanted.

I fall asleep sometime after dawn and wake up at two p.m. to my work alarm. A shower goes a long way to bringing my brain back online. Still, I'm moving more slowly than usual, and end up fifteen minutes late for my three o'clock shift.

As I walk in the back door, Owen's head pops out of the kitchen. He's trying to look concerned, but I can tell he's amused.

"I wasn't expecting you today," he says, approaching me cautiously.

I lift my brows. "Have I ever left you hanging?"

He shakes his head, then shrugs sheepishly. "Here's the thing, Rosie—the staff has been deflecting questions all day from wannabe music journalists. And there's a shifty guy with a camera camped across the street. Our regular customers are getting annoyed. Can you take another day off?"

I squeeze my eyes closed. "This keeps getting better and better." Opening one eye, I peer at my cousin. "I'll take the day, because I'm hungover on about ten different emotional and physical levels, but I'll be here tomorrow. I'll deal with the media. And if I can't, Breaking Giants will deal with it. Because *no way* is this shitshow messing with my café!"

Laughing, Owen grabs my arm and hustles me toward my office. "Try not to yell. The peanut gallery doesn't need anything else to gossip about."

I duck under his arm before he can push me through the doorway. "I'm not going in there. It's tainted. Can we switch?"

Owen rolls his eyes and follows me into his office, which is bigger and brighter, with two windows instead of one.

"I get it now," he says with mock gravity. "You staged all this drama for the sole purpose of snagging my office, which I won in a perfectly fair coin toss."

"Rigged," I mutter, but I'm kidding.

Flopping into his chair—it's nicer, too—I spin around a few times, bounce a little, then fiddle with a pen on his desk.

Owen crosses his arms over his chest, brow furrowing. "Rose. It's sunny and hot out. Go lay on a beach or some grass. And no, you can't get a start on next week's inventory."

"Why?" I whine. "Didn't Greta tell you I'm a little emotionally unstable right now? I got drunk *alone* the other night."

He snorts. "You're not unstable."

In a fair impression of Aunt Katherine, I say, "I crave harmony, and am therefore easily overwhelmed by sorrow and conflict."

He smirks. "She was bound to hit the mark eventually."

I throw the pen at him and pull my phone out of my back pocket. There are no new Facebook updates—because I deleted my account—but twenty-five missed calls from last night and this morning.

"Be warned, first thing tomorrow I'm changing my phone number. And making it private."

"I don't blame you," Owen says, then leans into the hallway as someone calls his name from the front. "Okay, I gotta go. Since you probably just woke up, I'll put in a food order for you and have someone bring it back. Then you're leaving, understood?"

"You're not the boss of me," I quip, but I'm smiling. "Thanks, coz."

"Sure thing."

When he's gone, I throw my feet onto his desk and stare out the nearby window, wondering if I dare go to a beach or park without shaving my head and wearing a mask. Realizing there's only one way to find out, I pull up a browser on my phone and type my name.

Ten minutes later, Christy knocks on the door with a bagged lunch and an Italian soda, and I'm still reading about myself with mixed awe and horror.

Moving around the desk, Christy peeks down at my phone. "Oh yeah, I read that one. Doesn't it say you're pregnant with Matt's baby or something?" When I don't immediately respond, she whispers, "Are you?"

Groaning, I close the browser and tuck my phone back in my pocket. "No, definitely not. We're not even —" I almost say *dating*, and substitute, "that serious."

Christy sighs dreamily. "You should totally have his babies."

I smile weakly and stand, collecting my keys and lunch. "Thanks for the delivery. I'll see you tomorrow?"

"Yep!" She chirps, flitting toward the door. "Hey, any chance you can get me an autographed CD when it drops?"

"Sure," I lie and make a beeline for my car.

10

CONFLICT OF INTEREST

When I arrive home, there's a gleaming black and chrome Harley parked in my driveway and a rockstar sitting on my front steps with his head in his hands. I'm not surprised; instead, a discomforting mix of satisfaction and anger stirs inside me. I want to drag him into the house and ravish him. I want to punch him in the face.

I park against the curb to avoid blocking his exit—because he's leaving immediately—and storm up the walkway. Julian looks up, unsmiling, and unfolds his delicious t-shirt and jean-clad frame to standing. Out of the corner of my eye, I notice Mrs. Thompson watering the flower pots on her porch two doors down and surreptitiously watching us.

Muttering, "Mrs. Thompson just saved your ass a beating," I brush past Julian and open the front door.

"Thank you, Mrs. Thompson," he murmurs, following me inside and closing the door.

Throwing my keys into a bowl in the kitchen and heading for the fridge, I ask without turning, "Would you like some water or a beer? Keep in mind that as soon as Mrs. Thompson goes inside, you're out of here. And you'd better hope no one else drove by and recognized you moping on my porch."

"I don't need anything, thanks," he says softly. "Rose, will you look at me? I have a few things to say, then I'll leave."

I close the fridge door and lean against it, crossing my arms over my chest. "Make it quick."

He mirrors my position, which isn't fair because *mmm tattoos.*

"I think you know I value my privacy." He waits for my nod. "I'm going to tell you something that no one outside my closest circle knows."

I lift a hand. "Seriously, don't. Plausible deniability."

He shakes his head. "I trust you not to repeat this."

I groan. "You don't even *know* me."

"I don't know your favorite color if that's what you're talking about, but my gut tells me you're a good person. Trustworthy. And given the wreckage I've caused in your life and the amends I need to make, there's something you should know first."

Wreckage.

Amends.

He sees the comprehension sweep over my face at the use of those words. Words I know well from being the daughter of an addict. Words used by people in recovery from alcohol and drug abuse.

A chill dances over my head, prickling my scalp. "How long have you been clean and sober?"

"Twelve years."

"Wow." I blink and do the math. "You were twenty?"

He nods, and I swallow back a tirade of prying questions, along with an utterly misplaced swell of grief for a mother who couldn't put together more than a month at a time without heroin.

Struggling for composure, I say, "That's amazing, Julian. A huge accomplishment."

He drags a hand through his hair. "Thanks, but, um, lately I haven't been doing too well. I haven't relapsed or anything, but I've been acting like an ass." He meets my gaze. "Especially where you're concerned."

"Amends accepted," I say, though my voice cracks a little. "Maybe you should, uh, call your sponsor?"

He cracks a smile at my fumbling guess. "I did. That's why I'm here. He said I had to tell you that it was really horrible of me, what I did to you. It was selfish to ask you to sing on the record then back out without an explanation. And kissing you while I'm engaged to Missy was... well, you were right when you said it was deplorable."

I shrug a shoulder, growing more uncomfortable by the second. The knowledge that Julian is an addict, even a recovering one, makes me want to crawl into a hole and hide. And cry. A lot. And maybe make appointments with twenty different shrinks.

"You're wondering if a part of why you're drawn to me is because I'm an addict like your mother," he says with eerie precision.

I don't even deny the being drawn bit, just shrug. "Maybe. But she never got clean. Not really. And you've been in recovery for twelve years. Obviously you're not the same."

I chew my lip and look around the kitchen, unable to meet his clear gaze.

"You can ask," he says softly.

My heart thumps hard, and I meet his eyes. "Was it heroin?"

He shakes his head. "Booze. I started drinking at fourteen when my dad split. Mom worked all the time, and a bunch of older kids lived in our apartment building. They felt bad for me and kind of took me under their collective wing. They'd let me have beers after school and would get me drunk on the weekends and make me talk to girls for them. Eventually, though, I was having daily cravings and begged and hustled for bottles. By the time I was sixteen, my mom couldn't ignore it anymore and dumped me in a state-run rehab."

The story keeps pouring out of him. No babbling, no shame, just honest facts about where he comes from. How he ran away from the rehab and crashed on couches, bounced through group homes, and lived on the streets until he was twenty. How he experimented with other drugs but always came back to alcohol. His overwhelming mental obsession and physical craving.

"I used to carry a little journal around with me," he says after a long pause. "I didn't know it then, but I was writing my first songs. Really, really bad songs."

I can't help smiling. "I'd pay money to read your bad poetry."

He grins, shaking his head. "Never gonna happen. I burned that crap a long time ago. Anyway, I was huddled up in a coffee shop downtown one day, trying to stay warm and dry for as long as possible before getting kicked out. There was this older man sitting at a table behind me. Long story short, he was my Eskimo."

I blink. "Your what?"

"It's something we say in the rooms. Your Eskimo is the person who introduces you to the idea that maybe, just maybe, there's a better way to live life than drunk and miserable. He took me to my first meeting and sponsored me until his death three years ago."

"I'm sorry," I say automatically.

He smiles softly. "Don't be. He saved my punk ass. Made me get my GED, go to college, and get a job so I could buy my first guitar."

"And the rest is history," I murmur.

"Yeah." He stares at the floor a few moments, then looks up at me through dark lashes. "Thanks for listening, Rose. I came here to try to make you feel better, but I think I got the better end of the deal. It's good to be reminded of where I come from, that everything I have today can vanish in a bottle."

I nod, even though I don't—can't—completely understand what he's saying.

"Thanks for trusting me," I reply, then clear my throat as discomfort seeps under my skin.

I wish I could say I feel better, too, but I don't. Knowing more about him has only complicated my feelings further. Even more than before, I want to ask him why the hell he's marrying Missy if he wants to kiss other girls. But it's none of my business.

None. Of. My. Business.

"Are you okay?" he asks haltingly.

"Yes." Then because I'm a stupid girl, I blurt, "You still haven't apologized for forcing me to make out with Matt."

Something shifts in his eyes, darkening them. I watch his internal struggle—hoping he loses, hating myself for it—but he rallies. "I made a mess, and you two had to clean it up for me. I'm sorry. I promise it won't happen again."

Well, there you have it.

"You're forgiven," I force out, then make a show of peering out the kitchen window. "Looks like Mrs. Thompson is gone, so you're clear."

Julian pushes off the counter and follows me into the foyer. I feel his closeness like an electric current on my skin, compounded by the knowledge that I'll never feel it again. Nor is it likely I'll see him again except at a concert. A safe fifty feet and a crowd of bodies between us.

"Rose," he breathes.

I realize I've been frozen with my hand on the doorknob for an inappropriate length of time.

"Sorry," I choke, and open the door a crack to peek outside. "No cameramen hiding in bushes. Good to go."

I step out of the way and open the door enough for him to slip out. He moves slowly enough for me to savor his scent, and pauses halfway across the threshold. Our shoulders brush, layers of clothing doing nothing to quell my body's instant reaction. *Wantneednow.*

"Listen to the B-side of the next single."

I stare uncomprehendingly at him. His lips compress, sunlight catching in his whiskey eyes.

"The song is yours. Just… I'm sorry about everything. You're amazing, Rose. The timing… I wish—"

The timing is inopportune.

Desire is gone in a flash. My low laughter surprises the hell out of Julian, who frowns in confusion.

"You know what I wish? That you hadn't said that." I've kept it together long enough. Too long, it seems, because I suddenly don't give a shit anymore. "Congratulations on your forthcoming nuptials. Have a great life."

I kick his boot out of the doorway and slam the door in his face. And listen with an empty heart to his footsteps walking away.

11

BEWARE THE FORTUNE TELLERS

Tuesday afternoon, three weeks and a few days after Julian's visit to my house, I'm cleaning the bakery case while The National croons through the café speakers.

The beautiful weather has held strong. Sunlight streams through Tullamore's tall windows, filling the space with diffused radiance. Ten or so patrons sit around tables or read in stuffed armchairs. Everyone's savoring the peaceful afternoon.

Less than a week after the photo-fiasco and charity event, the media forgot about me. Although a few pictures of Matt and I have shown up on gossip sites—I'm particularly fond of the one taken during our chili-dog eating competition—apparently our *dates* haven't been newsworthy. A visit to a tattoo parlor (for him), a bookstore trip (for me), and the newest action flick have rounded out our charade. They've also had the unexpected side effect of cementing our friendship.

Matt's good company. I kind of want to keep him. A joint custody sort of thing—Julian can be the primary friend, and I'd get him every other weekend. When I told Matt my idea, he laughed so hard he almost drove us off the road.

Unfortunately, the public's memory is longer than the medias'. Every few days people (young women, mostly) wander into Tullamore and ask indiscreet questions about me, Matt, or Julian. What these occasions have taught me is that not only is my staff protective, but our regular customers are, as well. No one's been asked to leave, but each time it happens someone makes it clear that my private life is private and questions aren't welcome.

I love my job.

Breaking Giants' new single came out Friday. Greta, a vinyl-junkie, bought it and says its amazing. I don't ask about the B-Side. Even though I want to. Really, really want to.

"Hey, Rose, can you watch the front for a minute?" asks Allison. "I'm going to run to the little girl's room."

"No problem."

I give the glass inside the cabinet one more wipe, then straighten and wander over to the registers with my rag. The counter is already clean, but I wipe it anyway because The National is singing about heart-break and I feel heartbroken. Over someone I don't really know, not sure I want to know, but can't stop thinking about.

Ugh.

"Can I order something?" asks an amused voice.

I realize I'm frantically scrubbing a spot on the counter that's been there more than a year. Flushing, I look up at the man standing opposite me. He's trying hard not to laugh, but his dark eyes are twinkling.

"Yes, sorry, I was…uh…"

"I get it. That damned spot just won't come out."

Surprised laughter bursts out of me. "I didn't kill the king, I swear."

He chuckles. "Lucky me. Usually that joke falls flat."

I shrug. "I majored in English Lit a million years ago. Lady Macbeth is a pretty memorable type of crazy." I pause in mock solemnity. "Wait, are you calling me crazy?"

"Nope," he replies with an easy grin. "Just a college professor making bad jokes."

I assess him and decide he can't be more than mid-thirties. "At U-Dub?"

His brows lift. "Should I be insulted or flattered by your skepticism?"

"Flattered," I say lightly. "All my professors were old and stodgy." Seeing a couple coming up to the register behind him, I get back to business. "What would you like, *professor?*"

He winces. "Elijah, please. How about a large drip with room, and…" he glances at the empty bakery case.

"Sorry, they're in the kitchen right now. What are you feeling? Cake? Cookie?"

"Surprise me," he says, and I look at him quickly, something in his tone tickling my female intuition. He's fiddling with the cup of table markers and pulls out one of the tarot cards. Surprise lights his features. "Prince of Swords."

I laugh to hide my immediate disquiet. "Yeah, that's a popular one."

For attractive men to pick out in front of me.

Elijah grins. "You know, I went to a fortune teller one time when I was in college. She said this was my card—it was some weird deck she was using. I've never seen it since."

"Thoth Tarot," I say weakly.

"Ah, that's it! Anyway, don't judge me, but I might have been drunk at the time. Not sure what the card signifies, but this guy looks impressive, right?"

I try to come up with something to say, but end up staring blankly at him until his brows pinch with concern.

"Are you all right? You're white as a sheet."

"Y-yes," I stammer, then give him an order total. "Let me get your coffee."

By the time I pour his coffee and return, Allison's back and taking care of the couple.

Elijah hands me cash and asks softly, "Did I say something to offend you?"

"Not at all," I say quickly. I give him his change and smile brightly. "I'll be out in a minute with your surprise pastry."

"Thanks." He glances down, then looks up with another smile. "Rose."

When he's gone, Allison gives me the side-eye. "He was flirting. Obviously he doesn't know you're dating a world-famous musician."

I mumble something inarticulate that I hope sounds like, "No, he wasn't," before heading into the kitchen to pick a pastry.

As I peer into various bakery boxes, I think about surprise treats, which is kind of a fun idea. I wonder if it would be marketable to have wrapped pastries on the counter, maybe at a special price, to move more bakery items during evening hours. I make a mental note to talk to Owen about it, then pull out one of my favorite muffins for Elijah—Blackberry, Lemon, and Thyme— heat it a little, then plate it.

I know—*know*—that Aunt Katherine and her mystical

mumbo-jumbo must, for sanity's sake, be taken with a grain of salt.

Yours will come, Rose.

Maybe not this *Prince of Swords, hmm?*

And I can't help wonder—is Elijah the English Lit professor the *right* Prince of Swords? Milliseconds later I give myself a mental slap and head out to deliver the muffin. And maybe I'll talk to Elijah for a few minutes just to… see where it leads. Not because of any Prince of Swords hoodoo, but because he's attractive and nice, and obviously intelligent.

Plus, I've never tried out the theory that the easiest way to get over a man is to get under a new one.

As I reach the main café, I pass Allison, who's chatting with a customer near the empty stage. Seeing me, she veers in my direction, pausing long enough to murmur, "Sorry, Rose. I was waaay off about that guy." Giggling, she continues past me to the registers.

I look across the café and see professor Elijah seated near the windows, holding hands with his boyfriend.

♩

"You really need to get laid," says Greta, earning a raised eyebrow from the seamstress crouched before her in a cloud of white tulle.

I don't look up from my phone. "How long should I wait before reactivating my Facebook account? Another week? Three years?"

"Are you even listening to me?" demands Bridezilla.

I give her my full attention. "Yes. I need to get laid. Blah blah. This isn't news to me. I almost asked a gay man on a date today."

She and the seamstress giggle, despite this being the third time they've made me repeat what happened.

At length, Greta composes herself. "When are you and Matt, um, you know…"

"Not for another couple of months, I think," I grumble.

"You can be discreet," she offers.

"Find me a hottie to be discreet with, and I'm all over it. Him. Whatever."

"Stop making the bride laugh," says the seamstress, smiling around the pins in her mouth.

"Yes, ma'am."

For the next thirty minutes, I shelve my personal drama and focus on the bride. The wedding is three and a half months away, and most of our conversations are beginning to revolve around the Big Day. I don't mind. Seeing Greta happy makes me happy, and I want to do everything possible to make sure things run smoothly for her. Even it if means wearing a lilac bridesmaid dress.

After the fitting, we head downtown to our favorite sushi restaurant and stuff our faces with rolls. Greta gets buzzed on Saki and rambles unendingly about a variety of wedding topics like RSVPs, catering, decorations, and the difficulty they're having deciding on a DJ or live band.

Halfway into a one-sided discussion on the merits of guestbooks, I feel a hesitant tap on my shoulder. Turning, I look up at a girl in her late teens or early twenties, trendy and pretty, with hair alternating between lavender and blonde.

She blushes, and stammers out, "R-Rose?"

Here we go.

"Yes," I say stiffly. "But—"

A CD case is thrust toward me. "Will you sign this?"

I stare blankly at my CD until Greta elbows me in the ribs. "Sure, yes," I blurt, "but I don't have a pen."

Lavender-Blonde hands me a black sharpie. Feeling like I'm in the Twilight Zone, I scrawl my name on the CD and give it back to her.

Beaming, she clutches it to her chest. "I can't tell you how much your music has helped me. Do you think you'll make another album anytime soon?"

My mouth opens and closes soundlessly.

Casting me a knowing smile, Greta answers, "She's

always writing music, so I'd say you can look for a new one by the end of the year."

"Awesome." She gives me a shy wave. "See you at open mic on Friday!"

Then she's gone, and Greta's gleeful cackle results in several dubious glances in our direction.

I shake my head in bafflement. "Oh my God, did that just happen?"

As Greta celebrates with another Saki, and our conversation returns to floral arrangements and potential reception dresses, I fight a growing urge to break the unspoken code of silence and tell a certain someone what just happened. Because I know he'll be tickled. And proud.

But really I just want to hear his voice and see if maybe there's a space inside him that still thinks about me. And wonders.

"You should call Greg!" says Greta.

A twist of self-loathing turns in my chest as I nod and promise to call him. Greg is who I should have thought of first. Not Julian.

Never Julian.

What the hell is wrong with me?

I shelve the question—and my unhealthy urges—as I drive Greta home. She invites me in for dessert, but I decline with excuses she doesn't buy but knows me well enough not to question. Owen greets her warmly at the front door. As I back out of the driveway, they wave and disappear inside hand in hand.

When I get home, I head straight for a pint of chocolate fudge ice cream. Four bites in, though, the urge becomes an itch. A burn.

Fuck it.

I text him.

> I was asked to autograph a CD today

Twenty seconds later, his reply comes.

> Rose? Your number is restricted. Send it to me.

I type the numbers and hit Send, my fingers shaking. I'd totally forgotten that I changed my phone number.

What if he's tried to call me?

Don't be an idiot, he hasn't called.

The phone rings in my hand.

12

SWEET UNDERTOW

*T*he Caller ID says *J. Asshole*. My heart tries to crawl out my mouth and down my spine. I sit there, staring at the name for at least four rings.

Answerthegoddamnphone Rose.

"Hello?"

"Hi," he says, and when I don't say anything else, he clears his throat. "Tell me about the autograph."

"Oh, uh… Greta and I were eating downtown, and someone tapped my shoulder. It doesn't happen much anymore, but I thought it was going to be a 'No Comment, leave me alone' moment." I take a breath. "But instead, this girl hands me my CD and asks me to sign it."

"Did you stare at her with your mouth open?" he asks lightly. "I did, the first time."

"Totally. Greta had to elbow me. Then I signed it, and she… she said my songs have helped her."

"Best feeling ever, huh?"

I feel myself grinning, full of delayed excitement and energy. "Yes. It took a while to sink in."

Julian laughs. "You're climbing the walls right now, aren't you?"

I pace from the living room to the kitchen, then down the hallway to my bedroom and back. "Yep. What the hell do you do when you feel like this?"

There's a weighted pause. "Something physical."

Air clogs my throat at the dark tone. Sensation rockets down, his voice sliding straight to my center.

Realizing I'm not saying anything, and he's not saying anything, I blurt, "Maybe I'll work on some songs."

"Good idea," he says, dragging in an audible breath. "Don't go yet, though. How are you?"

Before I can filter myself, I say, "I was flirting with and almost asked out a gay man today."

There's a small pause before Julian loses his shit, laughing hard and loud, complete with snorts and gasps for air.

"Are you serious?" he stops long enough to ask. Before I can reply, he falls into helpless laughter again.

"Glad I can provide comic relief," I grumble, but I'm smiling. I can't help it. The sound of his unreserved laughter, and the knowledge that I caused it, fills me with bubbly warmth.

"Okay, I'm calming down," he vows, taking deep breaths. "Whew. Thanks for that, Rose."

"Whatever," I snark. "So, how are you?"

"I'm… good."

Was that a hesitation? Did I imagine it?

If we were better friends—or friends at all—I would call him on it. But since I have no earthly clue where we stand, I say nothing.

In the following silence, my thoughts ping-pong amidst *Are we friends?* and *Can boys and girls who want to see each other naked be friends?* and *NakedmmmJulian.*

Then the subject of my fantasy says, "Actually, I'm kinda fucked up."

All thoughts vanish as my brain and body activate nuclear winter.

I must make a sound of dismay, because Julian immediately says, "No, no. Jesus, I'm sorry, Rose, I wasn't thinking how that would sound. I'm not loaded. Just having some creative issues."

A universe of tension and fear pours out of me with my sigh.

"Hey," he says softly, "are you okay?"

My libido is now six feet underground; logic runs cold and clear in my veins.

"Yeah, sorry about the freakout."

"It's my fault." He pauses. "If you ever want to talk about your mom, I'm here, okay?"

I laugh shakily. "I appreciate that Julian, but I really shouldn't have texted you."

"Don't say that. I'm glad you did. After you slammed that door in my face, I wasn't sure I'd talk to you again. And I—" He swallows back the rest of the words.

My fingers spasm on my phone. "I think I should go."

"Wait," he says urgently. "Did you listen to it yet?"

The B-Side.

"No," I whisper.

"Maybe you shouldn't," he murmurs, and the gravelly words instantly bring my libido roaring back from the dead. "I know what you're going to say, but I need to ask. Do you think we can be friends, Rose Cunningham?"

"Do *you?*" I ask incredulously.

"I know I want to see you again."

I slide down the hallway wall until my ass meets the floor. Closing my eyes, I wait for my heartbeat to get bored with my vagina and come back to my chest.

"Rose?"

"You're engaged," I whisper brokenly.

"Yes, but it's not… it's complicated. And I'm a deplorable human being, just like you said. I'd explain everything if I could, but I can't. I don't know how to stop thinking about you. Rose? I can't stop thinking about you."

Come over right now.

Nownownow.

With every scrap of willpower I possess, I tell him, "I can't do this."

"I know," he murmurs after a moment, "you're ten times the person I am."

"I'm not a cheater," I say, and it emerges sharp and bitter, tainted with childhood memories.

"I know," he repeats. "And it probably won't mean anything to you, but neither am I. This situation isn't—"

My brain hits the red. "Then why are you *marrying* her, for Christ's sake?"

"She's two months pregnant."

My head drops against the wall hard enough for stars to paint my vision. "Oh," I say, then—because *fuckthissucks*—I start laughing. Then, because I'm *easily overwhelmed by sorrow and conflict*, my eyes fill with tears.

"Rose, I… I don't think the baby's mine. In fact, I'm pretty fucking sure it's not."

"What?" I breathe. "Why don't you get a paternity test?"

"That's one of the complicated parts. First, she's in L.A., and I'm here, and Missy…" He hisses in frustration. "Shit, I'm really sorry, but I can't tell you more. I trust you, but this is her stuff, and—"

"It's fine," I say, sounding miraculously normal. "It's for the best. And I think it's safe to say we can't be friends, Julian. Because eventually I'm going to invite you over and bad things will happen."

He draws a sharp breath, and because he's my kryptonite, he says darkly, "Bad, bad things. Do you think about me, Rose?"

OhmyGod. Say NO.

"Yes."

He hums in satisfaction. "I think about you. The way you smell and taste. The little noises you make when you're turned on. I think about your hair in my mouth and on my pillow."

Magnetic, seductive voice, wielded without hesitance or mercy. *If I don't stop him now...*

"Julian—" I gasp.

"I think about that kiss, your legs wrapped around my waist, and I get instantly hard. Anytime, anywhere. I can be sitting in a fucking boardroom, and all I can think about is marking every inch of you my teeth and tongue."

I jerk involuntarily against the wall, my body going molten hot. I'm pulsing, careening toward a sparkling edge, and *I'm not even touching myself.* All it would take is his voice.

Holy shit.

"I made someone bring me your CD. I listen to it at

night." He pauses. "That throaty little hum you do on *Excess* gets me every time."

WHAT.

"You..." I start, shaking and poised to implode. I can't say it, though.

"Yes, I do," he says, with an edge of savagery. "Do you?"

My hand moves of its own volition, skating down my aching breasts to the juncture of my thighs. The added pressure, already intense from the seam of my jeans, hits *right there.* I try and fail to muffle my soft cry as I throb in ecstasy from his voice and the vivid mental picture of him stroking himself to my music.

When the ringing in my ears subsides, I hear Julian's harsh breathing.

"Tell me not to come over," he says sharply. "Tell me, or I'm getting on my bike right now."

Every cell in my body screams *YES,* but I whisper, "No, you can't. Please, Julian, I—"

"Okay," he sighs, and again, just a whisper, "Okay. Fuck. I should go." Self-deprecating laugh. "Kind of a mess over here."

My eyes burn. "I'm sorry."

"Don't be. Don't ever be sorry. Goodnight, Rose."

"Goodnight, Julian," I whisper, but he's already hung up.

♫

FRESHLY SHOWERED and curled in bed with a cup of chamomile tea, feeling warm and loose and surprisingly not conflicted, I open my laptop and search for the B-Side of Breaking Giants' latest single.

I don't find the song itself, but the lyrics pop up on more than a few private blogs as well as the band's major fan sites. My tea forgotten, I read Julian's words to me.

Fading footsteps like rain,
They wash out and away
The solace of night
And the promise of day

And here in the space between breaths I see
What could have become of you and me

Your voice in my ear
Or maybe my mind
A rose in a garden
I've waited to find

And here in the space between breaths I see
What could have become of you and me

And I want you to know
That I haven't let go
Of your laughter and eyes
Your sweet undertow

Maybe someday we'll find
Between breaths we'll see
What will become of you and me

Maybe someday we'll find,
What belongs to you and me.

I call Greta immediately. When she picks up, I demand, "Why didn't you say anything about the B-Side?"

She's quiet for a few beats. "I didn't think you'd want to know. Aw, Rosie, are you crying?"

"No," I sniffle, wiping at my eyes. "I shouldn't tell you this, but Missy is pregnant, and he doesn't think the baby's his, but for some reason she won't get a paternity test, and I think he's trying to do the right thing, only it's not the right thing—or maybe it is. How can I feel like this for someone I don't know?"

"Good Lord," she says. "Shit, Rosie, that's a train wreck."

"Tell me something I don't know."

She sighs. "Baby drama aside, to answer your question I think sometimes when we meet people we just *know* them. You don't have to be friends for years or date for months. Call it fate, or luck, or in the case of you and Julian, extremely bad timing. But obviously you're feeling more than just physical attraction. You've never been this bent out of shape over a man before."

I think of what draws me most to him, and she's right, it's not his body. It's his mind, his music. The complexity, the passion, the danger he represents. And the babbling, the panic attacks, the introversion and self-awareness. His daily triumph over the disease that killed my mother. His strength and moral compass—the compass I unknowingly knocked sideways.

"What a mess," I whisper.

"I don't know," muses Greta, "seems to me it's just life. It's easy to judge Julian—hell, I was first in line calling him a scumbag—but sometimes shit is just complicated. I'm not saying he's excused of all blame. He made some mistakes. But he's human, and we all make them. And that song. Whew. It's acoustic, and the emotion his voice is freaking unreal."

"Can I borrow the record? I only read the lyrics."

"Absolutely, but have a box of tissues handy."

"Ugh," I grunt, then chew my lips. "Greta? If I tell you something, will you take it to your grave? I'm serious. Not even Owen can know."

She pauses, considering my question seriously, which

is one of the reasons I love her so much. If she doesn't think she can do it, she won't lie.

Finally, she asks, "Is it something about Julian specifically? That doesn't affect your safety or the safety of anyone else?"

"Yes."

"Okay. What is it?"

I take a deep breath. "He's a recovering alcoholic. He got sober at twenty after a jacked-up childhood."

Greta's breath whooshes out of her; she gives a startled laugh. "Oh my God, it makes so much freaking sense."

I frown. "What does?"

"Don't take this the wrong way, but given your own childhood, it's no wonder you relate to him. In a way, you're both recovering from the effects of addiction."

I snort. "Okay, Dr. Laura."

"Hey, my soon to be mother-in-law is psychic. Maybe it's rubbing off on me. Should I start reading the cards and communing with spirits?"

I laugh. "God, no!"

"But seriously, I did mean what I said."

"I know," I say softly. "And you're probably on to something. I'm not sure it's a good something, though."

"Meh," she says, and I know her tiny shoulders just shrugged. "Like I said, it's complicated. But complicated doesn't necessarily mean bad."

"It did for my parents," I mutter.

"Yeah," she concedes, then yawns hugely. "Maybe try not to worry about it too much. Focus on you, honey. Do what you love, and the universe will take care of the rest."

"Thanks, Aunt Kath—I mean Greta."

She laughs. "Get some sleep. Talk tomorrow?"

"Yes. Love you."

"Love you, too."

13

THE JIG IS UP

Wednesday is my day off. I celebrate by staying in bed all morning—except for trips to the kitchen for coffee. As I luxuriate in the peace and quiet, distractedly flipping through a book I've been trying to finish for months, the patch of sky through my bedroom window becomes increasingly distracting. It's a cloudless sapphire, whispering tantalizing promises of a beautiful day.

Greta and Owen are working, and though I consider it, I decide not to call Greg. He told me he needed time, so regardless of my wishes that's what I'm going to give him.

After some thought, I throw on a bikini, cover it with a tank top and cutoffs, and call the one person I know will lay around in the sunshine with me. We've talked about it often enough. I also know she isn't working, because I'm the one who writes her work schedule.

But as I scroll to Allison's name, my phone lights up with an incoming call.

Matt Sullivan.

Brows lifting, I answer, "Hi Mattie."

"Bleh. I hate that."

"I know," I say sweetly. "I hope you're calling to break up with me."

"Actually, I am."

I pause in my bedroom doorway. "Really?"

He laughs. "Can you sound *any* happier about it?"

I grin. "Nope!"

"You're hell on my ego, Rose. I'm actually calling for another reason, too. I need a favor."

I shake my head even though he can't see it. "No. Nope. I'm maxed out on doing you favors, buddy."

"Pleeease?" he whines. "I think you'll actually like this one."

"What is it? I'm heading out to find a sunny patch somewhere, so make it quick."

"Perfect!" he yells, making me wince and pull the phone from my ear. "I'm having a barbecue at my place today and here's the thing—I need you to break up with me at the barbecue."

"Why?" I ask skeptically. "I thought we weren't doing anything public."

"It's not public. Close friends. I, um, want this girl to know I'm single."

Sighing, I sink into a chair at the kitchen table. "Matt, you're pretty much the friend I never wanted."

He laughs, then covers the phone to answer a question. A few moments later, he tells me, "Julian says he'll leave if you don't want him here."

Breathe, just breathe.

"No, uh, that's fine. He's fine. I mean—"

Matt cackles. "You guys are freaking ridiculous. So will you do this for me, Rosie Posie?"

I screw up my nose at his choice of nickname revenge. "Break up with you? With pleasure. Can I throw a plate at you or is this a teary-hugs kind of goodbye?"

"I don't care, just make it obvious," he says, then continues in a lower, oddly vulnerable tone, "I've liked this girl for a while now, and I think seeing me in a relationship has, you know, made her think I might be capable of commitment."

I hold my tongue with monumental effort, and ask only, "Is this girl over the age of twenty?"

"Yeah," he says, confused. "She's twenty-nine."

"Then she's a woman, Mattie-poo."

To my shock, he says, "You're right. Absolutely right. Rose, you need to stay my friend forever. You're like a little Buddha."

"Stop it," I say, fighting a smile. "Where do you live?"

He rattles off an address and says the barbecue is underway and to get there *stat* because the love of his life just walked in. I tell him I'll be there soon and hang up, then stare at my bedroom floor until my body stops feeling electrocuted.

A bundle of nervous energy settles in my belly and hardens. Changing my clothes ten times doesn't help. In the end, I put back on my original outfit because *screwitwhocares* and maybe I'll head to a beach afterward.

Putting Matt's address into my phone, I follow directions east on 520, across glittering Lake Washington and into the Clyde Hill neighborhood. It takes a little over twenty minutes from Fremont, which isn't nearly enough time to process my anxiety.

When my phone informs me I've arrived at my destination, I throw Siri a curve ball and drive past the house, meandering around the neighborhood for another ten minutes.

The homes that rise up amidst tall trees and lush landscaping are all gorgeous and huge, and the neighborhood's aesthetic is close enough to where I grew up that it feels nostalgic.

Floating in memories—for once, not bad ones—I drive back to Matt's place, a giant craftsman tucked at the end of a long, tree-shaded driveway.

"What is it with these guys and small parties," I mutter, parking behind ten other cars. Despite my whining, though, I'm kind of relieved to know it won't be *that* intimate. Like Matt, his future wife, Julian, his future wife, and me.

God I hope Missy isn't in town.

With that thought, I lock my car (probably unnecessarily) and walk up the driveway to the front door. As I'm debating the merits of doorbell versus knocking, a car door slams behind me.

A cheery voice calls, "It should be open!"

I turn, smiling at the woman striding toward me with a case of water in her arms and heavy-looking grocery bags clutched in the fingers of both hands.

"Here, let me help you," I say, meeting her halfway and reaching for the case of water.

"You're a lifesaver, thanks." She adjusts the bags, blowing pale brown hair out of her eyes. "Of course the guys organized a barbecue but forgot to buy condiments."

I laugh, eyeing the canvas bags. "That's a lot of condiments."

She winks. "There might be some eclairs, chips and salsa, and veggie burgers in here."

"A woman after my own heart," I say, grinning. "I'm Rose, by the way."

"Oh, I know who you are," she says, giving a throaty

laugh. "You're the poor woman the media put through the grinder last month."

I wince. "Yeah, that's me."

Clear, cornflower blue eyes fix on my face. "I think Matt's heart was in the right place, wanting to protect Julian, but I also think it's time Jules puts on his big-boy pants. You know what I mean?"

I flush, my mouth falling open. "I—no, I don't know what you mean."

If I've ever wondered, now it's official: I don't have a career in poker ahead of me.

"I'm Melody," says the sweet-faced brunette with x-ray vision. Her eyes roll with self-effacing humor. "I know, the name kinda set me up for being friends with musicians. My mom was a hippie."

"My mom named me after a tattoo on her ankle, so I hear that."

Melody and I share a giggle of camaraderie, and we're still laughing when the front door opens. Matt's eyes widen to almost comic proportions, veering between us. And the way he jerks forward, grabbing the bags from Melody's arms—while leaving the case of water in mine—gives me all the answer I need as to who he's trying to woo. And I definitely approve.

"What are you guys doing out here?" he asks, backpedaling into the house. "I mean, come in, please.

Uh, Rose, meet Melody. Melody… um, meet my girl-friend, Rose."

"We're way past that," says Melody cheekily.

I take in Matt's expression and share a meaningful glance with Melody. "He looks so scared," I whisper.

"What the hell, Rose?" he hisses.

Laughing, I tell him, "We can cut the act. I didn't tell her, but she knows."

I never imagined I'd be alive and present to witness Matt Sullivan, rockstar poster boy, utterly at a loss for words.

To my forever-glee, he blushes and stammers out, "Okay. Well, okay then. I'll take these to the kitchen. Thanks. Talk to you guys later."

He books it down a hallway.

"Oh man," I tell the woman beside me, "he's got it bad for you."

She winks. "I'm not done making him work for it."

A full belly-laugh escapes me, then dwindles swiftly to a wheeze as Julian turns a nearby corner and jerks to a stop. In a white t-shirt and jeans cut off below the knees, he looks like something I want to cuddle with on a blanket in the shade on a sunny afternoon.

Or whenever, wherever.

"Hi, Julian," chirps Melody, then my new friend-turned-traitor grabs the case of water from me and disappears down the hallway after Matt.

"Rose."

I swallow. "Julian."

His gaze devours me, lingering on my bare legs and the strings of my bikini top, visible beneath the straps of my tank.

My face is on fire, my knees weak, and all I can do is squeeze out a helpless, "Damnit."

His eyes snap to mine, then close. "I'm sorry." He swipes hands down his face, then peers at me over the tips of his fingers. "I'm going to stay at least ten feet away from you today. Okay?"

"Sounds smart," I say, nodding, while my inner-demon reminds me: *last night this man got you off with nothing but his voice.* The memory zings through me, teasing my core with aftershocks. Or pre-shocks, because if he keeps staring at me like this...

"I have a great idea," he says hastily. "Let's go find everyone else."

And because I have to know, I ask, "Is Missy here?"

His eyes narrow, melancholy clouding them. "No," he murmurs. "Matt and I wouldn't do that to you. Not again."

"Gee, thanks," I say, breaking eye contact to stare at the floor. My momentary lust has vanished, leaving raw nerves behind.

Why am I here?

Because of Julian.

Always Julian.

"I think… I'm gonna go."

He takes a step toward me. "What? I thought… That is—"

"Melody already knows, so it doesn't make sense for me to stay."

I don't belong here. With you.

"Please, stay."

I roll my eyes to the ceiling, blinking hard. The roller-coaster that has been my life the last few months is vividly clear to me. As is the truth that nothing has happened *to me*. I've been a willing participant.

I've developed a taste for danger, and I know that before long, I'm going to forget things that are important to me—like fidelity—and throw myself at Julian Ashburn. He is a craving beyond my control. A mental obsession.

"I'm addicted to you, Julian," I say, looking at him.

His eyes widen, then narrow, dark with promises of his body over mine. I clear my throat and take a cautious step back.

"What do they say in recovery? Something about the only cure being total abstinence?" He nods slowly, and I swallow. "We both know this is going nowhere. I have to get over you. And to do that I need to get away from you."

He takes another step, and my spine hits the front

door. I clutch the knob in my hand, ready to turn and bolt.

"And if I ended things with Missy?" he asks softly, tensely. "What then, Rose?"

I laugh humorlessly. "And started dating your lead guitarist's fake ex-girlfriend?"

He shakes his head. "I don't care about that."

Another step. He's close enough now that I can see his pulse hammering in his throat, racing to catch mine. And his eyes… ah, I can't even meet them, the look in them is so raw. And I know the question he's going to ask before he asks it.

"Would you be able to handle me being an addict like your mother? The fear that will always linger in the back of your mind? The fear that I'll drink again?" His head bends toward mine, lips grazing my ear as he whispers, "Or is all you really want to fuck me and get me out of your system? Because there's a bedroom ten feet away and I'm ready to go. That's all it has to be."

If there's a feeling more profound than shock, that's what slices through me at his words. Or maybe it hurts so much because it's a cocktail of *shock-disgust-arousal.*

Disgust wins.

"You're a real piece of work," I snarl, then tear open the front door and run down the driveway.

I don't look back, don't see if he follows, just jump in my car and get the hell out of there.

14

BRACE YOURSELVES

Could I? Could I be with an addict, even a recovering one? I don't know.

I don't fucking know.

When I drive into the cemetery parking lot, I don't question why my brain and body brought me here. I simply park and walk on autopilot to the gravesite I've only visited once, at thirteen years old, when the bodies were put into the ground.

PATRICK AND GRACE CUNNINGHAM

THEY LOVED MUSIC

THEIR DAUGHTER

AND EACH OTHER.

It's been over fourteen years since I threw the first handful of wet earth into their graves, and the ground shows no sign of its long-ago invasion. Crisp, mown grass covers the space before the massive headstone. There are several vases of whimsically arranged, partially wilted wildflowers resting at the stone's base; I easily recognize Aunt Katherine's handiwork.

'Find your mother! Find her, Rose!'

What if I had? What if I'd woken at the first ring of the house phone and answered? Would I have been able to reach my mother in time? Would I have dialed 911? Would paramedics have been able to shock her heart back to life?

I'll never know.

One evening when I was seventeen, Aunt Katherine, drunk on wine and sad, told me she'd dialed 911 herself when no one answered at our house the first time. But the dispatcher wouldn't send an ambulance because in her terror, Katherine hadn't thought to lie—she'd told the dispatcher she'd dreamed her twin's death.

I know she carries that guilt with her, just as I carry mine for not waking up sooner and answering the phone.

And my father... I'll never know, either, exactly what happened. What he was thinking. Why he carried my mother's unconscious body to his car and started the engine with the garage door closed.

The coroner reported no alcohol or drugs in his system, but he did have a sizable bump on his head.

Blood was found on a corner of the kitchen counter. It was determined he'd fallen while carrying my mother and suffered a concussion, and once in the car, had passed out before he could open the garage.

Why hadn't he called 911? Was it because my mother was already dead? Did he really pass out or was the thought of living without her too much?

I've mostly come to terms with the fact that the answers to these questions will never surface. But sometimes, like today, the old scars burn.

When I feel a presence beside me, and smell Aunt Katherine's perfume, I'm not the least bit surprised.

"Let me guess, the spirits told you where I was."

She chuckles softly. "No, actually. I come every Wednesday around this time."

I then notice the fresh flowers in her hands. Blinking my dry eyes into focus on her face, I ask, "Can I help?"

She smiles softly, eyes glistening as she hands me a bouquet.

Afterward, we sit for a while against the sun-warmed back of the headstone. I don't feel any pressure to speak and neither does she. We sit with our eyes closed, faces tilted to the sunlight. The silence is encompassing and restorative. Or maybe it's being close to my parents—the memory of them—and finally being able to admit that the inscription is true.

They loved music and each other.

And me.

In time, Katherine stirs and invites me home with her. I follow in my car, and we spent the rest of the afternoon in her small backyard drinking lemonade and playing a raucous game of croquet. And when the sun dips low, sending chills along my sunburned shoulders, we head inside to make linguini and salad.

We eat by candlelight, talking and laughing about nothing, though with the darkness a new awareness rises. That old scar flares, itching with painless heat.

Setting down my fork, I finally ask my psychic aunt the question that haunts me the most. "Did he commit suicide?"

Katherine lowers her glass of wine to the table. "No, Rosie. No. He merely panicked and was trying to get her to the hospital. He slipped in the kitchen and knocked himself out. When he came to, Grace was... she was gone. He couldn't accept it and got her into the car. Her seatbelt was on."

She frowns, staring into a world only she can see. Tears fill her eyes and roll silently down her cheeks. "He fought to stay conscious and got the car started. He was thinking of you. That he couldn't let you lose your mother."

The old scar splits open.

I sob.

For a long time.

Hours, it feels like.

Katherine helps me to the living room couch and holds me the entire time. Rocking me, murmuring, singing… all the things a mother does for her hurt child. Things my mother did for me when I was small. Before she started using. Before she disappeared into her addiction. Before the screaming fights, and the affairs, and the week-long disappearances.

"Let it all out," whispers Katherine.

And I do.

♪

MY SCHEDULE at Tullamore rotates weekly, but very rarely do I work an opening shift. I'm not what you'd call a morning person. But Owen has a doctor's appointment Thursday morning, so my alarm jolts me awake at the ungodly hour of four-thirty after a few restless hours of sleep.

Stumbling around in the near-dark, I throw on black leggings and a t-shirt and yank my curls into a bun. There's nothing to be done about my puffy eyes, and putting on makeup beyond moisturizer is simply not happening.

The streets are clogged even at five a.m., but the new dawn is stunning, streaks of brilliant white piercing the clouds and granting the world below rare clarity.

When I pull into the parking lot, Allison is waiting outside the back door. Unlike me, she's used to the hour. Behind retro tortoiseshell glasses, her brown eyes are clear, and her normally curly auburn hair is straight and shiny.

"Seriously?" I grumble at her. "You had enough time to flatiron your hair?"

"Yep." Watching me walk toward her, she struggles not to laugh. "Did you dress in the dark?"

"Huh?" I look down at my sneakers and black leggings—nothing wrong there—then realize my shirt is on backward. It's also white, mostly see-through, and I'm wearing a lacy black bra. "Good God."

Allison laughs. "That's what aprons are for. Come on, we've got a lot to do in an hour."

The next fifty minutes fly by. At ten till six, Gerard and a newer part-timer named Ritchie knock on the front door. Several customers linger outside, jonesing for their morning caffeine fix. Since we're ready to go, I leave the door propped open and flip the sign.

Then I take my last deep breath for the next three hours.

When the rush finally ebbs after nine o'clock, I sag

against a back counter and guzzle water. Allison finishes ringing up her current customer and joins me.

"Feeling any better?" she asks, a thread of concern in her voice that hasn't left since I took off my sunglasses and she saw my red-rimmed eyes.

"Yes, thanks," I say, smiling and fanning myself with a menu. "Besides feeling like I just showered. Without the actual showering bit."

She laughs. "It's definitely nuts in the morning. A whole different ballgame than evening traffic."

"I'll say. And I plan on leaving the insanity to you and Owen for all time."

Laughing, Allison wanders away to wipe down tables. I finish my water, then move to the bakery case to take stock of what needs replenishing.

Gerard, coming back from the kitchen, stops beside me with his phone in his hand. I frown. "You know better than that. No phones while on the clock."

"I know, I know," he says, and his tone narrows my eyes. He looks nervous, his complexion more pasty than usual.

"What's going on, Gerard?"

He scrubs fingers through wispy blonde hair, then shows me his phone. "I think you'll want to see this."

Focusing on the screen, I see it's an entertainment news article with the title, *Are Things Over for Breaking*

Giants Frontman Julian Ashburn and Country Darling Missy McKenzie?

I snatch the phone out of his hand and scan the article.

Are the men of Breaking Giants unlucky in love? A source close to the band has confirmed today that guitarist Matt Sullivan has split from Seattle songwriter Rose Cunningham. The parting was apparently amicable...

Blah blah blah. I skip down a bit.

...A close friend of the couple tells us that trouble has been brewing ever since their reconciliation. A large part of the problem is Missy's desire to take the relationship to the next level, and Julian's refusal to relocate to Los Angeles. This dynamic likely played a starring role in their initial breakup and might be rearing its head again.

The article continues, full of flagrant conjecture, then closes with a paragraph that makes my ears burn.

While there have been no whispers of infidelity in the relationship, the B-Side of Breaking Giant's newest single is causing a stir. Namely, it's the reference to a certain flower that has fans on both sides of the fence churning. That's right,

it's a Rose. Coincidence? Or has the flower sunk her thorns
into not one, but two members of the rock group?

"Motherfuckingfucker," I hiss. "This is a huge pop culture website."

Gerard squeezes my shoulder. "Sorry, boss. Anything I can do?"

I rub the space between my eyebrows. "No," I sigh. "At least this explains all the weird looks this morning." And the women clucking in sympathy at my makeup-free, puffy face.

"You want to take a break?"

I glance around Tullamore, noting curious looks from customers, most of whom avoid eye contact.

"Yeah," I concede. "I'll be back in ten."

Once in my office—Owen's office, technically—I find three missed calls on my phone. Two from Greta and one from Aunt Katherine. And two text messages, both from Matt.

What did Julian say to you yesterday?

Do I need to beat him up?

Improbably, the last message makes me laugh. Despite the shitshow of the last few months, I'm glad I met Matt. I really hope things work out for him and Melody.

Slumping into Owen's chair, I text him back.

Nah, don't ruin his pretty face. Did you see the trashy article?

I don't read that crap. You shouldn't either.

At the casual dismissal, a weight lifts from my shoulders. And thank God, because I desperately needed the reminder that nothing good comes from emotional investment in what strangers think of me—a lesson I learned the hard way in high school. The rumor mill is inescapable, and for the orphaned daughter of parents suspected of committing suicide, it's also vicious.

My phone vibrates with a new message.

I'm taking Melody on a date tomorrow night

I smile.

Awesome. Happy for you!

Thx, Rose

At a knock, I look up to see Allison in the doorway. "Um, Rose? We have a problem."

Her anxious expression pulls me to my feet. "What kind of problem?"

She steps inside and closes the door. "I just overheard Gerard talking to a customer about you. Something about a picture of you that he wants to sell." She winces. "He said you were more interested in Julian Ashburn and his girlfriend than upset over breaking up with Matt Sullivan."

We stare at each other for a few long moments, our expressions mirroring equal levels of betrayal and disappointment.

She finally says, "I know Gerard is struggling to make ends meet. I think… shit, I'm pissed off, and you're probably a thousand times more pissed, but I guess I feel kind of bad for him, too."

I take a deep breath that does nothing to abate my feelings of hurt, anger, and helplessness.

"He could have asked for more hours," I murmur, scanning Allison's face as if for an answer. "I didn't know."

"Don't blame yourself," she says firmly. "We're paid well. Really well. Why do you think there's a stack of applications two-hundred deep on the corner of your desk?"

I squeeze my eyes shut. "Okay. Thanks for letting me know. Can you send him back here, please?"

She nods. "What do you want me to do about the guy he was talking to?"

I shrug. "Just let him go. I don't want a scene."

"You got it," she says and leaves to fetch Gerard.

The following conversation is brief. He doesn't defend himself; nor does he exhibit much remorse. I ask him to show me the photos—I look horrible, haggard and sad—and when I ask him to delete them, he does.

Though I manage to stay professional, it's painful to witness his apathy. He's worked here close to a year, and Tullamore's small staff feels like a family. To me, anyway. But if I know anything, it's that a person's perspective is their reality. I have no choice but to respect that Gerard's priorities are obviously different from mine.

The only explanation he gives is that when he realized whoever took those photos of me and Julian months ago had likely hit a big payday, he couldn't pass up the opportunity of cashing in himself.

And that's it. He doesn't threaten to sue for wrongful termination—which he'd lose, as he breached his employment contract—but merely asks when he'll get his last paycheck in the mail.

We shake hands, I wish him the best, and he leaves. I go back to work, my heart a little heavier and my eyes a little clearer.

15

FREEFALL

*A*fter the shit day I've had, the Lotus Lounge in Fremont is precisely what I need. Crowded, dark, and loud. The band on stage is one of my favorite local acts, an indie group with enough melody and spunk to keep me moving.

Greta thinks I'm crazy for going to see bands by myself, but for me, sometimes there's nothing better in the world than being alone and anonymous in a sea of people.

The energy onstage is contagious, and all around me are smiling faces. Feeling a part of something bigger than me, I lose myself in the collective rhythm, cheering and screaming along with everyone else. The vibe is so great that the band does three encores, and even after the last one we all keep screaming for more.

Eventually, the female lead singer laughingly begs us

to stop, and with good-natured whining, we cut them some slack. They just rocked the house down for two straight hours. After a final thank you, the house lights come up, and the band starts packing up their gear.

Luxuriating in the afterglow, I linger, chatting with a couple of women about the show. I'm happy and calm, enjoying the camaraderie and my rediscovered peace of mind.

Then one of the women whisper-yells, "Betsy! Is that Julian Ashburn onstage?"

"Shut up," gasps Betsy, turning fast.

And sure enough—because today clearly required a *fuckyouRose* exclamation point—it's Julian. He's sitting on an amp chatting with the band's drummer, a giant of a man with a bald head and arms the size of tree trunks.

"Oh my God, Sarah, we have to talk to him," gushes Betsy, and grabs us both, hauling us toward the stage.

I plant my feet, but she has a seriously viselike grip, and seconds later it's a million years too late to hide.

"Rose?" asks Julian, brows raised in surprise.

My companions stare at me like they've never seen me before. Finally, Sarah connects the dots. "Rose Cunningham? No way!"

Feeling the pressure of Julian's gaze, I force a smile. "Hey, Julian. These ladies would really love to say hello to you."

His eyes flicker to the women and back to me. I can't

read his expression, which is partially shadowed. At length, he says, "Sure, absolutely," and walks downstage, hopping to the floor.

As the women babble and stare at him, salivating with glazed eyes, I wonder if I wore a similar expression the first time we met. And if the blind adoration of his fans irritates him because it's at such odds with how he views himself.

Then I decide I don't care.

Clutching the remains of my musical afterglow, I say, "Betsy, Sarah, it was great meeting you guys. See you around, Julian."

I. Will. Not. Run.

I manage to keep my promise to myself and once outside, decide the walk home will be good for me. The heatwave has loosened its hold. There's a nip in the night, but it feels good on my flushed skin.

My walk stays peaceful for ten minutes before my brain is hijacked by *JulianJulianJulian*. The craving rears up, seizing control of my mind.

I want to run back to him, the urge so primal that my steps slow. With the last of my sanity, I shake my head roughly and pick up my pace.

By the time I reach my driveway, my vow is toast and I'm running. Taking the front steps in one leap, I attack the lock on my front door like someone's chasing me. Only its just my mind, and there's no escape.

I finally have the key in the lock when the unmistakable sound of a Harley roars down my street. My fingers spasm and the key falls. Limbs heavy and tingling, I slowly turn.

Julian pulls into my driveway with a protest of tires. He's off the bike seconds later, helmet on the ground and striding toward me like Hell's on his heels. Then I'm in his arms, flattened against the front door, my body exploding with sensation as his mouth devours mine.

I don't know who finds the key, who opens the door, but we make it inside.

He pauses long enough to ask, "Rose?"

I grab his hair in my fists and drag his face back to mine. He answers my demand with a needy groan and possessive sweeps of his hands, capturing my breasts, my hips, my ass, before lifting me away from the wall.

"Bedroom, now," he growls, and I point. He walks through the dark house with me in his arms, and after some fumbling and a few near collisions with walls, he finds it.

We fall onto my bed. Urgency robs us of grace as we tear off clothing as fast as we can. My nails score his back. His teeth imprint my shoulder. He is heat, and movement, and *perfectmorenowplease*.

"Please, please," I chant, and hear a condom foil rip. He settles between my thighs, which quiver in welcome.

"Fucking hell," he breathes. "Last chance to kick me out."

I answer with my fingernails on his ass, and his first thrust is hard and deep and drives straight to my body's limit. I cry out, arching to accommodate him.

Yesyesyes.

He moves like a man possessed, fucking me with such single-minded focus I feel simultaneously worshipped and sundered. My body is his. And when he grabs me under the legs, lifting and rolling so I sit atop him, I sacrifice myself to the same passion. I make him mine.

"Rose."

I open my eyes and absorb a vision I know will be imprinted in my memory forever. Julian beneath me, sweaty and real and *inside me*, one hand on my hip, the other curved around the back of my neck.

His eyes are locked on mine, the look in them more naked than our bodies. I move faster, needing, *needing…* his jaw clenches, abdomen flexing as he effortlessly matches my pace.

"We're perfect," I whisper.

And he says, "You're perfect."

I touch his face, then guide his hands to my breasts as I shift to a slower, deeper rhythm. Searching… *there.*

Julian closes his eyes, whispering something I don't catch. I feel him grow thicker, harder, and I know he's close, struggling for control. And the knowledge makes my own body quicken.

My climax is shattering, lightning bright, and *loud*. Julian hauls me to his chest, fingers tangling in my hair, and swallows my cries. His hips jerk hard and go still, and against my sensitive inner flesh I feel his release.

I collapse on top of him, my cheek against his shoulder, and relearn to breathe. Our hearts are pounding so hard I'm not sure which beat belongs to whom. A cool breeze flows like a blessing over my naked back, lifting goosebumps.

Belatedly, it occurs to me *why* there's a breeze.

My open window, of course.

Swallowing past a throat gone raw, I gasp, "Oh my God, the neighbors."

Julian's chest shakes with silent laughter. I slap his arm, but there's no force in the blow.

"At least the curtains are closed," I continue, torn between hilarity and embarrassment. "Was it that bad? Am I going to be known as the Harlot of Fremont? Most of my neighbors are elderly. Poor Mrs. Thompson."

Unable to hold it in longer, Julian bursts into laughter. He shifts onto his side, gathering me in his arms, and I frown up at his grinning face.

Smoothing the sweaty hair from my temples, he finally composes himself enough to say, "Rose Cunningham, you are *loud*," then starts laughing again.

"This is horrible," I laugh-groan. "At least tell me I had enough brains not to scream your name."

He's still laughing. "I don't know. I don't care. All I know is that I've never seen or heard anything sexier in my life. You're an animal, Cunningham."

This time there's more force in my slap. "You're the animal, *Ashburn*. What happened to romance? Candlelight and massage oil?"

He's laughing so hard now I wonder if I should fear for his health.

"Stop," he gasps, "I can't breathe."

I wriggle into his side, seeking warmth—and if I'm honest, imprinting myself with his scent.

"Oh well," I say with a hearty sigh. "I guess that stuff only exists in romance novels."

He bites my neck, laughter turning into a growl, and suddenly I'm flat on my back. His arms cage me as his fingers roam my features, sliding across my cheekbones, my jaw. Tracing my lips and temples.

My heart stutters at the reverence in his touch, then kicks hard as he gently kisses my mouth. Upper lip, then lower, and each corner, before kissing me slow and deep, our tongues lazily exploring.

When he finally lifts his head, I raise my brows in expectation.

He grins. "Not yet, wildcat. Soon. In the meantime, where do you keep the candles? I hear they're necessary for romance." One hand wanders down my belly, tickling as it goes. His smile turns wicked. "Besides, I want to see what I'm eating."

Oh, have mercy.

♪

AT THREE IN THE MORNING, we make a meal of pancakes, eggs, and hash-browns, the latter almost inedible because there might have been a fifteen-minute detour to the couch.

Julian sits in boxers at the kitchen table, sipping tea and watching me. I'm across from him, wearing underwear and an oversized t-shirt, stuffing my face with a second helping of pancakes slathered in maple syrup.

"Has anyone told you that you eat like a caveman?" he asks dryly. My reply is a grunt, which makes him grin. "Where do you put it all?"

Around a mouthful of carbohydrates, I say, "Good genes. Besides, I just burned a bajillion calories."

His smile transitions to smugness. "I'll say."

I point a fork at him. "Has anyone ever told you that you're an insatiable madman?"

Julian sets down his tea and snags my free hand,

pressing a kiss to my palm. "Actually, no. Frankly, tonight's—"

"Debauchery?" I offer.

He cocks a brow. "I was going to say brilliant, sweet, uninhibited love making—" I giggle. "—Hey! I'm trying to be romantic!"

Laughing outright, I abandon my pancakes for his lap. Despite my aching muscles (and other parts), my body instantly warms. Taking his face in my hands, I press our foreheads together.

"It's almost four o'clock in the morning. I think we should forget romance and take a shower together. A *dirty* shower. Then, if I'm going to be at all conscious during work tomorrow—er, today—I need to sleep."

His hips flex up, earning a fluttery exhale from me. "You're the boss," he murmurs, one hand sneaking beneath my t-shirt and up to palm and knead my breast. His mouth veers to my neck, nibbling, as his other hand navigates south.

When he finds me already aroused, he groans. "Let's shower after."

"Mmm," I agree, shifting so he can pull aside my underwear and his. I feel him thick and blunt at my entrance and twitch helplessly in need.

"Damnit," he hisses, head lifting, expression strained. "I'm out of condoms. Do you have any?"

The heavy hand of reason descends on my shoulders.

Standing to adjust my undies, I tell him, "I don't think so, but let me look." Then I see what's exposed beneath me. My thoughts scatter. Spreading his knees, I kneel hungrily between them.

Julian is unmoving above me, eyes bright and fixed on my face. I wait for the canned *You don't have to* line, but he surprises me with the quiet words, "I want to fuck your mouth, Rose. More than anything."

My newly awakened inner sex goddess preens and gleefully complies.

We make it to the shower eventually, after Julian carries me back to bed and returns the favor with gusto. We're both so tired that we sloppily wash, then stand listlessly in each other's arms while the hot water turns cool. After heroic efforts to towel ourselves dry, we make it back to bed and fall into a naked heap, passing out almost immediately.

I don't hear him leave.

When I wake up at noon to my alarm, I reach for him before I'm fully conscious. And at that moment, when my hand finds empty space, I feel the heaviest, most pervasive disappointment of my life. It steals the air from my lungs, jerks my knees protectively to my chest.

Because although my mind had known he'd slip away, my heart had hoped he'd stay.

♫

THE WEEK FOLLOWING what I come to refer to as the Seven Hour Mistake is one I hope to look back on someday and recall only the vaguest details: long work days, poor sleep, overconsumption of chocolate, and compulsive sheet-washing. Not the messier details, like almost chopping off my hair, considering my first tattoo, and listening to the untitled B-Side on repeat while I sob in the shower.

And sending tens of text messages that go unanswered. Or that, when I finally gather the courage to call him, it goes immediately to voicemail.

And I definitely don't want to remember Aunt Katherine's impromptu arrival at my house in the middle of the night—in the midst of a tearful cookie fiasco—to inform me that the message of the tarot remains the same.

The timing is inopportune.

16

BREATHE

$\mathcal{A}$t Tullamore on Friday afternoon, a week and a day after the Seven Hour Mistake, I take advantage of a lull in customer traffic to watch a summer thunderstorm play war-games in the sky. I'm thinking about collisions and timing and consequences, but there's no poetry.

No music.

I wait for my mother's voice to remind me that love kills art, but it doesn't come. I muse that maybe instead love is so powerful it can *interrupt* art, at least for a while, either while the spirit soars in happiness or works to heal and endure.

The front door creaks open, wind gusting wetly inside before the man entering hurriedly swings the door shut. Pulling down the hood of his coat, Greg wipes his face with the backs of his hands then passes fingers through his short, damp blonde hair.

When he sees me out of the corner of his eye, he turns with a smile. A familiar smile, full of warmth and mischief—one I've missed terribly.

"Hey, Rose," he greets, sidling around tables to join me at the far window. "Do you have a minute?"

I lift my brows. "What's up?"

"Well, I noticed last week at open mic that your CDs have all sold…"

I blink hugely. "They have?"

He shakes his head chidingly. "You're the absolute worst."

I nudge his shoulder. "Just kidding. I'm not that clueless." Narrowing my eyes, I add, "Are you offering to produce another album for me?"

He nods. "Full length this time. Ten to thirteen songs, all original. I want to bring in a band for some of the tracks, mix it up with a heavier sound for *Feline Tendencies*. Maybe a violin for *Decay*—"

"Whoa," I interrupt, my hand flying up between us. "Are you serious?"

"Dead serious. I know you have at least three albums worth of songs stacked in that head of yours. I've seen the sheet music for a few that you've never played at open mic but I know will be fucking amazing."

Staring into his determined eyes, I ask, "What brought this on? I sold a hundred CDs over several months—it's not like I'm rolling in demand over here."

He chews his lower lip, and finally blurts, "I got a new job. I'm working at Icon, and I played your EP for one of the big producers, and—"

"Icon?" My scalp prickles. "As in the studio where my mother recorded?"

He smiles. "Yeah. And Pearl Jam, Deathcab, Dave Matthews, Breaking Giants, Johnny fucking Cash... Yes. And Jonas said even though we're booked from now until Armageddon, he'll make space for you. And cut some of the fees. He even said he'd review our final tracks and make suggestions."

"Because of my mother," I whisper.

"Maybe in part. But trust me on this, Rose, if he thought your music was crap, he wouldn't have made the offer. This guy is the real deal." He gives a comical shudder. "He scares the hell out of me."

"Okay."

He blinks, swallows, and asks slowly, "Okay?"

I nod. "Yes. Let's do it."

Greg's hoot of victory startles most of Tullamore's patrons, including Owen, who yells from behind the register, "Pipe down, this is a respectable establishment!" which in turn triggers laughter from nearly everyone.

I yell back, "I'm recording at Icon!"

Owen's mouth drops open, and a second later he hollers, "It's about damned time!"

Christy squeals, Ritchie throws his hands in the air, then everyone in the café is smiling, laughing, and clapping.

Because I'm going to record an album at Icon Studios. Because they're happy for me. And because they can't see the painful squeeze in my ribcage as I have the sudden urge to tell Julian, then remember that he got what he wanted.

I'm out of his system.

♫

THE NEXT SEVEN weeks pass in a blur. Goodbye July and August, hello September. My days are full of work and helping Greta with the wedding, as October 1st is rapidly approaching.

There are final fittings, tastings, and tours. Finalizing of the vows, music, guest list, hotels for out-of-towners, honeymoon details, and oddly, the most time consuming and aggravating finalization of all: seating arrangements for the reception. Greta doesn't morph entirely into Bridezilla, but there are a few close calls requiring Sakiinterventions.

Nearly all of my remaining spare time is a juggling act of caffeine, songwriting, and trips to Icon Studios in Belmont. Greg and I audition and hire a violinist, a percussionist, and two more guitarists. When a track calls for piano, I play it myself.

The work is hard, oftentimes excruciatingly so, and exhausting, especially since our hours in the studio are random and many times limited by the scheduling of bigger acts. But little by little, one song at a time, the album takes shape.

Sometime in August, Breaking Giants' new album is released. I barely notice (okay, I notice) when their new material floods the radio with single after single, garnering acclaim left and right. They perform on all the late night shows, amping up interest for their upcoming U.S. tour.

I'm happy for them.

I am.

Only, there's still a jagged place inside me that won't heal. It wakes me up in the middle of the night with memories of his touch. Fingers in my hair. Tattooed arms and ridged, pale stomach and whiskey eyes locked onto mine as he...

You're perfect.

On one particularly bad night, I almost burned the

kitchen chair, the couch he bent me over, and the head-board marked by my fingernails and teeth.

At around the four-weeks-of-silence mark, I couldn't stand the pain anymore and talked to Aunt Katherine. I spared no details about the Seven Hour Mistake. For once, she didn't have any advice from the mystical world; instead, the mix of sympathy and nostalgia on her face convinced me it was time to pull on my Big Girl Pants.

After all, the past belongs in the past. And maybe someday I'll feel nostalgic—like Aunt K does for her own private memory—about my single, glorious night of mind-blowing, body and heart wrecking sex with a rockstar.

Until that day comes, the most I can do is be happy for Breaking Giants' success, avoid gossip columns like the plague, and make my own music.

And apparently, my alleged spirit guides are all about timing because on a Friday evening in mid-September (seven weeks and one day after the Seven Hour Mistake), Greg walks into Tullamore an hour ahead of open mic night with a single, unlabeled CD case in his hand and a grin on his face.

The album is finished.

I squeal and run around the counter, launching myself into his arms. He spins me a few times, then to the amusement of the steadily growing crowd, waltzes me around the area before the bakery case singing *We Are The Champions* by Queen at the top of his lungs.

As we pass Owen, my cousin snatches the case from Greg's fingers. "Is this it? It's finished?"

"Yep," says Greg, bringing us to a halt.

From across the café, a young woman who looks vaguely familiar calls out, "Rose! Is that the new album?"

When she smiles, I realize it's Lavender-Blonde, only she's recently dyed her hair bright blue. She looks as ecstatic as I feel, and the connection warms me to my toes.

"Yes," I tell her, laughing. "You wanted it, you got it."

A couple of our regular open mic acts approach, and Greg and I spend the next thirty minutes chatting with them about recording at Icon, and the indomitable (and frankly terrifying) Jonas Smart, who tweaked four of the twelve tracks before giving his imperious Nod of Approval.

When it's time to set up for open mic, Greg disappears with folksy flower girl Kelly West, who he's been happily dating for the last two months. I draft another regular to handle setup so I can take a quick break.

Clutching my unnamed CD, I swing by my office—which has been cleared of *residual energies* by Aunt K—and grab my phone, then step onto the back patio for some air. It's cold and empty, the iron chairs locked to the tables, the sunshades tied tight. The rain has let up a bit, but I stay out of its reach under a wide overhang.

Leaning against a damp wall, I unlock my phone and update my Facebook status with the news. I don't have a personal account anymore, but at Greg's urging made the requisite artist's profile. I have a whopping eight hundred and forty-six followers. Ten more than yesterday.

"Eat that, Breaking Giants," I mutter, snorting as I review recent activity.

Notifications start streaming in for likes and comments on the news that the album has wrapped. Glancing at the time, I decide to savor them later and pocket my phone.

Inside Tullamore, the celebratory air lingers, affecting everyone. Chatter is loud, laughter louder, and Owen is dropping free pastries on tables, telling everyone his cousin is a recording artist. Greg and Kelly are back, looking flushed and cuddly as they unpack their instruments. The sights, the smells, the sounds... I'm home. Everything is exactly as it should be.

Until my phone buzzes in my back pocket.

And I pull it out

and see a text message

from *him.*

Congrats, Rose. Can't wait to hear it

And my heart just

sort of

disintegrates.

"Rose?" asks Christy, concerned face wavering before mine. "What just happened? You started swaying! Are you okay?"

I blink hard. "Yeah. Just dizzy for a second."

And angry.

Sofuckingangry.

Owen appears like magic. I grab his arm, needing something solid to hold onto. He knows the whole ugly story, and all I say now is, "Look at this."

I hold up the phone. He reads the message, eyes narrowing. "He's got a lot of nerve," he says, gaze veering back to me. "How did he even know?"

I shake my head roughly. "No clue. I just updated my Facebook status... Matt's girlfriend Melody follows my page. Maybe she told him?"

"Kind of odd timing, don't you think?"

From behind me, Greg asks softly, "Rose? Uh, you're talking about Julian? About that... There's something I need to tell you."

Turning slowly, bracing for the whole fucking world to go sideways, I meet Greg's worried, apologetic eyes.

"Spit it out. Right now. But if you say that Julian in any way, shape, or form influenced the making of this album, I'm going to freaking *murder* someone."

Greg swallows, eyes darting to Owen—who's almost as furious as I am—before coming back to me.

"I'm sorry. So sorry. He made me swear not to tell you until it was all done, and I've hated lying to you, but he got me the job—"

Something inside me snaps.

17

HELLOGOODBYE

hen the body experiences a powerful enough stressor, it's flooded with cortisol, epinephrine, and endorphins. The first two are most recognizable as heralds of the fight-or-flight response. They accelerate the heart and respiration, enhance hearing and vision, and even make your liver release sugar to give you a boost of energy. Then there are endorphins—*ah, beautiful endorphins*—which help block out pain of an impending attack.

Or the pain of launching one. Like right now, as my fists pound relentlessly on the unyielding wood of Julian's front door.

When it suddenly opens, I allow myself one second to feel the impact of his presence. *Imissyouadoreyouhateyou.* Then I punch him in the face. It's a beautiful punch. He howls, his glasses go flying, and *thank you endorphins* I don't feel a thing.

"Jesus, Rose!" he cries, stumbling back with a hand to his mouth. "You split my fucking lip!"

"I should split more than your lip, asshole!" I yell, then blink as I try to make sense of my statement, and finally follow up with, "Like your head!"

Bent forward with his hands braced on his knees, Julian spits blood on the lovely wood floors. He grunts, and I see his torso shaking, and when I realize he's laughing my vision goes a charming shade of red.

Taking three steps into the house, I shove him hard, watching in satisfaction as he tumbles into a console. A bamboo plant falls on his back, and a picture frame clatters to the floor.

"Bro, she's beating you up," says a mild voice.

I glare down the hallway at Breaking Giants' drummer, Nick Henderson, who looks like an attractive cross between a NFL linebacker and a computer nerd. He's eating rather noisily from a bowl of popcorn as he watches us.

"Hi, Nick!" I say brightly. "We haven't been introduced. I'm the girl your frontman fucked over, fucked, then fucked over again!"

Nick spits out popcorn to release a laugh. "Oh, I know. Our publicist almost had Julian's balls on a plate when she found out he spent the night with you."

"*What?*" I snap, then shake my head. "I don't care."

"Rose—" Julian begins, now sitting upright against a wall and prodding his bloody lip.

"Shut up!" I snarl, then point at Nick. "Go away. Your buddy and I need to have a conversation."

"Sure thing," he says, then gives Julian a *Clean This Up* look before disappearing with his popcorn.

"At least close the front door," murmurs Julian.

I kick it closed, then rub my throbbing temples. The bad news about elevated stress responses is that when they disappear, it feels like you just ran a race without the satisfaction of a finish line.

"Let me guess," he says, sighing, "Greg told you I put in a call to Jonas at Icon."

I sink onto a padded bench opposite him. "I don't get it," I whisper. *Don't cry don't cry.* "Why would you do that to me? Knowing how it would make me feel?"

He puts on his glasses, then lets his head thump against the wall. "You're so talented. I didn't want you to hold yourself back because of your mother, what happened to her..." He licks his lower lip, already swelling noticeably. "Just think of it as one professional helping another. It's not unheard of, you know."

"Is that what it was?" I ask bitingly. "One professional helping another? Or did you just feel guilty about cheating on your fiancée with me?" Angry again, I stand up and make a show of looking around. "Or, wait—are you married yet? Where's the wife? I'm sure you're looking forward to raising another man's baby!"

He doesn't move, but his eyes turn to ice. "You're way out of line."

"Are you kidding? *I'm* out of line?" I yell, then freeze, heaving, as I'm consumed by a moment of clarity.

Just like me, Rose.

"Oh my God, why am I even here?" I whisper brokenly at the ceiling. Looking down at Julian, I tell him, "I'm sorry I hit you. That was completely not okay. And I'm sorry for what I said about Missy. But most of all, I'm sorry about that night."

"I'm not," he says, and pushes himself to standing.

His gaze is too penetrating, too full of the man I'd thought he was. The kind of man who would have chosen me, no matter the bad press. Unless…

"The baby's yours, then?" I force out.

He stares at me in naked anguish. "I don't know. But if it is? I can't just abandon her. She's… struggling."

I have a sudden flashback to the limo, and Missy chugging champagne. When he'd told me she was pregnant, I'd figured maybe it was sparkling cider. But now…

I gasp. "She shouldn't be drinking."

Ire flashes in his eyes. "I know that. Don't you get it? Of all the people on earth, *I know.* She has a team supporting her in L.A., sponsors and life coaches, fitness and nutrition experts. But it's a delicate situation. I can't leave her!"

"I understand," I say, and I'm proud of how calm I sound.

I edge toward the door, needing an escape. Needing away from this emotional earthquake that *wontfuckingstop.*

"Rose," he whispers, "please. I haven't been *with* Missy in months. Since before you. Before us. The relationship is a sham, a public front to hide her problems. As soon as she has the baby, I'm out."

I realize his admission should mean something to me. He isn't with her. He doesn't love her. We're not cheaters. But I'm numb.

Words don't change anything.

"I need to go," I say, and reach for the door.

He grabs my arm—not hard, but not gently, either. Turning me toward him, he stares down at me, eyes burning with vulnerability and frustration, confusion and fear. I flinch from the visceral impact.

"I have to protect that baby, Rose, whether or not it's mine."

I nod. "I hear you. I just wish… maybe you could have told me. Maybe I would have understood two months ago, too."

"I'm sorry," he breathes. "For me, that night wasn't a mistake. It was the best night of my fucking life.

Goddamnit—if I couldn't have all of you, if I couldn't give you all of me, I couldn't stay. Don't you get it? You and me, we're not walks on the beach and romantic dinners. We're a supernova. A fucking black hole."

I'm falling, but don't know if his words are wings or a cement floor.

"You don't know that," I say faintly.

"What did you want me to do?" he asks, giving my arm a little shake. "Ask you to be my mistress while in public I'm playing dutiful fiancé to Missy? Hide you? Like I'm *ashamed?*"

My eyes fall closed as the situation sinks in. "No, I guess not."

His calloused fingertips lift my chin. "I miss you. I miss you every day. I'm sorry."

The hand on my arm softens, floating to my shoulder, then cupping the back of my neck. I don't want to feel anything. But of course, I do. Earthquakes and supernovas. Awareness pulses through me, tingling and hot.

"I'm sorry," he says again, and I feel his breath on my lips.

I open my eyes and see his, close, full of yearning and a dangerous, forbidden question. His scent envelops me, his broad shoulders blocking out everything else.

I'm in a tiny electric world just big enough for two, with a man who is impossibly complicated, incomprehensibly perfect. A black hole.

"Your lip…" I say pointlessly.

He shakes his head, smiling a little as he brushes his mouth over mine. My body unfurls from the inside, blooming into a pulsing, focused need. I moan and he matches the sound, surging forward, yanking me up and into his arms.

I wrap my limbs around him as tightly as I can, as though if I try hard enough, I can pull him beneath my skin and keep him there. Safe and happy.

Julian takes a set of stairs two at a time, walks swiftly down a hallway I don't see, and turns into a dark room. The door is kicked closed behind us. He finds a switch on the wall, and a floor lamp in a distant corner comes on.

We fall onto a bed in a surreal parallel of the last time. Only this bed is his, and his kisses are slow and drugging instead of frenzied. He worships my ears, my throat, and finally my breasts through shirt and bra. When I'm panting and writhing beneath him, he buries his face in my chest, breathing deeply.

"Sunshine."

I thread my fingers through his hair, holding him close, and the sharp edge of arousal fades against the steep bluff of contentment. Tension slowly leaves his body. We stay this way, in the shadows and silence, for a long time. I almost fall asleep, and I think he drifts off once or twice.

Then his fingers move lazily under my t-shirt, pushing it up. I lift my arms, and the fabric slides over my head, sailing off the bed. My bra follows, then shoes and pants, all with a leisurely pace that's somehow more overwhelming than urgency. I manage to get his shirt off and jeans unzipped before he gently guides me back down.

He hovers above me in the near dark, teasing my skin with flicks of his tongue. My shoulders, ribcage, and finally my aching breasts. Each tug of his mouth, nip of his teeth, sends bolts of awareness down my center until I'm twitching and *dyingpleaseplease*.

"Tell me," he says, in the dark voice that ignites every pleasure circuit in my body.

"Julian, I need you," I whimper. His head dips to my belly button, and his tongue traces a thin line down, down... "I need your mouth. On me. Now."

"That's my girl," he murmurs, settling between my trembling legs. "So beautiful."

His tongue makes long, sweeping passes, then delves purposefully. My back comes off the bed, a ragged cry tearing from my throat.

Humming into my flesh, he lifts his head long enough to say, "I think about this all the time. Being right here. Listening to *that*."

And then there's no more talking.

When Julian's satisfied that I've had no less than two

orgasms complements of his mouth and fingers, he finally gets rid of his jeans and boxers. Feeling like useless putty, I lie sprawled on the bed and watch him roll on a condom.

Not a bad view. At all.

When he settles above me, I feel the odd sense of imprinting again—like I am being indelibly marked by him. Every inch of me.

The feeling fades as he slides into me, anchoring me wholly to the present.

"Perfect," he says.

My hips surge against his until he growls, and at last, unleashes his passion.

And it is, just as he said, *perfect*.

♪

THE HOUSE IS dark and quiet as, several hours later, Julian walks me to my car. We've barely spoken since our final, explosive bout of sex. I think both of us know there's nothing to say because there's *too much*.

He gives me one last kiss through the open window of my car, grunting a little at the contact.

"How's your lip?" I ask, and see his soft smile in the dark.

"Hurts like a bitch," he admits. "How's your hand?"

"Same. I'm so sorry." I shake my head. "I don't know what came over me. I've never hit anyone in my life."

His smile widens, then he grimaces and touches his lip. "I think I deserved it." Our eyes meet in a moment of gravity and clarity. "I want to see you again. Now, tomorrow, yesterday…" He shakes his head helplessly. "But I can't ask you to—"

"I know," I say, smiling bravely as I memorize the shape of his face, the outline of his body in the night. About to lose it, I turn on the car and put it in reverse. "I'm, uh… I'll miss you. Take care of yourself, Julian."

Not waiting for a reply, I back out of the driveway. I take a final look at him—tall shadow, a single hand raised in goodbye—and drive the empty streets home.

18

NUCLEAR FALLOUT

October 1st dawns cold and clear, the sky a brilliant shade of Happily Ever After. By nine a.m., I'm on my third cup of coffee and nibbling my way through a muffin at Aunt Katherine's kitchen table.

The other three bridesmaids trickle in over the next hour, toting garment bags and chattering a mile a minute. They're sorority sisters of Greta's, and although they've always been nice to me, when I'm around them I can't help feeling like Greta's slightly odd sidekick.

When they ask to see my maid of honor dress, I realize my designation isn't necessarily a bad one. A few weeks ago, Greta finally conceded that lilac was not my color *at all*, and we went shopping again.

As the women *ohh* and *ahh* over the pewter, floor-length sheath, I silently thank Greta for being the awesomest best friend in the world.

"It's so… couture," says Tracy, running a finger over one of the artfully shredded layers.

"Very *you*, Rose," says Jackie, trading a meaningful glance with the final bridesmaid, Lindsey.

On the other side of the kitchen, Aunt Katherine smirks. I hide a smile as I cover the dress, thank the ladies for their compliments, and refill my coffee.

Greta arrives not ten minutes later in a flurry of hair-curlers and bags. Her conservative socialite mother is right behind her, lobbing suggestions on the day's time-line despite the schedule Greta and I made and printed last week. To her credit, Greta is blissfully unaffected, ignoring the running commentary as she flutters around the room giving kisses.

The next hours fly by in a haze of mimosas, laughter, a few sobs, and flying shoes. Greta's favorite stylist comes and goes, perfecting her makeup and hair. By the time three o'clock rolls around, we're all dressed except for Greta, who won't step into her gown until we reach the venue.

When the limo hired by Greta's parents pulls up outside, there's an eruption of chaos as we gather together everything we need—and a bunch of stuff we probably don't—and pile inside. Two blocks down, we realize we forgot The Dress and have to turn around. Thankfully, it's the only near-catastrophe of the day.

The venue is a historic downtown hotel that Greta

has dreamed of being married in since she was a kid. The smiling wedding coordinator meets us outside and guides us to the bridal suite, where we spend the next hour alternately calming Greta and serving cocktails to her mother.

In a brief moment of respite, I hide in the bathroom with my phone to respond to Owen's most recent message, which is more or less the same as all his other messages today. After assuring him that everything's fine and running smoothly, I scroll through my contacts and call Matt.

"Hey," he answers. "You didn't spill the beans, did you?"

"Nope," I say, grinning. "She's going to flip out. I can't thank you enough for this, Matt."

"My pleasure, Rosie Posie. We're packing up and should be there in about thirty minutes. The hotel has been really accommodating with security. She won't have a clue until the reception."

I do a little dance against the bathroom counter. "Ah! So exciting. And you swear Julian's okay with this?"

After a pregnant pause, he says in a low voice, "Rose, you know he'd do anything for you."

I blink hard, squeezing the phone against my ear. "Yeah, okay. Thanks."

We hang up. I straighten to smooth the gown over my hips, then head back into the suite where Greta is anxiously waiting. A photographer approaches, letting us know it's time for the maid of honor to zip up the bride's gown, our figures framed by the beautiful baroque window.

♫

THE CEREMONY GOES off without a hitch. After, there's pictures, more pictures, and so much smiling my face starts to hurt. But it's a good hurt—the happiness I feel for my two favorite people is poignant and nigh overwhelming. It helps offset the knowledge that in just a few minutes, I'll see Julian for the first time in more than three weeks. Since punching and *I'm sorrys* and incredible sex and *goodbyes*.

When it's time for the bridal party to enter the reception, my skin starts humming in anticipation as we line up before the couple. Attendants open the doors and the first chords of Breaking Giants' *The Next Day* float to our ears.

It takes four seconds before Greta screeches and grabs my shoulder. Biting my lips, I look over my shoulder with wide, innocent eyes.

"You bitch!" she squeals and starts jumping up and

down, tugging on a laughing Owen's arm. She whacks his shoulder. "You knew!"

He gives her the biggest grin and kisses her soundly. "Only because I overheard Rose talking about it in her office one day."

"Surprise!" I say, which is all I have time for before the best man and I make our entrance, and there on the stage of the whimsically decorated ballroom sits Julian on a stool with a guitar and a microphone stand, singing about forever-love and tomorrows.

It's a hard call who's getting more attention, Julian or the entering bride, but I don't think Greta cares. Instead of heading to the bridal table or greeting any of the cheering guests, she leads the way to the stage. Front and center with Owen, she happily sways in time to Julian's liquid-velvet voice. Because she's the bride and gets whatever she wants today, we all follow, and soon enough most of the guests have abandoned their tables for the dance floor.

Just before the second chorus, the rest of the band walks smoothly onstage, taking up their instruments without fanfare. And with the perfect timing of a group who's played together live for years, the song lifts from acoustic to a rousing electric symphony.

Julian stands, his voice coming stronger, harder for the final third of the ballad. He smiles at Owen, winks at

Greta, and then his gaze roams until it finds me. And the final chorus is mine.

> *From last night till forever*
> *I'll follow you blind*
> *because no matter when*
> *you'll always be mine*
> *To the place we begin*
> *where in the end we'll stay*
> *to the back of tomorrow*
> *and every day, always.*

THE CROWD CHEERS. Greta starts crying, prompting bridesmaids to whip out tissues, and I stare at Julian. Julian stares at me, then snaps out of it and turns his attention to the microphone.

"We are Breaking Giants," he says with a smile for Greta. "On behalf of Matt, Nick, Jackson, and myself, I want to wish Greta and Owen the happiest of forevers. Enjoy your dinners. We'll be back for the first dance."

He blows Greta a kiss and disappears offstage amidst another resounding cheer.

I mingle for a few minutes, feeling out of sync and fuzzy, before Owen passes me and says, "We won't be mad if you disappear for a few."

I grimace. "Thanks. I, um, want to say thank you to the guys in person."

He grins knowingly. "Uh huh."

A security guard lets me through the side door. I wander down a short hallway, then see a sign taped to a door. *Wedding Band*. Trying not to laugh at their demotion from superstardom, I knock.

Matt opens the door, which swings closed as he steps into the hallway. "Rosie!" he cries, lifting me into a hug.

"Mind the gown, jackass," I laugh, and he puts me down carefully. "You guys are getting food, right? I told them—"

"Yep, yep," he says, and when I glance at the closed door, he takes an unsubtle sidestep to block it. "So, any changes to the setlist? Or, uh…" When I just stare at him, he deflates. "Shit, I can't lie to you. Your eyes are like freaking lasers."

I palm my stomach, which is suddenly fluttering. "He doesn't want to see me? It's okay, I'll just—"

The door opens, and before Matt can reach back and slam it shut, I hear laughter. A woman's laughter. It sounds familiar, but I can't place it.

Then it clicks.

My stomach drops. Matt's expression probably mirrors mine—wide-eyed and pale.

I stammer, "W-what's she doing here?"

"She's in town for the weekend and wouldn't take no

for an answer," he says with strain. "I'm sorry, Rose. But she's…"

"Six months pregnant and engaged to Julian," I whisper, then slap a palm to my face to stifle a burst of inappropriate but totally irrepressible laughter. "And hanging out with him at my *best friend's wedding* because the universe fucking hates me."

There's more hilarity than rancor in the words, and Matt offers a wavering smile. "Yeah, that damned universe…" he trails off, wincing.

I wave a hand dismissively. "It's all good. Tell them I stopped by. Or, on second thought, maybe you shouldn't." I rise up on my toes to kiss his cheek. "Thanks again for doing this."

Then I head back to the party.

I'm not super proud of how the rest of the night goes. I allow the best man to refill my champagne too many times. I laugh too loudly at his jokes and flirt too brazenly. And during Breaking Giants' last song of the evening before the DJ takes over, I even let him kiss me. It's sloppy and regrettable, but when I hear Julian's voice go momentarily harsh, I feel perverse satisfaction.

I don't drink any more after that, and really, I can't blame the champagne. Or Julian, even. I'm the one hanging on. Unwilling or unable to move on despite repeated, overwhelming evidence that I'm wasting my time waiting for him. Waiting for the tides to change. For the spirits to have a new message: *Now, he's yours.*

They don't. They won't.

But I still can't let go.

Aside from kissing Owen's best man, I don't embarrass myself or anyone else. I celebrate, I dance, and even give the most amazing toast *ever* to the happy couple. At eleven o'clock, all hundred and fifty of us make a tunnel and throw confetti onto the newlyweds' heads as they run out of the ballroom toward the waiting limo.

It's absolute magic.

Twenty minutes later, as Aunt Katherine and I are packing up the bridal suite, I find my phone where I left it on the bathroom counter. And five minutes after that, Katherine finds me sitting on the floor with my legs splayed, crying like I just lost all hope in the world.

And I have.

Because his text message reads:

The baby's mine

19

_____

WHIPLASH

*I*n November, local radio stations start playing *Excess*, which is so punchy and satirical it's an instant hit. By the end of the month, I've performed in venues throughout Washington and as far south as Eugene, Oregon. I'm interviewed on UW's independent radio and the mainstream alt-rock station, and because of the generated buzz, by early December I'm being courted by several indie record labels. For now, Greg is handling my management, as it became clear early on that I suck at self-promotion.

By necessity, I've had to cut back on my hours at Tullamore, which has been both a blessing and a curse. Despite the whirlwind of performing multiple times a week, of write-ups and praise from local magazines and critics, I'm in an emotional limbo.

The life of a musician is being offered to me, and what *should* be a no-brainer isn't. Because I'm not, in fact, my mother, to crave the spotlight and attention. And I really do love my life, running Tullamore and satisfying my need to perform once a week at open mic.

The alternative is nonstop touring. Seedy hotels and cramped vans. Slinging merch to make enough money for said hotels and cramped vans. I vacillate day to day. Greta thinks I should stay. Owen and Greg think I should go all-in.

Aunt Katherine is resoundingly silent.

One lonely night in the second week of December, I make the mistake of calling Melody for advice. We've struck up a friendship and meet a few times a month for dinner or cocktails. She and Matt have made it past the honeymoon phase of their relationship and are firmly in the *shit just got real* portion. It makes for some interesting, laughter-filled ladies' nights.

When I call her, I'm twenty bites into a pint of ice cream, sitting in my dark living room and staring at my blazing fireplace. What should be a cozy winter's night is turning into a pretty depressing one. Beginning with the horrible error of playing the infamous B-Side, and ending with Melody's efforts to help.

"I was talking to Matt about where you're at with the touring thing," she says in her rapid-fire way, "and he thinks you should just come out with them. They have openers for most legs of the tour but are still auditioning for the first leg."

I whistle softly. "Aren't they cutting it a little close?"

She laughs. "Yeah, well, the boys are as picky as teenagers with pimples."

I grimace. "Nice, Mel."

"It's true! Julian's a mess and can't make a decision to save his life. Jackson and Nick say they don't care, then throw in opinions at the last possible second to derail everything. Matt's eyeball-deep in his Mother Hen routine trying to make everyone happy. And of course, he's failing." The last is said with a bite.

"That sounds ominous," I say, hoping to steer the conversation toward her.

"Nice try," she quips. "You and Breaking Giants are a match made in music heaven. You know it. I know it. At the very least, it will give you huge exposure. You'll be signed in an instant! Sure, you'll have to headline tours eventually—that's the life, after all. But you'll have way more freedom and way fewer roach-infested hotel beds."

I shudder. "I appreciate what you're saying, Mel, but it's not a good idea. It's actually the *worst* idea. I haven't spoken to Julian in months. And isn't Missy due pretty soon? What if she goes into labor?" I make a gagging noise. "I mean, time heals some wounds, but I'm not a fucking robot."

"Are you still in love with him?"

Ah, Melody, straight for the gut shot.

I haven't actually said the L-word in reference to Julian, but Melody throws it around like it's a given. Maybe it is. Maybe I do love him. What I know for certain is that I'm still addicted, still in withdrawals, and despite being on a few relatively nice dates with nice men, I fall asleep at night with a head full of Julian Ashburn.

"It doesn't matter," I answer her question. "What matters is that there's static between us. The kind that doesn't just fade with time."

Melody explodes, "This is fucking *bullshit!*" Her vehemence is so off the charts that I pull the phone from my ear and stare at it. With barely a pause, she yells, "I have told that asshole a thousand times what a horrible mistake he's making. Missy is a lying, cheating, conniving, superficial twat! That baby is *not* Julian's. It's probably her skeevy trainer's spawn. He didn't even ask for proof of paternity. He just *took her word for it.* For an alcoholic who spent his childhood hustling, he's the most gullible sonofabitch I've ever met!"

Heaving for air, she falls silent. I tentatively lift the phone, my hand shaking so hard it takes a few tries to get the device to my ear. I have no words—too many words—and my tongue is sealed to the roof of my mouth.

"Rose?" asks Melody softly. "I'm so sorry. I shouldn't have freaked out like that. Matt and I had a fight today, and I'm PMSing. God, I'm so sorry."

"It's okay," I croak. "I can't—there's no way I can go on tour with Julian."

She sighs. "I know. And I completely understand. I'm sorry, I just really hate thinking about Julian throwing his life away for some warped sense of nobility linked to his childhood trauma. I wish I could get through to him. That *someone* could get through to him. He just needs the right push."

Melody, I discovered early in our friendship, has a Masters in Psychology.

"Yeah," I say noncommittally, then with relief, see Aunt Katherine on my Call Waiting. "Mel, I gotta run. Try not to castrate Matt tonight. He loves you."

"I won't," she says. "Talk to you later?"

"Yep. Bye." I switch calls. "Aunt K?"

She doesn't say hello, opening with, "The spirits told me to tell you: *Say yes*."

My stomach sinks like a ball of lead. "Huh? What are you talking about?"

"Not sure," she says lightly. "It's just been repeating for the last twenty minutes. Driving me bonkers, actually. *Rose—yes—say yes.* On and on. Tell me that means something to you."

I stare at the shadows on the ceiling. Then I stare into my melting pint of ice cream. Finally, I yell at the spirits I don't even believe in: "Are you fucking kidding me?"

Aunt Katherine says, "That doesn't sound good."

"Why am I even considering this?" I ask redundantly. "On the word of rainbow garden fairies, no less?"

"That's rather insulting," she replies with affront.

I sigh. "Sorry. I can't believe I'm saying this out loud, but I think your Psychic Friends Network wants me to yank my own heart out of my chest and go on tour with Breaking Giants."

"Oh! That sounds transformative, Rosie!"

Biting hard on my lower lip, I mutter, "You say transformative, I say emotionally fatal. Tomato, tomahto." My phone beeps against my ear. Glancing at the screen, I see Matt's number. "Am I in a vortex? Is there a mystical alignment of *fuckyouRose* stars and planets happening?"

"Um, nooo…" says my Aunt.

"Gotta go, Aunt K, love you," I say, then answer Matt's call. Before he can say anything, I blurt, "Fine, I'll do it!"

"Do what?" he asks, voice loud against chaotic background noise. There's yelling. Car doors slamming. *Is that a siren?* "Rose? Are you alone?"

"Yes, why?"

"Can Greta or Owen come get you?"

The world beneath me cracks like unstable ice, shifting and rocking. Before he speaks, I know; the fear, the devastation in his voice. I remember it. I *lived* it.

"Tell me," I whisper.

"Julian's been in a motorcycle accident."

20

FLASHBACKS

When Owen pulls up outside UW Medical Center's Emergency entrance, there's already a dense crowd gathered, mostly contained by hospital security and several police officers. Media and fans and paparazzi, all hoping for glimpses of famous faces or snippets of gossip from inside. It's an eerily familiar scene.

I feel thirteen years old again, only my father isn't on failing life support inside, Aunt Katherine doesn't have her arm around me, and Owen can't fill the role because he has to park the car.

Before I make it ten feet toward the entrance, I'm spotted. Lights and flashing cameras rush my way. A padded microphone is shoved in my face before a hospital security guard saves my ass, stepping between me and a rabid reporter.

"Are you Rose Cunningham?" he asks. His eyes are kind; I notice that much.

"Y-yes."

"Okay, come with me."

I keep my gaze straight ahead, fixed on the guard's black jacket, as he leads me through the emergency room to the ICU. Outside the signage-heavy automatic doors is a small group of people. Matt looks up and sees me, his face crumpling.

Missy sees me a second later.

"What the hell is she doing here!" she screeches, pointing a finger at me while cradling her rounded belly with the other arm. Her finger swings to the guard. "Get her out of here, right now. She's not welcome."

All around us, conversations die sudden deaths.

Matt steps forward, expression thunderous, but Nick clamps a hand on his shoulder and shakes his head. Easygoing, popcorn-eating Nick, who's known among Breaking Giants' fans as eternally devoted to his two loves—drums and smoking pot—plants himself in front of Missy.

Big body shaking visibly with the force of his emotion, he snarls, "Shut your mouth. Her name was the first fucking word he said when he regained consciousness. How about you try this on for size, Missy? *You're not welcome.* We're his family. You're just a soul-sucking parasite standing between our brother and what he wants. So why don't you and the baby everyone knows *isn't his* get the fuck out of here! Now!"

Although Nick isn't physically threatening her, his words are dangerous enough. Matt and Jackson grab his arms and march him to the nearest empty seat. All around the waiting room, people stare. More than a few are busily typing on their phones.

Strangely, all I can think is, *That poor child.*

Beside me, the security guard mutters, "Really glad he didn't get violent," and from the nurses' station, I hear the murmured words, "Cancel the alarm, we're fine… Yes, I'll tell you later."

From the corner of my eye, I see Melody enter the room. Her gaze trips from a visibly shaken Missy, to the men currently kneeling in front of Nick, and finally to me.

"You're here," she says, rushing forward. "Thank God. Did you go back yet?"

Matt stands and walks quickly to me. "Come on, Rose. He's going into surgery any minute."

My hand firmly in his, Matt leads me through the ICU doors, nodding at several nurses and another security guard. Buffeted on all sides by moving personnel and machinery and hushed voices and brave families, I'm mostly numb again by the time we reach a private bay manned by the head of Breaking Giant's security team. I don't know his name, but recognize him from the day at Tullamore when he blocked the crowd from surging inside.

He nods at us. "Good timing. They're about to take him."

I hear a raised voice, thick with pain and slurred. "I said *wait*. She'll come. Don't… stick me… that!"

I don't hesitate, ducking around the thick curtain. "Are you Rose?" asks a harried nurse, and I nod. "Praise Jesus. Come here. Put your hand on his right shoulder. He can't see you very well, but he'll hear your voice."

Julian…

Oh dear God…

One eye is black, swollen completely shut, the other clotted with blood. Half his face is discolored and swollen beyond recognition. Contusions and scrapes—some superficial, some deep and weeping—cover his arms and chest, and a thick pad rests on one side of his abdomen. His neck, one leg, and both arms are in stabilizing braces. Bloody bandages and gauze litter the bed as two nurses work on his other leg… I see a gush of fluid my vision goes a little wonky.

The nurse who praised Jesus takes pity on me and grabs my arm, pulling me around her and placing my palm on Julian's naked shoulder. His skin is blistering hot.

"Julian," I say, but no sound comes out.

"Rose," he whispers, twitching. Turning his face as

best he can, he slurs, "Can't see. Torn retina. Fucked... Sorry."

Seeing how much it hurts him to speak, I say quickly, "Don't talk."

"...you," he breathes, "—tay?"

Another nurse, currently emptying a syringe into an IV bag, says, "He's asking you if you'll stay."

Say yes.

Like there was ever any doubt.

"Yes," I tell him. "I'm not going anywhere."

The fight goes out of him with a rattling breath.

"We're good to go," says one of the nurses, stepping away from his leg.

A doctor in a white coat throws back the curtain. "Mr. Ashburn, time's up, we need to get you to surgery now."

Julian doesn't say anything, his head rolling away from me. The nurses fly into action, bundling chords for the portable units, unlocking the bed. I'm pushed perfunctorily out of the way, my hand slipping from his shoulder, as they wheel him from the trauma bay toward glistening silver doors.

When I'm standing alone in a sea of bloody gauze, a scream begins building in my belly, rising through my chest to my throat. Matt, entering the ICU from the other side, sees me and immediately starts running. He catches me as my knees buckle, muffling my wail with his shoulder. Half-carrying me, he takes me back to the waiting room, where *Thank God* I see Owen, and I stumble into my cousin's arms and fall apart.

♫

HE'S in surgery for ten hours. A few hours in, we're ushered to a smaller, private waiting room. People come and go—family and friends with food, snacks, and blankets, a frazzled woman who I decide must be the band's publicist, a teary older man who I recognize as their manager, and various security and police. Missy, who disappeared after Nick's outburst, hasn't returned.

We get periodic updates throughout the night, and finally, just after dawn, the head surgeon appears. Weary but clear-eyed, she tells us how lucky he was that he was wearing a visored helmet, that the car that hit him wasn't going any faster, and that when he was thrown from the bike after impact, he landed on dirt instead of asphalt.

Lucky lucky lucky.

He required tens of stitches. Suffered a mild concussion. Fractured his left femur, wrists, and four ribs. Six broken fingers. Detached retina. And finally, severe enough abdominal trauma that they'd had to remove his spleen.

We listen to it all, and only Jackson asks questions. Expected time in the ICU. Rehabilitation. Whether he'll regain full mobility in his wrists and fingers. Because although the question might sound self-serving, we all know what it means for someone who makes a living playing guitar. It's not about the money—Julian could probably retire whenever he wants—but it's very much relevant to his life's purpose and passion.

The surgeon gives what answers she has, deflecting the ones requiring too much speculation. *It's too early to say. He's young and strong.*

When she's gone, Matt asks, "Rose? Do you want me to take you home for a while? She said he won't be receiving visitors any time soon."

"No," I whisper.

Melody brings me shitty coffee and a stale croissant, demanding that I consume both. When she's satisfied I'm at least trying, she drops wearily into the chair next to mine.

"Nick really messed up when he went off on Missy. It's all over the internet." She pauses. "For the record, this was *not* the push I was hoping for."

Improbably, I laugh—a rusty, half-deranged sound. Then Melody starts giggling, and Nick lifts his head with a frown. "What's wrong with you two?"

Melody sticks her tongue out. "I can't believe you

handed Missy's ass to her when I was out of the room. Couldn't you have waited?"

Nick snorts, then wheezes out a laugh that sounds only marginally less spastic than mine. Rubbing his face with his hands, he mutters, "Shit, I really said those things, huh? In public?"

Matt snorts. "Blew the fucking lid off, dude."

Jackson, splayed on the floor with a pillow on his face, offers, "He was calling it all off, anyway." His voice is muffled, and it takes a few seconds for the words to work through my haze of sleep deprivation.

"Say what?" I blurt.

Jackson flips the pillow so it's under his head. Bloodshot eyes find mine. "I stopped by Julian's yesterday. We were supposed to go for a run. There was no answer when I knocked, but the door was unlocked so I let myself in." He fluffs his pillow and stares at the ceiling. "I heard them arguing. About proof of paternity? I guess Julian's lawyer got his hands on the document."

"And?" snaps Matt.

Jackson shrugs. "It's what we all thought. The baby's not his. He was pretty torn up about it. Missy was screaming. She threatened to drink if he left her." He shudders. "It was freaking brutal, so I got out of there. I should have stayed. He needed someone."

"Don't do that to yourself," says Nick hoarsely. "Not

your fault. It wasn't anyone's fault. Slick road, hydroplaning car. Motorcycles are fucking dangerous."

"Is the other driver okay?" I ask softly.

Matt nods. "It was a family. They're fine. Traumatized for sure, but walked away."

Melody clears her throat. "Have we heard anything about—that is, do we know from the tests…" She trails off, looking helplessly at Matt.

"No," he says mutedly. "We haven't heard anything."

"Heard what?" I ask.

Matt's gaze meets mine, then drops. "Whether or not Julian was drinking."

"No way," says Jackson sharply. "No fucking way he threw away thirteen years on that hag. Right?"

No one says anything.

21

GRAVITY IS A BITCH

Julian stays mostly unconscious over the next few days. When he is awake, the painkillers and trauma make for interesting, often hilarious conversations. At one point, Matt reports that Julian's convinced he's an oxygen farmer from Hawaii and has to get back before his animals turn into aliens.

I laugh with everyone else, but secretly wish I had a similar story. Although I've seen him, he hasn't said much, and I've left each time not knowing if he even knew I was there.

It takes a week for the swelling around his uninjured eye to dissipate enough for him to see; the other still boasts a patch as it heals. The bruising on his face is severe—a mere sliver, I know, on the spectrum of his pain.

Two weeks after the accident, I stop by before work, hoping he'll talk to me beyond superficial chitchat, that he'll acknowledge in some small way that things are different between us.

I'm jittery from too much coffee and not enough sleep, my clammy fingers twitching around an ornament for the little Christmas tree set up in the corner of his private room.

Taking a steadying breath, I knock on the door. An unfamiliar, older man answers.

Steel grey eyes only a few shades darker than his hair scan my face, pinging from one area to the next in an impersonal appraisal. It's mildly unsettling, but when he asks, "Rose?" I realize he was matching me to a verbal description.

"Yes," I say uncertainly, then point over my shoulder. "I can come back."

From inside the room comes Julian's voice. "No."

The man opens the door, giving me a smile that under other circumstances likely transforms his face to downright jolly, but today is tempered by solemnity.

"I'm Steven," he says, shaking my hand. After a small pause, he adds, "Julian's sponsor."

"Ah," I say, because *whatelsedoyousay?* and glance at the bed.

Julian is sitting upright, expression pinched as he wiggles the fingers of his left hand. A black brace covers his forearm, wrist, and thumb. The eye patch is finally gone, and the bruising on his face has mellowed from black and purple to shades of yellow and green.

He looks alert, and broken, and beautiful.

I clear my throat. "Hi, Julian."

His eyes dart to me before returning to his fingers. "Hey, Rose. How are you?"

"Um, good. How are you feeling?"

"Okay."

Why is this so awkward?

Stuffing down the desire to flee, I glance at Steven. He's frowning expectantly at Julian, who still won't look at me for more than a second. Discomfort prickles under my skin. The beginnings of a panic attack slither through my belly.

"Julian," prompts Steven.

Julian sighs and lowers his arm, then turns his head to stare out the window. "Here's the deal, Rose. I wasn't drinking the night of the accident. But I wanted to. I was considering it."

I swallow hard, glancing at Steven, who says, "Now, Jules, don't scare her. Tell her the rest."

"I was heading to a meeting when I crashed." His lips twist sardonically. "I'm still *technically* sober, though the constant morphine feels, uh, risky."

"But you have to have it," I say quickly. "Julian, you have broken bones—"

"No one's saying he shouldn't be on medication," interjects Steven gently. "But as alcoholics, no matter how much time sober we have, the use of mind-altering substances can trigger cravings. It's going to be a delicate road while he recovers, both from his injuries and prolonged use of painkillers."

Gently factual tone. Perfectly sensible words. But I hear what he's not saying; I can read the sympathy in his eyes well enough. Tingling numbness spreads through my chest, panic supplanted by shock.

"Julian…" I take a helpless step toward him. "Please, don't—"

"I have to," he whispers.

"Why?" I ask, too loudly. "I'd *never* stand in the way of your sobriety. You know that! I can help!"

His eyes close. "You can't, Rose. Not with this. My life has gone too far off the tracks already. I need to get my head on straight and get through this."

Without you.

Because you're part of the problem.

The unspoken words ring between us, slamming straight into my heart.

A soft sound of misery escapes me. "At least look at me as you throw me away. Can you please look at me?"

He doesn't.

Fighting tears, I move away from the bed, turning blindly for the door. I make it into the hallway. Halfway to the elevator, Steven catches up to me. At the touch of his hand on my shoulder, I jerk, twisting away from him.

"I'm sorry," he says softly.

"Get away from me," I hiss. "Whatever you told him, it's bullshit. I could have helped. I was willing..." I clamp my lips shut as they begin to tremble.

Steven sighs sadly. "All I told him is that he needs to clear away the things that stand between him and his recovery. That's it."

"Great," I snap. "Thanks for letting me know I've been reduced to the classification of *thing*."

He winces. "I'm sorry, poor choice of words. Please try to keep in mind what he's been through, is going through now, and what he'll be enduring over the next months, and consider that maybe he doesn't want to expose you to all the ugliness."

I laugh caustically. "Oh, it's too late for that."

Turning my back, I toss the glass ornament of a music note in a nearby trashcan and jab the elevator button.

♫

THERE ARE some things no amount of booze, yoga, or ice cream can fix. This is one of those things. Even knowing this, I can't handle the level of the emotional pain I'm feeling right now. Somehow, I have to blunt it. I don't do drugs, so…

I choose temporary denial.

I drive to work. I put on my floppy Santa hat and smile. I. Do. Not. Stop. No breaks except to scarf food and chug espresso. Thank fairies and Christmas elves, it stays busy from three until ten.

When the last customer is gone and the closing routine complete, I send Christy and Ritchie home. Once they've left and the doors are locked, I connect my phone to the sound system and crank up the volume on PJ Harvey's 1993 masterpiece *Rid of Me*. Then I move all the tables to the side and mop the floors. Clean the windows. The bathroom. The bakery case.

I alphabetize and refill all the jars holding loose leaf teas. I scrub at the little bits of residue built up on the registers' keys. And when I knock over the tin with table placards in it, and the Prince of Swords sails up and smacks me in the face…

I don't lose it.

I calmly collect the cards and put them back.

When *Rid of Me* has played in entirety four times, I take a break to drink some water and find a new sound-track. Sitting on the back counter, I debate between Nirvana's *Nevermind* and The Clash's *London Calling*.

My phone buzzes with an incoming call. Owen's name flashes on the screen, and I answer.

"Quick, pick one. Clash or Nirvana?"

"Are you at Tullamore?" he asks, sounding tired and irritated.

"Yes. Why? I'm cleaning."

There's a long pause. "It's almost three in the morning, Rose," he says evenly. "The alarm company just called me to report that the alarm wasn't set tonight."

"What? How come they call you first?"

"Rose!"

His yell finally punctures my denial, sinking into my overtired, emotionally bankrupt self. Sudden, immense fatigue sags my shoulders.

"Sorry. I'll close up and head out."

"Are you okay?" he asks in a low voice.

"Yep. Go back to sleep. Sorry to have woken you."

He yawns loudly. "Okay. Love you. Drive safe."

"Will do."

I hang up and shove my phone in my back pocket, then put all the tables back, store my rags and the mop in our small cleaning closet, gather my keys and coat from my office, turn off the lights, set the alarm, lock the door behind me.

Get in car.

Start car.

Drive home.
Crawl into bed.
Darkness.
Peace.
Sleep.

Was that my alarm?
Work!
Have to—

"Hush, Rose. Sleep."

Sinking.
Sleep.
Peace.

Too bright in here.
Too much light.
Can't—
Ah, darkness. Better.

Floating.

Brokenlegsbrokenheartsbroken.
What could have become of you and me.
youmeyoume
What will become—

NO!

"There, there, child. Just let it out."

Sinking.
Dark.
Empty.
Sleep.

♫

"Rose," says Greta gently, "You need to get up now."

"No. Can't."

"Honey, you've been in bed for two days."

"Nooo… Wait—what?"

Opening my eyes takes a monumental effort. Greta's face comes slowly into focus. She's sitting on the edge of my bed and behind her stand Owen and Aunt Katherine.

Owen looks nervous and worried. Aunt K, unruffled as always, shrugs a little and says, "I told them you were fine."

My cousin's lips pinch. "Two days in bed is not fine. No matter what the spirits say."

Katherine rolls her eyes and walks to my window, twitching back the drapes. "Merry Christmas Eve, Rose."

"Aren't you pagan?" I ask hoarsely.

She shoots me a reproachful look. "I accept all religions, as you know."

Owen rolls his eyes in a perfect imitation of his mother, and I snort. Greta smiles widely at me, taking my hand in both of hers.

"There you are," she murmurs. "We were so worried."

Yawning, I turn my head to stare at the ceiling. "I missed work."

"Forget Tullamore for a minute," says Owen tightly.

Greta says quickly, "Don't mind him, he was scared for you. You missed work and weren't answering your phone. Katherine called and told him you were fine, but today he couldn't take it anymore."

I have a foggy memory of a voice, arms holding me while I wept, and meet Aunt K's clear eyes.

"You stayed with me. Took care of me."

"Of course," she says softly.

Blinking hard, I whisper, "Thanks." She nods. "Owen, I'm sorry I worried you."

He sits heavily on the bed beside Greta. "I'm the one who's sorry. I knew something was wrong when you were at work so late. Cleaning? For God's sake, you hate cleaning." He peers at me from around his wife's shoulder. "What happened?"

The memories don't rush back or flood my mind or anything so dramatic. They never went anywhere, to be returning now. So I tell them the truth.

"Julian dumped me before we ever went on a date," I say, and before any of them can open their mouths, I continue, "It's for the best. He needs to focus on his rehabilitation, not us. Me, whatever. Plus there's all the fallout from the accident, his now ex-fiancée, the band's tour being postponed… Honestly, it's kind of a relief not to feel like the girlfriend in the corner anymore. Maybe I can finally move on."

After a moment's silence, Greta asks, "Do you mean any of that?"

I give her a tired smirk. "Some of it." I clear my throat, which feels suddenly tight. "Really, what have I lost? There wasn't anything to begin with. Potential, maybe, but that's it. Right, Katherine?"

She turns again from the window, her expression inscrutable. She seems to weigh her words, then offers simply, "That's right."

Right.

Nothing to lose, nothing lost.

Done.

22

KEEP MOVING

SIX MONTHS LATER

"*T*hank you, San Francisco, goodnight!"

With a final wave, I step off the small stage and unstrap my guitar. Behind me, the applause continues as the stage lights dim, then slowly transitions to chatter. Greg takes my guitar with a grin, and Brody and Aiden move past us to begin breakdown.

"You were on fire tonight, Rose," says Greg, giving my arm a squeeze. "Ready for home?"

Wiping the sweaty hair from my forehead, I smile. "So ready."

After six weeks on the road, the thought of my own bed is halfway to a spiritual experience. I also miss Tullamore, and Owen, Greta, and Aunt K. We have two more shows in Oregon as we head north, then a homecoming show this Friday in good ol' Fremont.

"Me too," he agrees. "I'm gonna check on Juliet. We'll hang for a while, then pack up the merch and hit the road. Cool?"

"Yes, thanks." As he turns, I grab his arm. "Greg, thank you. For everything. Coming on tour, managing me, producing the album. I couldn't have done any of this without you."

Eyes softening, he grabs me in a quick hug. "It's been my pleasure." Drawing back, he winks. "We've come a long way. I love you a lot, and I'm happy to report it's completely platonic."

I laugh, and he gives me a mocking salute before jogging away. Snagging a bottle of water, I watch Brody and Aiden moving efficiently, wrapping chords and packing instruments and equipment.

Brody, a recent college grad, is a brilliant pianist. I'm unbelievably lucky he harbored a secret desire to play keyboard for a touring band. And Aiden...

Fighting the urge to fan myself, I watch the muscles rippling in his back as he lifts an amp. He's on loan to me from the Seattle band Full Stop, on hiatus from touring while their frontman's heavily pregnant wife waits to go into labor. Again, it was luck that brought us together.

Greg and I were having a terrible time finding a drummer, and a few weeks before we were scheduled to head on tour, I threw out during open mic that I was looking for one. Aiden was at Tullamore that night, and the rest is history.

As if he can sense me watching him, Aiden glances back at me. One tawny brow cocks, a teasing grin lifting his lips. I return the smile. We've been dancing around our sexual tension for weeks, neither of us wanting the complication it brings to a cramped tour van and nightly performances.

When we get back to Seattle, though…

I haven't been with anyone since Julian, and though my heart still thumps with desire and hurt when I think of him, the rest of me is ready to replace his mark with the hands of someone new. Specifically Aiden's. I've heard about the stamina of drummers for years; it might be time to find out if the rumors are true.

I entertain salacious thoughts for a few more minutes, then finish my water and head onstage to help with carrying the gear out back. By the time we have the van loaded, Greg and Juliet—formerly known as Lavender-Blonde—begin bringing out boxes of merch.

Normally after shows, I spend time at the table meeting and chatting with new fans until the venue flashes closing lights. But I didn't sleep well last night, and I'm beyond tired. There's also a telling tickle in my throat, one I'm hoping stays at bay for a few more days.

"People were still showing interest," says Juliet as she

hands me a box. "We could hang for another thirty minutes if you want."

"Nah," I say. "It's already pretty late, and our hotel is three hours north. Is that super selfish of me? I really just want to sleep."

"Not selfish at all," she says quickly. "Honestly, I'm kind of relieved."

"You did three encores," adds Aiden, squeezing my shoulder briefly, "and you've been performing almost every night for weeks. No one's going to blame you for not sticking around tonight."

"We're almost done," says Greg, heading toward us. "Rose, hop in the van and relax. I'll wrap up with the venue."

I don't argue, climbing into the middle seat and grabbing a pillow to prop between the window and my head. I doze off for a bit and wake up when everyone piles in. Aiden's in the driver's seat, Greg's riding shotgun, and Juliet and Brody are in back with me.

"Everything good?" I ask, yawning.

"Don't worry your pretty little head," says Aiden. "Get some rest."

Juliet finger-jabs me in the ribs. I roll my eyes at her, then close them and drift, letting the vibration of the road relax my mind.

I'm not quite asleep when I hear Juliet ask, "Can you turn it up a little?"

Aiden whispers, "She's sleeping."

"No, I'm not," I say groggily.

The volume on the radio increases until I hear a woman speaking.

"This is Danielle Shoemaker for Alt Talk. If you're just now joining us, my guest this evening is a man who needs little introduction. Grammy-winning, double-platinum recording artist Julian Ashburn of Breaking Giants—"

Greg mutters, "Turn that shit off."

Juliet whines, "Why? I want to hear it."

Greg glances back at me. I sigh and say, "Whatever, it's fine."

Aiden looks questioningly at me in the rearview, but I drop my gaze before we make eye contact.

"—talk about the accident. You've been working hard with physical therapists to regain full mobility in your fingers and wrists. How's that going?"

"Really good, Danielle. It's been a hard road, but I can finally report my hands are back to hundred percent."

Even with the power of his voice dimmed by radio waves, I'm still affected. Closing my eyes, I feel a damnable stirring, which escalates to a low throb as he keeps talking.

"My focus right now is rebuilding core and leg strength. I probably won't run a marathon anytime soon—" Laughter, both from Julian and interviewer, *"but then again, I have an amazing team of trainers and therapists, so anything's possible."*

"That's wonderful news for the fans, Julian. I remember clearly when the story of your accident broke. There were prayer circles and vigils all over the place. A lot of people were pulling for you."

"I know. I feel really blessed to have the support I do, both from my inner circle and the wider circle of fans.

"Can you tell us—any word yet on new tour dates?"

"It's looking like September or October for the start of the tour. Nothing is fixed in stone yet, but I'd say within the next couple of weeks we'll be ready to release some rescheduled dates."

There's a significant pause. Even before the interviewer speaks, I'm relatively certain where she's headed.

"I know how rare it is for you to grant interviews, so first and foremost, I want to thank you so much for talking with me. Now, to avoid getting hate mail for not asking what's on a lot of minds, can we veer to the personal for a moment?"

Julian chuckles, but I can tell it's forced.

"Go ahead, Danielle."

"Now that you've had some time to heal, physically and emotionally, is there a special someone in your life we should know about?"

In the ensuing three seconds of silence, every nerve in my body goes hyperaware.

"I'm not seeing anyone, no."

"Not even Rose Cunningham? Rumor has it she was at the hospital every day after your accident."

Juliet gasps.

Greg mutters, "Oh, she went for it."

Aiden's head jerks up as he asks, "Did she just say—"

Brody laughs. "Dude, has your head been under a rock for a year?"

On the radio, I almost miss Julian's response, but Greg cranks up the volume.

"Rose was, and is, a close friend of the band. She's an incredibly generous and loving person, and I'll always be grateful for her support in those first weeks."

Danielle, who probably realizes she'll never interview Julian again after this, says leadingly,

"It sounds like you care about her a lot."

"I care about all my friends."

Julian's voice holds an unmistakable thread of steel. There's an awkward pause, then Danielle rushes to close.

"Thanks for humoring me, Julian, and for taking the time to speak with us tonight—"

Greg flips the channel.

I lean my head against the pillow and close my eyes. Beside me, Juliet and Brody share a few whispers, while silence reigns in the front seats.

Generous and loving.

Close friend.

Grateful for her support.

The words cycle through my head, triggering varying degrees of hurt, hilarity, resignation, and yeah, I'm still a little angry.

When we reach the hotel, we lumber like zombies through registration and disappear into our respective rooms. Juliet and I normally share, but tonight I have one to myself. I shower quickly and throw on pajamas, then sit on the edge of the bed. Five minutes later, there's a soft knock on the door.

Opening it, I look up at Aiden. His hazel eyes scan mine, a little frown on his brow.

"Are you dating Julian Ashburn?"

"Nope."

"*Did* you date Julian Ashburn?"

"Nope."

He drags a hand through his dark blonde hair, gazing past me. "Were you…" he trails off, probably realizing the question he wants to ask is inappropriate.

I answer anyway. "Yes. A few times last year."

He nods thoughtfully, and his gaze drops to my eyes, then to my mouth. "Okay."

My brows lift. "Okay?"

"Can I come in?"

I smile and grab a fistful of his shirt. "Yes."

Whadda ya know... the rumors are true.

23

SHORT-CIRCUIT

At the Lotus Lounge on Friday, I take a peek around a thick curtain to see the crowd. To my excitement and terror, it matches the level of noise. On the shadowed stage, Aiden, Brody, and Greg are finishing setup. Near the front of the venue, Juliet is selling merch before the show.

My itchy throat is now verging on a sore one. I've been drinking copious water, sucking on lozenges, and popping Vitamin C for the last two days, but my warmup wasn't the greatest. I know I shouldn't push it and have already worked out in my mind which songs will require a lower register to avoid strain.

I'm not worried, exactly, but this is my home court, and nerves get amplified when you know a bunch of people in the audience. Greta, Owen, and Aunt K are out there somewhere, as well as Allison, Christy, and at least one record label scout.

From behind me, I hear a familiar rapid-fire voice. "Rose! Is that you lurking in the curtain?"

Turning with a laugh, I throw my hands up before Melody can hug me. "I'm sick, careful."

"What?" she cries in dismay. "Oh, no! Are you okay to perform?"

I jab a thumb toward the stage. "Not sure there's much of a choice at this point."

She grimaces. "Well, the good news is that little rasp makes your voice super sexy."

I snort. "Gee, thanks. I guess I can just sex the audience to death, then."

A tall, shadowed figure approaches. My heart trips, then resumes its rhythm when Matt's face becomes clear. "What are you two yammering about? I heard my favorite word."

Melody grabs his arm as he moves to hug me. "She's contagious."

Matt frowns. "Oh, shit. That sucks, Rose." Glancing over his shoulder, he calls, "Hey Julian, Rose is sick!"

FULL.

SYSTEM.

FAILURE.

Melody mouths, "Sorry."

I suck in air too fast and abruptly bend in half as a coughing fit consumes me. A strong, warm hand strokes down my back, fingers lingering on each subtle ridge of my spine. My tank top is a worthless barrier; I flush from head to toe.

I'd know his touch anywhere.

"Just breathe," murmurs Julian.

Eyes watering, I jerk to standing and step a little away, hoping my instinctive defense goes unnoticed. By the clenching of Julian's jaw, it doesn't. But his feelings are my lowest priority at the moment. Mine are over-whelming enough.

He looks leaner, sharper, his hair buzzed close to his head. Still beautiful. And so, so dangerous. As the lights flicker on stage, I see a small scar on his jaw, and another one high on his chest, glistening dully beside the v-neck collar of his black t-shirt. He opens his mouth, then closes it, gaze dropping to the ground.

"Rose, you okay?" asks Aiden, his arm sliding around my shoulders. "Here, drink some water."

I sip from the bottle, sighing at the relief in my throat.

"You shouldn't be performing," says Julian, staring fixedly at me.

What do you care?

"I'll take it easy," I reply, then look up at Aiden. "Time?"

It takes a few seconds for him to stop glaring at Julian and focus on me. "Five minutes."

"Aiden, she can't sing right now," Julian snaps.

I stiffen, frowning. "You two know each other?"

They don't say anything, and I look past Julian to Matt, who's wearing an odd, defeated expression. When I glance at Melody, she's inspecting a fingernail.

In the dark.

Fighting uneasiness, I laugh. "Where's the elephant?"

Aiden says tightly, "I was Breaking Giants' drummer once upon a time. Right, Julian?"

"*What?*" I blurt.

Then I start laughing.

Because *whatthemotherfuck.*

And, WHY ME.

And, *Does no one see how funny this is?*

"Rose, are you okay?" asks Melody worriedly.

Wiping my streaming eyes, I nod, then fall into another round of giggles.

"I just… it's so… Whew!" Finally reigning myself in, I point at Aiden, and I'm only half-joking as I demand, "Was this some weird revenge shit?"

Aiden frowns. "No, Rose. Jesus. Why would you think that?"

"Because she's not stupid," growls Julian. A second later, Matt takes his arm, drawing him back a few feet.

Julian shakes off his grip and points menacingly at Aiden. "I swear to God, if you hurt her—"

"Fuck you, man," snarls Aiden.

"Stop!" yells Melody, loudly enough that I can hear the noise decrease in the front row. "You're both acting like idiots."

Aiden huffs and turns away.

"You're right, we are," says Julian, his shoulders relaxing. "Aiden, I apologize."

Aiden grunts.

Julian sighs, looking at me. "I'm sorry. I'm just worried about you singing. If you don't mind, I'd like to stay offstage. If you need my support, you can wave me out, okay?"

I blink, confused. "Support?"

His eyes bore into mine. "I know your songs, Rose." There's no trace of arrogance in his voice. Just quiet admission.

Floored, I nod. "Okay."

Greg darts across the stage to us. "What's going on? We've got an impatient crowd out there."

They're clapping and yelling, the general din slowly resolving into one repeated word. The stage lights go dark.

"Rose! Rose!"

Aiden gives my forehead a swift kiss. "Showtime," he whispers, then jogs onstage.

I take another few swallows of water, then a slow, deep breath. My gut is churning, my thoughts erratic, and for a moment it feels like the world is falling apart.

Behind me, Julian says, "I'm here."

And *goddamnit*, the words melt away my anxiety, surrounding me in an indefinable sense of safety.

My kryptonite.

And, at this moment, my saving grace.

I glance back at him. "I hate you," I say, but unfortunately, my tone says something different.

I'm not sure he hears me, but then he says, "I know. But I'm still here."

I nod, take another breath, and walk onstage.

♪

THE FOLLOWING AFTERNOON, I lie bundled in blankets on my couch while Greta putters in the kitchen, heating homemade chicken soup and baking my favorite apple pie.

Aunt Katherine is keeping me company in a chair by the window, a pile of knitting on her lap. Another new hobby, but one that hopefully lasts long enough for me to score a few scarves. Beyond her, rain spatters against the window, and the afternoon light is dimmed by the storm.

"It's so good to be home," I sigh.

Aunt K winces. "There's a hyena in your throat."

I scowl. "Thanks."

She points a knitting needle at me. "I wish you'd told me your throat hurt. I would have brought you a remedy to clear it right up." I close my eyes so she can't see them roll; her remedies have *never* worked, and invariably taste like shit. "Even so, the concert turned out rather lovely, don't you think?"

My scowl doesn't dim. "I only made it through three songs."

She clucks her tongue. "That's not true."

I groan. "Three songs *unassisted*."

She smiles blithely. "Are you sure you've never sung with Julian before? Even with your voice at half-strength, your duets were enthralling."

"You're killing me," I grumble, tossing onto my side so that I face the back of the couch.

She's right, though. When my voice started failing, all it had taken was one glance for Julian to come onstage. While the crowd went nuts at the sight of him, he set up a second mike and retrieved two stools, unceremoniously plopping me onto one of them. He left me with my guitar, merely settling next to me like it was the most natural thing in the world, and nodding at me that he was ready.

He wasn't lying, either. He knew every word to every song, and exactly how to support my struggling vocal chords. In between songs, he chatted with the audience while I sipped water, summoning the full magnitude of his charisma for my benefit.

And my utter bafflement.

Greta enters the living room, trailing mouthwatering scents. "Do you want your soup in here or in the kitchen, Rose?"

I roll over and sit up, dragging a blanket with me. "Kitchen." I look at Aunt K. "You coming?"

She bundles her knitting into the bag at her feet. "Actually, I think I might head home. If that's alright?"

Taken a little aback, I say, "Sure, of course."

She gives me another smile, gathers her things, and leaves the room. When I wander into the kitchen, Greta's brows are raised.

"Why did Katherine just tell me I need to leave?"

"What? I don't know. You definitely don't have to leave."

The doorbell rings.

Greta and I stare at each other. "Are you expecting someone?" she asks.

"Uh, no."

Frowning, I head into the foyer, hoping it's not

Aiden. I don't know where we stand after last night, and frankly, I'm not sure I want to stand anywhere with him. The notion that he might have only wanted in my pants because of some old grudge makes me queasy.

The peephole shows me the back of a tall man's raincoat, a raised hood obscuring his head. Sighing, because I figure it must be Aiden after all, I open the door a few inches. The man turns to face me, and my heart gives a rusty thud.

"Can I come in?" asks Julian.

Clutching my blanket around my shoulders, I step outside and pull the door closed at my back. "Why are you here, Julian?"

He licks his lips; under the porch light, I see a flush bloom on his cheekbones. "It probably feels like déjà vu, but I need to make amends to you."

I sigh, pinching the bridge of my nose. "I know it's been six months, but I don't think I can handle rehashing everything right now. I'm good—I mean, I'm pretty much over it. You. But... I don't feel that great. Bad cold, obviously..."

I trail off as the door behind me opens. At first, I'm relieved to be saved from my downward spiral of awkward, but then Greta slips past me like a fairy in flight, bounding down the stairs into the rain.

"Call me later, Rose. Love you! Give Julian some soup!"

Watching her retreating back, I mind-yell, *Traitor!*

"I know you don't feel good," says Julian gently. "I won't stay long."

I finally move my gaze back to his face. His lovely, earnest face. "Fine," I snap. "But only because it's cold as tits out here, and I want soup."

His smile lights up his eyes.

Damnit.

24

REVELATIONS

*A*fter hanging his coat on the peg I point out, Julian follows me into the kitchen and sits at the table. In *that* chair. Grimacing internally, I head to the stove. Beside the big pot of chicken soupy goodness are two empty bowls, two spoons, and two napkins.

"She's turning into Katherine," I mutter.

"What's that?" asks Julian, but I shake my head. His chair scrapes back. "I'm so sorry, do you want some help? Sit down, I'll get your soup for you."

I shoot him a glance that freezes him in his tracks. "Sit." He bites his lips on a smile and does as I say. "Are you hungry?"

There's that stupid sexy flush again. "Kind of, but—"

"There are already two bowls out," I interject, "it's not a problem."

The problem is carrying two full bowls of soup with a blanket draped around me. I ponder the problem a minute too long, then decide *screw it*. He's seen it all, anyway, and I'm feeling sick and punchy, and the idea of making him uncomfortable is appealing.

As I'm carrying the bowls to the table, Julian clears his throat. "Uh, Rose…"

"Deal with it. It's pajamas." Kind of. If a black silk camisole and buttery soft leggings qualify.

"Aren't you cold?" he asks with strain.

Pleased to have elicited a response, I set a bowl in front of him and drop the napkins and spoons to the table. Claiming my own seat, I say mildly, "The thermostat is set to seventy-five degrees as per my aunt's insistence. Unless you're a robot, you know very well it's hot as Hades in here."

"Okay, sorry."

We eat in silence for a few minutes.

"This is really good soup," he offers.

"Mmm," I reply.

Another few minutes of silence.

"How's your throat?"

"I sound like a jackhammer. What do you think?"

"I think you sound adorable when you're sick."

Ignoring the flutter in my abdomen, I put my spoon down and cross my arms over my chest. Julian takes a final bite of soup, then does the same. We stare at each other, me with barely contained resentment, him with solemn acceptance.

I break first, lowering my gaze to the table. "You look good. Healthy. How's your leg?"

"Aches sometimes, but thanks, I feel good. Scarred and weird and different, but good." He gives a soft laugh. "I'm probably in better shape now than I've been in years. I've been working every day with a trainer and physical therapist—"

"I know. I heard the interview."

"Oh." He scratches the stubble on his jaw. "You did, huh?"

"She really pissed you off, didn't she?"

He nods. "She completely blindsided me with the personal stuff. It was firmly in the 'do not ask' demands we gave her."

I make a noncommittal noise, fiddling with my napkin.

"How was the tour?" he asks.

Fed up, I say sharply, "Are we going to chitchat all night? Because I'd rather stab myself in the eyeballs. And there's no way I'm having sex with you. So if that's what you're after, you can kick rocks."

His eyes flare with amusement, though his expression stays somber. "Rose, I'm not here for that. I want to make amends."

"So, go ahead."

He stands up and walks out of the kitchen. I stare after him, frowning, but he returns a few seconds later with a thin, folded newspaper. Instead of bringing it to the table, he tucks it under an arm and clears the soup bowls and utensils to the sink. Then he places the newspaper directly in front of me.

It takes a few moments to make sense of what I see—not that it makes any sense at all.

Before me is the front page of *The Seattle Times* from February 19th, 2002. Exactly one week after my parents' deaths.

A huge color photograph stretches beneath the title *The Price of Fame and The Legacy of Addiction*. The photo is of thirteen-year-old me throwing dirt into the gaping hole where my parents' coffins rest. I'm all wild curly hair, pale skin, and huge eyes. It's hard to read the expression on my face. If anything, I look desensitized.

Jerking my gaze up from my image, I whisper roughly, "What is this? Why do you have this?"

"I was eighteen when they died," he says softly. "Living on the streets and singing with a borrowed guitar for money to eat. I passed a newspaper stand and saw the photo. I stole the paper."

I touch the crease, worn almost flat by time. The paper itself looks delicate, faded. I shake my head in confusion.

"I don't understand. Why?"

Julian shrugs. "Why did I take it? I don't know. Maybe some part of me knew I was going down a dark road and the article felt like a warning. Something I needed to remember. What I do know is that when I got sober and had a place to live, I kept it pinned to the wall over my bed. It stayed there for years. Every time I wavered in my sobriety, doubting my alcoholism because of my age, or because I couldn't relate to people, or was rejected by a woman, or embarrassed myself, or wrote a crappy song…" He takes a breath. "That photograph reminded me of who I was, where I came from. And what could happen to my daughter someday."

A drop of wetness hits the corner of the newspaper; I blink at it, belatedly realizing it's a tear. Sitting back quickly, I grab a napkin and wipe my eyes.

Finally, I manage, "This is a lot to take in, Julian. I'm not sure what to say."

"You don't have to say anything, just listen. You've always been this figment in my life, a symbol of something I was equally drawn to and wanted to avoid. The promise of a happy life and the threat of an alcoholic death. But for as long as I can remember, I've wanted to protect the girl in that photograph. And instead, I hurt her. Repeatedly. I made her hate me."

I whisper, "I don't hate you."

"I hurt you, Rose. I did exactly what you accused me of. I threw you away. Because I was afraid."

Blinking back a new surge of tears, I have a sudden memory of something Aunt Katherine once said. When I asked—or thought about asking—why Julian kissed me the first time.

Fear. Doubt. Hope.

And it makes sense, now. In a way that's almost incomprehensible.

He continues, "When we met that day at Tullamore, the second I looked across that counter I knew who you were. And I wanted you. More than I'd wanted anything in my life. Even sobriety, the band, peace, family. Everything. It scared the shit out me. Then Missy called, wanting to get back together, and I... I made a mistake. The first of many."

"Julian," I breathe, shaking my head. "I can't—this is too much."

"When Missy told me she was pregnant, I was elated. I've always wanted to be a father, to be for a child what your parents couldn't be for you. It blinded me to the truth. The truth of her, you, and myself. I started acting out of fear and impulse—"

"Stop. Stop. Stop!"

I throw my chair back and stand, stalking across the room to the sink. Gripping the cool steel rim in my hands, I stare out the window. It's dark outside, the rain making halos of house lights across the street.

Humorless laughter bubbles in my throat. Bowing

my head, I close my eyes and grit my teeth until the urge passes.

"I thought you were going to say 'sorry I was a dick' and I could say, 'okay bye forever' and that would be it."

I hear him stand. I tense, but he doesn't move closer to me.

"Tell me what to say to make this better, Rose. Please."

"You can't!" I yell, spinning to face him. "Don't you get it? I cared about you, you sonofabitch. *A lot.* And now you tell me all this?" I wave a hand at the newspaper. "I'm a symbol? Of everything you want and everything you lost, or could lose, or whatever. What am I supposed to do with that? Tell *me*, Julian! How is this fair? Or okay, or right?"

"It's not," he breathes. "But it's the truth. And what I feel for you is real, and perfect—"

"Don't you fucking say that," I snarl, striding across the room to jab a finger in his chest. "You don't get to say shit like that to me. Not now, not ever."

My voice cracks and fades, my throat on fire from what I just put it through. And Julian... Julian watches me with sympathy, and sadness, and acceptance.

"Rose, let me fix you some warm salt water. You should take a shower, too. Lots of steam."

I think I could have handled just about anything but his kindness. The edges of me fold into themselves, crumpling down until I'm made small. So small. The girl in that photograph again, the living legacy of addiction. A survivor, but only because I had no choice.

Sobbing, I reach for him. Not because I want him, but because I need *someone*. Human contact. Confirmation that I'm still here, still me.

Julian sweeps me off my feet and carries me to my bed, sitting down with me in his arms. I cling to him, shaking with the force of a grief that will never truly fade.

Because of my lost voice, my cries are silent, but their force manifests in other ways. He doesn't once loosen his hold, though, doesn't even flinch as my fingers clench deeply into the muscles of his shoulders and arms.

Finally, after minutes that feel like days, my tremors ease and the storm within me passes.

"I'm sorry," I rasp against his throat, the skin damp with my tears.

"Don't speak," he says, and shifts to guide me back onto the pillows. "I'm getting you saltwater."

He leaves the room. I hear him in the kitchen opening cabinets, running the water. By the time he returns, I've managed to prop myself against the headboard. As he approaches the bed, I see his slight limp, which only reminds me of that terrible day, those terrible words, and brings a fresh flood of tears to my eyes.

Julian's been in a motorcycle accident.

Quickly wiping my wet face, I scoot aside so he can sit. When I reach for the glass, he shakes his head and carefully holds it to my lips.

"Gargle and spit." I glance from the glass to him, frowning, and his lips twitch. "It's your own backwash. Do it."

Afraid of hurting my vocal chords further by speaking, I take the easy road and gargle, spit, gargle, spit until he's satisfied.

"Should I leave so you can get in the shower?" My head shakes before my brain can tell my body to shut up. He must see the panic in my eyes, because he says, "I'll stay. Are you tired?" I shake my head. "Come on, then."

He stands up, offering me his hand. His *brokenhealed* hand. I take it, letting firm, strong fingers grip mine and leverage me up.

"You have to put on a different shirt," he mutters, leading me down the hall into the living room. With clear relief, he grabs a blanket from the back of the couch and wraps it around my shoulders. "Sit down and find a movie. I'll bring you pie. No ice cream though." I groan, and his eyes flash, bright and laughing, to my face. "No dairy until your throat heals."

Huffing, I sit and turn on the television. I scroll aimlessly through the guide until I spy *Arsenic and Old Lace* and quickly select the movie. If Julian doesn't like it, he can suffer.

Returning to the living room, he says, "Oh man, I love this movie. Cary Grant is hysterical."

Figures.

Handing me a bowl with pie in it, he sits on the other end of the couch. I glance from the bowl to him.

He notices my look. "Bowls are better for pie. Just mash it all together and scoop it up."

I stare at him another moment, then look down.

"You always eat your pie like this, don't you?" he asks quietly.

I nod.

Eyes on the television, he says with quiet precision, "Perfect."

The broken half of my heart tingles, waking up from dormancy. Like an atrophied muscle, it hurts. Tears once more pool in my eyes and leak down my cheeks.

"Say the word, Rose, and I'll leave."

I lift my head and look at him.

Just… look.

Clear eyes, full of self-awareness and depth, are whiskey-dark right now as they watch me. Faint lines fan from them, more than were there at this time last year. Sloping eyebrows are currently raised in question, and his long, straight nose has a new bump from being broken. On his jaw, a thin scar interrupts the stubble near his right ear. Lastly, I gaze at his firm, generous mouth, punctuated by the promise of a dimple on the left.

"Do you want me to stay?" he murmurs.

Rose—yes—say yes.

I don't speak, but I mouth the word. He smiles softly, then settles back to watch the movie and eat his pie.

And I do the same.

25

SO IT GOES

Sunday is spent doing laundry, unpacking from the tour, and babying my throat with steam and saltwater. By the time night begins creeping over the city, I'm exhausted and hungry, but there's nothing in my fridge except pie and soup. Since I ate the former for breakfast and the latter for lunch, I'm craving something different.

My voice is back—barely—but I don't want to push it, so I text Greta and wait for a response. Ten minutes later, I acknowledge she must be at work, so I text Melody.

Hungry and sick. Feed me

Can't sry. Dinner with Matt's parents.
Hiding in bathroom.

I snort.

> Can't wait for the story. Call me tomorrow!

Will do

Next, I try Aunt Katherine, who doesn't respond, then Allison, who's on a break at work. Then Greg, who's no doubt sick of my face, but might feel sorry enough for me to bring me sustenance. No go—he's with Kelly, which means he's probably naked. And naked makes me think first of Aiden, whose calls and texts I have yet to respond to, and then of Julian, who kept his clothes on all night and his distance, too.

We watched black and white movies until I fell asleep on the couch sometime after midnight. He tugged me to my room and tucked me into bed, then left with the ominous parting words, "I'm not done making amends to you."

I couldn't reply, but I'm pretty sure he got the message my glare was sending.

Fiddling with my phone, I pull up Aiden's number. Then I hesitate, my thoughts skittish as I walk down the hallway to the living room. I flop onto the couch and stare at the ceiling light, which unfortunately doesn't yield any insights.

Weird drama with Breaking Giants' aside, I like Aiden. He's level-headed, sweet, and he busted his ass for six weeks on tour with me. We have awesome chemistry, mutual respect for each other as artists, and sex with him (all two days of it before I got sick) was great. Easy.

Not explosive, or primal, or the least bit raunchy. No headboards were injured. No hair pulled. No teeth marks in skin or nails scratching or *Rose Cunningham, you are* loud.

"Shit," I whisper, knuckling my eyes against memories that, even nearly a year later, are vivid enough they could have happened yesterday.

I threw you away. Because I was afraid.

Julian's words float back to me, igniting old hurt and fresh anger. I was moving on. I was getting over him—I *was* over him—before he once again barged into my life and turned it sideways.

Singing my own songs with me. Showing me that newspaper. Accepting my abuse while I sobbed in his arms. Saltwater kindness. Mashing my pie and laughing as on the television, Cary Grant deals with his crazy family. Looking at me with eyes that hold new gravity, born of his accident, his long rehabilitation.

The rehabilitation he hadn't wanted me to be a part of.

Sitting up, I text Aiden.

He's at my house an hour later with burritos and cold

medicine and flowers. We eat and flip through channels on the television, and I make him finish Greta's pie.

After, despite his protestations—albeit weak ones—I lead him into the bathroom and fill the big tub with hot water and lavender scented bubbles. We undress each other slowly, kissing skin as it's exposed, until I forget about Julian again.

I wake up much later, in the dark of my bedroom, consumed by anxiety from a dream I can't remember. Reaching across the sheets, I touch Aiden's warm arm. He murmurs something and shifts away.

As I slowly relax and begin to drift back to sleep, I remember a snippet of the dream. A tarot card lying face up, signifying its bright, fully actualized aspect.

The Prince of Swords.

♫

Nursing a cup of tea at Tullamore the following Saturday afternoon, I stare across the table at Melody.

"I don't know," I say doubtfully, "I'm not sure it's a good idea."

She squints at me. "You never think anything's a good idea at first. It's just a birthday party."

"Julian's birthday party."

She shrugs. "Look, I know you guys have more baggage than a 747, but it's going to be a huge party. At least a hundred people. You don't have to talk to him except to say 'happy birthday bye.' Matt and I want you to come. We miss you. The weather is finally warm. Just think of it as any other summer party."

I hold up a hand to halt her tirade. "I don't think Aiden's going to like me going. I don't want to fuck this up. He's nice."

She groans. "Nice. Yuck." At my scowl, she grins. "Sorry. And you're right, he probably won't like it. But you should still come. I'll be lonely."

Rolling my eyes, I finish my tea. The café is busy around us; outside, the weather is warm and clear. A perfect day for a party.

I think back to the voicemail Julian left me earlier this week, haltingly inviting me to his birthday party. His thirty-fourth. But only if I was feeling better. And if I wanted to come. It was okay if I didn't, but he didn't want me to feel excluded.

Ugh.

At length, Melody casually asks, "Has Aiden told you why he was kicked out of the band?"

My shoulders bunch. "I haven't asked," I admit.

"Huh."

I narrow my eyes. "What does that mean?"

She blinks innocently back at me. "Nothing. Just surprised. Don't you want to know?"

"Not really," I mutter.

"Okay."

We stare at each other.

Finally, I sigh. "You're a pain in the ass, Mel."

She grins, fully aware that I'm conceding defeat. "I know. How about we drop your car at your place? We can get ready at mine and head to the party in…" She glances at her watch, "an hour? Just enough time to get you buzzed on daiquiris and convince you to wear the smallest bikini I own."

"What? Hell no," I protest, then see the wicked glint in her eye. "Stop it. Stop it right now."

Laughing, she stands and grabs her purse. "You do know I always get what I want, right?"

She doesn't wait for a reply, flouncing toward the front door. I let her have her moment of imagined victory and wave goodbye to Christy and Allison before following.

An hour later, Melody finally accepts that I won't wear the indecent, silver, sorry excuse for a bathing suit she forces on me. She does, however, demand that I change my requisite jeans and t-shirt.

After some haggling—and my second daiquiri—I leave the house wearing shorts that are probably making my father roll in his grave and a flowing tank top that despite its loose fit, is almost as risqué as my silk camisole.

At least I'm wearing a bra.

It isn't until we pull off the exit for Mercer Island that the reasonable half of my brain wakes up from its coma. But by then it's too late, and minutes later we arrive at a ginormous gated property with cars stacked in the driveway and against all surrounding curbs.

Melody pulls to a stop beside a valet stand and smiling young men open our doors.

Feeling a little numb, and a lot nervous, I follow Melody to the open gate where a woman stands with a clipboard.

"Names?" she asks.

"Rose Cunningham and Melody Finnegan."

The woman's gaze snaps to me, then roams down the clipboard. "Cunningham." A scratch as she checks off my name. "And Finnegan." Another scratch, and a bright smile. "Enjoy the party, ladies!"

Melody links her arm through mine and saunters up the driveway. The massive front doors are open, allowing thumping music and loud chatter to reach our ears. Small groups of people mill on the manicured lawn and flow in and out of the house.

As we walk up steps toward the door, I look up. And up.

"Who's house is this?" I ask.

"A label exec's," she says, then giggles. "Wait till you see the pool. It's ridiculous."

Melody, who was here yesterday with the party planners, guides me confidently through the throngs toward the backyard. We step outside onto a covered patio that runs the length of the house.

People are everywhere. Draped on lounge furniture, clustered around a state-of-the-art outdoor kitchen, laughing and dancing and having a good time.

> *Tick tock when it stops*
> *I'll fall into the deep*
> *After all, the world is small*
> *and when it's dark I'll sleep*

"Come on, I see Matt," Melody chirps, and drags me forward again.

A shirtless Matt is sitting on the edge of a spectacular pool, shaped like a kidney bean with sapphire water. A huge jacuzzi is nearby, packed with people. Most of the women strolling around are wearing bikinis that make the silver one look conservative.

"Ladies!" cries Matt when he sees us. He leaps to standing and gives Melody a kiss, then crushes me in a hug. "Thanks so much for coming, Rose. It means the world to him."

My stomach does a queer dive. Laughing forcefully, I

step out of his reach, cursing the fact I let Melody railroad me into taking one car. Glancing around, I wonder if I can slip away and hide in a room somewhere until she's ready to leave.

"Oh, there's Julian," says Melody, then yells, "Don't break anything, birthday boy!"

Turning my head, I see Julian standing on the far side of the pool about to dive in. And, like every other woman in the backyard, all I can do is stare.

Before the accident, Julian had a great body. I should know. Now, after months of physical training, he's… breathtaking. Corded, lean muscle everywhere. Washboard abs and that defined V low on his torso that women cream their pants over.

To add torture to my private hell, he's already wet, water dripping down his sculpted chest, over assorted tattoos, through the faint trail of hair leading into his black board shorts.

I am not immune.

Not by a long shot.

But what lands the hardest punch isn't his droolworthy physique, but the new scars. None of them are large or detract from his virility, but I nevertheless see them immediately. The right side of his chest. Left, high by his shoulder, and another near his ribs. And the little line on his abdomen from surgery.

When I finally drag my gaze up, the impact of

Julian's eyes on me feels physical. Then he smiles, gives me a little wave, and dives into the pool.

Blinking, I return from the border of spontaneous combustion and look at Melody.

She's grinning. "I think fifty women just murdered you with their eyes."

"W-what?" I stammer, but sure enough, when I look quickly around I see baleful glares being cast in my direction. And they make me wonder what expression Julian was wearing before I looked up.

"Melody, you're freaking relentless," chides Matt, throwing his arm around my shoulders. "Come on, Rosie Posie, let's go find you a drink."

"Good idea," I say, and let him lead me away.

26

FELINE TENDENCIES

Matt abandons me a little while later, but only after finding me a safe group of people to hang with. Ensconced on an outdoor couch next to Nick and his girlfriend, I slowly relax and even begin to enjoy myself. We're merely three among many watching a violent game of ping-pong between Jackson and one of Breaking Giant's production crew.

Much to the delight of everyone, Nick is playing sportscaster for the event, booming out updates every few seconds.

"Ah, a brilliant shot by the wily Jackson Everett! Ladies, take note—he wields paddles in the bedroom with even more skill!" The crowd cheers, women yelling approval.

Jackson flushes, shaking his head.

"You're so mean," I tell Nick, but I'm laughing.

He grins through a new, thick beard. "Jackson's shy. Just doing my bro a favor."

When someone sits on the arm of the couch beside me, I open my mouth to offer to shift down. Then I see a chiseled calf muscle, and my gaze wanders up to black board shorts, and then to *abs in my face*.

Julian smiles down at me. "Hi, Rose."

"Hi," I say, then clear my throat because *breathless*. "Happy birthday. It's today, right? July 1st?"

"Yep," he says, glancing at the game before turning back to me. "Do you want anything to eat?"

"No, um, I'm okay," I say, then because I suck at lying, I blush.

Julian's smile widens. "You're hungry. Want a burger?"

"I, uh—"

Whiskey eyes flicker to my mouth. "I could probably get you pancakes if you'd prefer."

I want to fuck your mouth, Rose.

The sudden memory is kerosene on a flame. I'm pretty sure my pupils dilate with the force of my arousal because Julian sucks in a sharp breath. He shifts on the arm of the couch and quickly stands. His expression darkens for a moment, then like clouds passing, brightens again.

"Come on, let's get you some food," he says, offering me his hand.

There are people watching us, Nick and his girlfriend Kat among them. Nick says cheerily, "Hey Rose, if you bring me back a burger I'll let you open for us on tour."

"Nick!" snaps Julian.

Thankful beyond words for the diversion, I laugh and stand up. "I'll get you one. No bribery required. Kat, how about you?"

She shakes her head, smiling. "I'll just eat half of Nick's."

"What? No way," he protests, then at Kat's sweet smile, he deflates. "Of course you can have half my burger, sugarplum." Out of the corner of his mouth, he hisses at me, *"Two burgers."*

Laughing, I nod and turn around, running smack into Julian's warm, naked chest.

"Sorry," I gasp, jerking backward.

He laughs. "Not the most graceful, are you, Cunningham?"

I frown up at him, but it's taking effort to hold in a smile. "Whatever, *Ashburn*. Time to eat."

He swallows. "Yes. Okay. Burgers."

On that awkward note, he turns and walks through the crowd. When we're swiftly separated by moving bodies, he stops and grabs my hand, placing my palm on his shoulder.

Throwing back a grin, he says, "Safety chain."

"This does *not* feel safe," I mutter, though thankfully my admission is swallowed by the noise around us.

I do my best not to stroke his smooth skin, but it's a freaking battle. And when he stops abruptly, and I careen into his back, the press of him against my breasts and stomach ignites a longing so deep and vast, so far beyond rational thinking, that it feels like a crime to ignore it.

People press around us, talking and smiling and wishing Julian a happy birthday. But here, in the small space of the universe occupied only by us, his hands come back and seize my hips, holding me to him. The pressure in his fingers isn't demanding, or overtly sexual, but it's Julian touching me. Liquid warmth surges between my legs, and my hips twitch involuntarily.

Julian's fingers clench, branding skin below the hem of my shorts.

And I finally wake up.

I snatch my hand from his shoulder and step backward, mumbling, "Sorry," to the person I crash into.

Turning blindly, I push through the crowd toward the house, continuing with a litany of *Sorry, Sorry*, as I fight the tide, and rising claustrophobia, and *JulianJulianJulian*.

"Rose!"

I hear his call, the frustration, the appeal, but I don't stop. Can't. I make it into the house, down a long hallway toward the distant light signifying the open front door.

As I pass another hallway, Melody calls out, "Rose?"

I start running. Out the door, down the driveway, past the gate. I don't stop until I'm several blocks away. Yanking my phone from my back pocket, I dial the only person I know for sure isn't working or busy.

"Hey, sexy," answers Aiden.

"I need you to come pick me up on Mercer Island." I sound breathless, panicked. Before he can say anything or ask why the hell I'm on Mercer Island, I tell him the address of the house to my left.

He asks, "Are you safe?"

"Yes," I gasp.

"Hang tight. I'm not far. Be there in ten to fifteen."

He hangs up.

Sitting on the curb beside an ornate mailbox, I pull my knees to my chest and drop my head. Images and sensations cascade through me. Teasing grin. Golden molasses eyes. The babbling introvert gone—the frontman charisma aimed like a spotlight on me. Making me feel unique and precious. Desired. Like the luckiest woman in the world.

I thump my forehead against my knees.

"Rose."

My stomach clenches; I don't lift my head. "Go back to your party."

"I'm sorry."

Frowning, I look up. "Stop saying that."

He must have fled straight after me because he's barefoot. Sunlight teases the tattoo on his left pectoral, an antique pocket watch set to the time 2:12.

He says with quiet intensity, "I want you in my life, Rose."

I shake my head, feeling that deranged laughter clogging my throat again.

"What did you call us? Oh, right. Supernovas and black holes."

"I said that, yes," he admits, "but I'm not the same person I was then."

"Neither am I. And in case you forgot, I'm seeing someone."

"I know," he says mutedly. "I want to be friends. Can we try? Please?"

My muscles spasm, sending me to my feet in a fit of rage and need and helplessness. So I say what I know will hurt him, because it's the only way to protect myself.

"The only friends you want to be are the kind that fuck. Right, Julian? Cause we're so, so good at it. But you know what? Aiden's good, too. Better, even. Because there's no lying, or cheating, or shame and guilt."

He jerks, taking a half step back. His expression shutters, eyes emotionless and dark.

"You're sleeping with him," he says flatly.

"Yes!" The laughter finally releases, bitter and *wrong*. "What did you expect? Did you really think I'd wait for you? After what you did to me? I'm over you. I don't want you anymore."

"Okay," he says, his voice low and hard. "You've made your point."

I deflate. "Good."

He gives me a tight smile. "I'm glad you got all that off your chest. I hope this means we can function in a professional capacity from here on out."

I blink, my mind fogging. "What?"

His smile sharpens. "You're being signed by our label, and you're coming on tour with us in two months."

"The hell I am," I whisper hoarsely. "I don't know what garbage you're spouting—"

He takes two quick steps, bringing us face to face. "You're going to sign a contract with Indigo because you're not stupid. And you're coming on tour for the same reason."

"Is this more twisted amends bullshit?" I ask, and instantly feel a spike of shame.

His eyes flash darkly. "I didn't ask them to sign you—do you think I want to get punched in the face again? A scout has been tracking you."

A car turns the distant corner, and I recognize Aiden's SUV. Julian follows my gaze, then his eyes lock on mine.

Before I can read his intent, he reaches up and sinks his fingers into the hair at the nape of my neck, tightening them until I suck in a startled breath of lust and self-loathing.

Tilting my face up until I have no choice but to stare into his burning eyes, he murmurs, "You're right. I don't want to be friends, and the thought of Aiden touching you makes me fucking crazy. But rest assured, I know when you're lying. The two of you don't compare to *us*, and someday soon I'm going to obliterate all traces of him from your body."

Then his grip vanishes and he's gone, jogging away, back to his party.

A car pulls to a stop behind me, and a door opens. "Rose?" asks Aiden cautiously. "Was that Julian?"

I nod, as yet unable to face him.

"Is there something I should know?"

PullittogetherRose.

Dragging air into my lungs, I plaster a smile on my face and turn. "I'll explain in the car. I have some pretty incredible news."

♫

WHEN WE ARRIVE at my house, Aiden follows me up the front steps. I unlock the front door with my spare key but turn before he can follow me inside. His brows lift, and in his eyes lingers suspicion and hurt, neither of which I could fully alleviate with my fumbling explanation in the car. Sure, he didn't hear Julian's final words to me, but he saw well enough our near-intimate stance.

Feeling reckless and sharp-edged, I blurt, "Why did they kick you out of the band?"

He takes a step back, frowning. "It was a million years ago. Why is it important?"

"If it's not important, why don't you just tell me?"

He drags a hand through his hair, eyes sliding away from mine. "Creative differences. Julian wanted to take the band to melodic la-la land, and I wanted to stay hardcore."

Surprise and dismay filter through me at his bitter tone. "Melodic la-la land, huh? If that describes Breaking Giants, what am I, bubble-gum pop?"

"No," he snaps.

"Why are you so angry?" I ask quietly.

He releases a long sigh, but his shoulders stay tense. "Look, Rose, I really like you, but I'm not at a point in my life where I want a lot of complications."

I blink a few times. "I'm sorry, I think I just side-stepped into Crazytown. Are you breaking up with me because I asked why you left Breaking Giants?"

"Breaking Giants, Breaking Giants," he mocks. "I swear to God, it's all I hear. And now Indigo Records is probably signing you, and you get to piggyback to stardom on Julian-fucking-Ashburn's glittery wings."

Completely turned off by his sudden shift from nice to nasty, I hold up a hand to stall further venom. My emotions, already chaotic from Julian, twist and turn like a tree in a hurricane.

"You know what, Aiden? Forget it. This is obviously a mistake."

Shoulders slumping, the fire leaves his eyes. "I'm sorry. You didn't deserve that. I just have a raw nerve where Julian is concerned."

Rubbing the space between my eyebrows where a headache looms, I say as evenly as I can, "Let's talk in a few days, okay?"

He knows I'm calling it quits, and I see both resignation and relief in his eyes.

"Okay, Rose. Take care. And good luck."

I wave goodbye as he walks down my driveway and hops into his car. Then he's gone, and I'm back where I started. Alone with a head full of thoughts I don't want to think and a body full of unnamed need. Only the need does, in fact, have a name.

Once I'm in the house, I call Aunt Katherine. When she answers, I say, "She was right. I'm just like her. Maybe it's not heroin, but it's an addiction just the same. I'm ready for some freaking treatment. What do I do?"

There's a long pause. "Oh, honey, it's not an addiction. At least, not in the way you mean."

"Then what the hell is it?" I cry.

Gently, she answers, "It's love."

27

HALF-PAST NEVER O'CLOCK

Thursday morning, I have the coveted meeting at Indigo Records. At Greta's insistence, I bring her father with me. A spritely man in his sixties with his daughter's blonde hair and green eyes, he happens to be a fancy downtown lawyer with a soft spot for me.

Also with us is Greg, still my acting manager, as well as a surprisingly young and easygoing label executive, the scout who saw me in California and tracked my progress on tour, and the label's straight-faced lawyer.

We've moved past the wooing stage to the nitty-gritty. As legal jargon gets tossed back and forth across the conference table, I hear echoes of conversations overheard between my parents.

Copyrights and licensing. Royalty rates. Exclusivity.

Twelve-month contract with the expectation that I record at least one full-length, commercial album.

On and on it goes, until the sound of my name jolts me from a daydream involving bubble bath and chocolate.

"Rose, now that the paperwork is out of the way, if you don't mind I'd like to invite Julian Ashburn into the room."

The words, spoken by the executive who looks like a surfer at his day job, snap me out of my daze. Though my impulse is to ask why, I already have a suspicion.

Plus, I'm being grown up and polite.

"Absolutely," I say.

Mr. Exec—aka Cory Donovan, aka owner of Mercer Island mansion—pushes a button on a small console and trades words with a receptionist. Less than a minute later, I see Julian walking down the hallway toward the glass-walled conference room.

Wearing dark jeans, a faded t-shirt beneath an unzipped hoodie, and his glasses, he looks completely out of place and at the same time, totally at home. As well he should. Before Breaking Giants' astronomical success, Indigo was a small fish in a big pond. Now they swim easily with the sharks.

When Julian sees me watching him, he smiles broadly, with absolutely no trace of our last interaction. Wishing I was as unaffected, I straighten in my chair.

He enters the room like the superstar he is, shaking hands with everyone, then bending down to give me a squeeze around the shoulders and a peck on the cheek. Fast. Platonic.

You know, because we're *professionals*.

When he sits beside Cory near the head of the table, he catches my eye. Responding either to the dark humor in my gaze or the sardonic tilt of my lips, he winks and shakes his head chidingly. I slowly unclench my teeth and paste on my *excited to be here* expression.

Julian rocks back in his chair, lacing fingers behind his head. "Rose, congratulations. Cory wanted me to come down this morning to personally invite you on tour with Breaking Giants this fall."

Even though I'm not surprised, I still feel the impact of the words. How could I not? They're the equivalent of winning the musical lottery.

I'm suddenly breathless, my wide eyes and the tremor in my voice unfeigned. "Thank you. What a huge honor, Mr. Donovan. I'm blown away."

"You're very welcome," he replies magnanimously. "As I'm sure you know, it's not entirely altruistic. Your musical styles complement each other, and a lot of Breaking Giants' fans have already heard your name. It just makes sense."

It does make sense. To capitalize on Breaking Giants' fanbase to launch a new act. And squeeze every drop of rumor and conjecture out of Julian's and my past to sell out venues.

Well, at least he's honest.

"I understand," I say, smiling brightly. "It's a good business decision and we'll all benefit. I'm grateful to be working with a label that cultivates creative freedom while protecting the bottom line."

Julian whistles. "Cory, you sure you want to take that on?"

Cory laughs. "I'd expect nothing less from the daughter of music greats."

The meeting wraps a few minutes later. Handshakes and smiles all around. I say goodbye to Greta's dad, then gather my things and wait near the door for Greg, who's chatting animatedly with Cory like he just found his new best friend.

Citrus and sandalwood.

"Congrats, Rose. Really."

I look up at Julian, then away, unable to maintain eye contact. Aunt Katherine's pronouncement is still ringing in my ears and bones. I'm not sure what to make of it yet; or rather, I'm not sure it changes anything.

Regardless of Julian saying he's not the same person he was last year, I still think his own pronouncement remains painfully relevant. *Supernovas and black holes.*

We've hurt each other, over and over. Just like my

parents. And there's no guarantee that the cycle is broken. Or can be broken.

"You look so sad," he whispers. "What can I do?"

Blinking hard, I smile. *Professionals.* "Take Greg and me to lunch to celebrate?"

Julian nods. "Of course."

From across the room, Greg asks, "Rose, do you mind if I hang here? Cory's going to hook me up with Breaking Giants' manager, Phil."

My smile freezes. "Sure, not a problem."

Julian says softly, "I know just the place to eat."

♫

"Basilico?" I hiss at him as we walk into the iconic downtown eatery. "Aren't we a little under-dressed?"

Julian smirks down at me. "Who cares?"

"Ah, that's right," I say dryly. "You're Julian Ashburn."

His eyes flare with laughter. "And you're Rose Cunningham. Time you start acting like it." To the maître d', he says, "Two, please. Front patio, if available."

Looking surprised, the man replies, "Of course, Mr. Ashburn. Right this way."

"You eat here a lot?" I whisper, mindful of the growing interest from the other diners, mostly upper-crust urbanites having power lunches over wine and risotto. As Julian holds the patio door open for me, I elaborate, "In public?"

"No," he says easily. "I normally eat in a private room in back."

To that, I have no response. It isn't until we're seated on the patio—very much in view of the other patrons and the bustling street—that I understand he's doing preemptive advertising for the upcoming tour.

On the one hand, I admire his business savvy. On the other, I feel a little used.

Taking a sip of water flavored with fresh mint, I say blandly, "You're full of surprises, Ashburn."

"Mmm," he replies, eyes on the menu. "You have no idea."

I jerk forward. "What does that mean? Did you call the press or something?"

One eyebrow cocks up. "You think I'd have to?"

I give the tables around us the side-eye, gauging their occupants' interest. Most seem oblivious or mildly disdainful of our attire. Then my gaze flows to the sidewalk, partially obscured by an awning and separated from us by two empty tables.

There, amidst flowing foot traffic, I see a young

woman standing stock-still, her mouth open as she stares at us.

"Do you want some wine?" asks Julian. At my sharp look, he shrugs. "It won't bother me. The guys drink around me all the time."

"Shouldn't you lower your voice?" I whisper.

He laughs, settling back and lowering his menu. Dancing eyes scan my face. "You're wound tighter than a two dollar watch. Relax."

"A two dollar watch?" I echo. "What are you, eighty-five?"

His smile softens. "It's something my friend used to say before he died."

His first sponsor.

"Ah, okay." I shift in my seat and take another sip of water, then glance at, but don't read, the menu. "So I'm tense. Can you blame me? Whenever we're in the same place at the same time, bad things happen."

I instantly realize my mistake.

His eyes narrow, darkening dangerously. "Bad, bad things."

Unstoppable heat floods my cheeks, my mind happily providing an assortment of memories for my sensory pleasure. Sweaty skin and gasping moans and my hair in his fists. Perched on my knees, my fingers digging into the headboard. An ice cube melting on his tongue, on my...

"Stop flirting," I hiss.

"Is that what I'm doing?" he asks, propping an elbow on the table and resting his chin on his palm. "What were you just thinking about?"

"Nothing."

"You were thinking about us, weren't you?"

"No."

I'm saved from further response by our server, who asks Julian if he wants his usual, and when he nods, I say, "I'll have the same."

"Very good, madam." With a slight bow, he retreats inside the restaurant.

Julian gazes thoughtfully at me. "You seem different today." A pause. "Less antagonistic."

Drumming my fingers on the edge of the table, I shrug. "This is business, and we're professionals, right? And if we have to be stuck on a tour bus together, we need to learn how to get along."

His lips twitch. "There's no way you're coming on our bus. You'll have your own." I frown, and he leans back in his chair with a grin. "First, I don't think you'd appreciate what happens a lot on there. And two, I can't sleep that close to you."

Awareness frissons down my spine; with effort, I focus on his first statement.

"What happens a lot?" I repeat, then my eyes narrow angrily. "Matt can't possibly think he can cheat on

Melody while on tour. I'll fucking flay him. And Nick? He really didn't strike me as that kind of guy."

Julian lifts a hand, laughing. "I'm not talking about that. I'm talking about four guys in a small space, with one bathroom, acting like assholes."

"Ah," I say, understanding. "Smelly."

He chuckles. "To put it lightly."

A few minutes later, our server returns bearing steaming plates of sweet potato gnocchi. It's excellent, and we eat in companionable silence until the growing disturbance outside becomes impossible to ignore. The other diners are trading confused glances, though a few are avidly watching the progression of the crowd.

On the sidewalk, people are snapping pictures of us with their cell phones. When Julian glances over, several of them shout his name. He doesn't seem the least bit bothered, unhurriedly scooping up the last morsels of his lunch.

For as long as I've known about Breaking Giants, I've known about Julian's loathing of public attention. But maybe, as he said, he's not the same person he was before the accident.

Thinking about the day at Tullamore when the sight of the crowd outside had triggered a panic attack, I eye him for signs of anxiety.

There are none.

Sitting back, he asks me, "Are you finished?" I nod,

and he signals our server, who looks both flustered and excited about the attention. "Henry, can we leave the back way?"

"Of course," he says.

When we stand, the shouting from the sidewalk increases. As we head into the restaurant, Julian faces our audience and waves.

"Thanks, guys, have a great day."

His hand settles on my back, sliding proprietarily down to the curve just above my ass. My knees go liquid, but when I stumble, he shifts to support my body with his. Behind us, the crowd's noise doubles in intensity.

"Asshole," I mutter.

His lips graze the hair over my ear. "We're going to sell out every single show. Glance back and give them that sultry look you so do well. Smile and wave."

I have no idea what look he's talking about, but I do as he says, smiling and giving a brief wave. Seconds later, we're inside the quieter confines of the restaurant.

The head of Julian's security—Randy, I found out at the hospital—nods from his station just inside the front door. Behind him, people press against the glass.

"Your car's out back," he tells Julian, tossing him a set of keys.

"Thanks, Randy."

Our server leads us down a hallway, through a

kitchen of staring people, and out a back door. In the narrow alley, a sleek Audi waits.

"Sorry for the disturbance, Henry," says Julian, shaking the man's hand.

Henry, who I'm starting to think might be the manager, just grins. "Not a problem, Mr. Ashburn."

Julian winks, then strides around the car to open the passenger door. Taking the hint, I follow and slip into the cozy leather seat. The door closes, and he rounds the hood, sliding behind the wheel.

He starts the car and puts it in gear. "Sorry you didn't get dessert."

I roll my eyes. "It's not a requirement at every meal for me or anything."

"Uh huh," he says cheekily, then navigates us out of the alley and onto the busy downtown avenue. "Do we need to go back to Indigo for your car?"

"Greg drove, so I'm good."

He hesitates. "Do you want me to take you home?"

The arousal that's been simmering since I saw him walking down the hallway at Indigo flares. *Home. Bed. Now.* I smother the impulse with moderate success.

But I also don't want to say goodbye to him yet, the conviction unsettling in its magnitude.

"Can we just drive for a while?" I ask.

He smiles. "Yes."

28

CREST

Several hours later, after a relaxing stop at Alki Beach and a quick detour for gelato in Ballard, Julian pulls into my driveway. He leaves the car running, and we sit for a few minutes in silence, our seatbelts still on and tension ratcheting in the space between us.

I tell myself repeatedly to get out of the car but can't make my body obey. Nor can I look at him, though I feel his gaze, heavy and searching on the side of my face. That old need rises, clogging my airways and scattering my thoughts.

Finally, I muster enough brain cells to speak. "Thanks for lunch and gelato. And, um, everything."

"Of course. Do you—that is, are you seeing Aiden tonight?"

"No," I whisper, then clear my throat. I consider lying

but decide I can't be that petty. "We ended things on Saturday. It was mutual."

He's silent a few moments. "Did he tell you why we kicked him out?"

"Yeah. Creative differences."

He huffs a caustic laugh. "My ass."

My stomach sinks. "What do you mean?"

Julian sighs, pulling off his glasses to rub the bridge of his nose. "When we were just starting out, Matt's little sister Erin would come on tour with us and sell merch. Aiden seduced her, and they fooled around for a while. She was in love, but he... Let's just say his appetites weren't satisfied by one woman at a time."

My mouth drops open. "Oh my God. How old was she?"

He frowns a little. "She's twenty-eight, so... nineteen, twenty? She was devastated. Dropped out of school and everything. Doing great now, though. She's a vet up in Bellingham."

I grimace. "So that's what creative differences means."

Julian sighs. "It was a long time ago. We all made our fair share of mistakes. We were young and stupid, and there's a lot of feminine attention that comes with being in a touring band. It can be overwhelming, especially for a bunch of horny twenty-five-year-olds."

"You don't have to make excuses for him, Julian."

"I'm not, but eventually I had to deal with the anger and let it go." His gaze flows over my face. "You okay? About the breakup?"

I snort. "Stop it."

"Stop what?"

"Pretending you care," I say flatly. "If we hadn't already parted ways, that stunt at the restaurant today would have ensured it."

He hesitates. "Should I apologize even if I'm not sorry?"

I can't help laughing; Julian grins back at me, and I groan. "Will you stop being so damned nice? It's driving me nuts."

"You'd prefer I was mean to you?"

"Maybe," I say soberly. "It would certainly make it easier to keep hating you."

His eyes twinkle. "You don't hate me. Resent me, yes. But you should probably just forgive me because resentments are like drinking poison and hoping the other person dies."

My brows lift. "Some recovery wisdom for me, eh?"

He doesn't smile, and the sparkle in his eyes darkens to something different. Something that makes my body come alive and divorces my mouth from my brain.

"Do you want to come in?"

He watches me a moment. "More than anything in the world. But I'm not going to."

An ache spreads through my chest and burns in my cheeks. "Oh, okay," I say lamely, then unlatch my seatbelt, grab my purse, and open the door. "Thanks again. Um, bye."

He gently grabs my arm, freezing me in place as his eyes scan mine. "Don't think for one second that I don't want you. But I'm not messing this up again—this time, we're doing things the right way."

His gaze drops to my mouth and his jaw clenches; when his eyes come back to mine, there's no doubt what he was just thinking about.

He finishes, "But I'm also not going to be deterred. So unless you do something stupid like fall in love with some other guy, this," he waves a finger between us, "is inevitable. You know me better than most. You know how I am when I want something."

"Determined," I whisper, struggling to catch my breath, to not launch over the seat.

Nodding, he releases my arm with a tender stroke. "Enjoy the rest of your day. Can I call you tomorrow?"

Swallowing hard, I realize this is the moment that changes things. Everything. And it all hinges on my answer to his simple question.

"Yes."

I don't linger to bask in his wide smile, exiting the car and heading up my front steps. Julian waits until I've unlocked and opened the door before waving and backing down the driveway. I watch him go, then sag against the doorframe.

While the still healing half of my heart whispers, *What have you done?* the other half of me pulses with an emotion I haven't felt in months.

Hope.

♫

GRETA, curled up on one end of my couch the following evening, chews thoughtfully on a roasted almond before asking, "Did he call you today?"

My cheeks heat. "Yes."

"Aaaaand?"

I shrug. "We talked about finding a new drummer for the tour. He has a couple of people in mind. And, um, possibly writing a song together."

Greta sighs happily. "You're going to marry him. It's destined."

I throw one of my almonds at her. "Not helping."

She laughs. "I know, but it's like a fairytale."

I grunt. "I don't know any fairytales that are quite as dark and twisted as this one."

She unwinds a leg to poke me with a pink toenail.

"You say dark and twisted, I say fraught with challenge and triumph."

"Oh God," I groan. "You have to stop hanging out with your mother-in-law."

She giggles, sitting forward to put down her cup of almonds. "Owen and I looked over the rescheduled tour dates. I think we're going to fly down to see you play in San Diego."

I instantly perk up. "That's awesome! Late September, yeah? I can check to see if we have a free day following. I'd love to hang out with you guys."

She nods, looking down and picking at the hem of her sweater. "We're kind of torn, actually. We've always wanted to go to Austin City Limits, too. But, um, I'm not sure about timing, and with my work schedule, and Tullamore…" She trails off, and I see her chin quiver.

Alarmed, I lean across the couch to touch her knee. "What's wrong?"

She bursts into tears and wails, "Nothing's wrong! Everything's wrong!"

Grabbing her by the shoulders, I pull her into a hug. My mind is racing between *What did Owen do?* and *Holyshit Greta never cries—what do I do?*

Stroking her back, I say, "Whatever it is, just tell me. We can get through it together."

"I'm pregnant!" she bursts out, then sobs into my shoulder like the world is ending.

My first reaction is swift joy, followed by equally potent confusion. In the pause between bouts of wailing, I say, "Um, Greta? I thought you guys wanted kids..."

"We do," she says, hiccuping and wiping her face on my shoulder. "Just not *now*. My birth control failed. Freaking Katherine knew before I did. The other day she asked me if I wanted pickles—*I hate pickles*—and I suddenly wanted a stupid fucking pickle! And then when I got home, I threw up the pickles and took a test. And *two pink lines!*"

Meltdown round two commences.

By the time she quiets, I'm trying my best not to laugh. Because I know she's happy, but also scared and overwhelmed and annoyed that Katherine spilled the mystic beans.

"You're laughing at me, aren't you?" she grumbles, finally quieting.

Leaning back, I can't stop a grin from overtaking my mouth. "I'm going to be an auntie!"

Eyes red-rimmed and still leaking, she laughs weakly and nods. "Sorry. I'm really happy. Overjoyed. Probably already hormonal."

"Nooooo," I say dryly, then palm her flat stomach. "How many weeks? Can I come to your doctor's appointments? Can I name her or him?"

She laughs, smacking my hand. "Seven weeks or thereabouts. I have my first appointment next week. But

I think Owen wants it to just be us. If you come, then Katherine—"

"I totally understand," I say quickly.

"Thanks, Rosie."

"Aww, come here," I gush, grabbing her again. "I'm so freaking happy! What do you want for dinner? Pickles?"

"Ha Ha," she says, then pauses. "Pizza. With lots of meat."

"You got it, preggers."

Giving her a kiss on the head, I jump off the couch and head for my phone to place an order at our favorite pizzeria. When I return to the living room, Greta's on a phone call.

"Sure, I'll ask her. Okay, love you. Talk to you soon."

I wait for her to hang up. "Was that Owen?"

"Yes. He said he tried to call you, but you didn't pick up."

Glancing down at my phone, I do indeed see two missed calls, but no voicemails.

"Everything okay?"

She winces. "Tullamore is slammed and two people called out sick. Allison can't come back in because she's already maxed out on overtime, and it's Friday, and there's no else—"

"It's okay," I say, laughing. "I'll get dressed. Pizza

should be here in a half hour." I point a menacing finger at her. "Don't you dare eat the whole thing."

"Don't worry, I'll save you some crust."

I show her a certain finger and leave her giggling in the living room to change my clothes.

As good as celebratory pizza and movies with Greta sounds, I'm actually pretty excited to put on an apron. I miss the energy of the café, the feeling of usefulness and purpose. I dress quickly, throw my hair into a ponytail, and with a final goodbye to Greta, jump in my car and head to Tullamore.

Before leaving on tour, I'd handed my café keys off to a newly promoted Allison, so although I park in the back lot, I jog around to the front door.

The café is glowing with activity in the evening light, the usual open mic crowd in full effect. As I approach, I see Kelly on stage, laughing and strumming her guitar. I spot Greg's short blonde dreadlocks in the front row, as well as Juliet's hair—formerly blue, now purple. Christy darts back and forth from the espresso station to the bakery case, and Owen is hustling like a madman behind both registers.

Watching my cousin, I think of my tiny tadpole niece or nephew, and happiness surges in my chest.

Sound and warmth flow over me as I open the door. Faces glance my way, familiar ones waving in welcome. Moving quickly past the line of customers waiting to order, I veer around the counter and take up position beside Owen.

"Thank God!" he says, wiping a forearm across his sweaty brow. I give him a conspiratorial wink. His grin is immediate. "She told you?"

I nod as I wave the next customer up. "She said I can pick the name."

"What?" he barks.

Pointedly ignoring him, I focus on my customer. "Hi, what can I get you?"

Ten minutes later the line is manageable. I escape before Owen can grill me and move to assist Christy in making drinks. She squeals at the sight of me and throws her arms around my neck.

"I'm so excited you're here!"

"Me too," I say, smiling and nodding at the espresso machine in front of her. "Been partaking of the goods?"

She nods her head spastically. "I couldn't help it. It's the most perfect night!"

I laugh. "Okay champ, you're cut off."

Applause fills the café as Kelly wraps up her set. "Thanks so much," she says, "and now, the moment you've been waiting for…"

A cheer erupts. More than half the crowd stands, yelling and whistling. Feet begin pounding on the floor. Startled, I glance up at the still-empty stage, then at Christy.

"What the hell is going on?" I ask over the noise, musing idly that if her smile gets any bigger her face is going to crack.

"Surprise!"

My head turns towards the stage so fast a muscle in my neck tweaks. A man sits down on the solitary stool. His finger taps the microphone.

"Hey guys, my name is John Doe."

29

EXCESS

*J*ulian either doesn't know I'm here or is purposefully ignoring me. He settles onto the stool, adjusting the strap of his guitar. Incognito doesn't work for him anymore, but he's trying: black hoodie, beanie, and glasses.

"Okay, okay, pipe down," he admonishes, and the excitement of the crowd falls from a boil to a simmer. "Thanks for having me tonight." Another cheer rises then falls. "As some of you know, a little over a year and a half ago, I asked one of the owners if I could perform here at open mic. You were such a great crowd, I had to come back. I wrote a song. Wanna hear it?"

Screaming.

Julian laughs. "All right, here you go."

And then he begins to play, *brokenhealed* hands moving confidently, swiftly as the complex melody unfolds. It's painful, and hopeful, and arrestingly beautiful.

Then his voice comes, strong and sure, and I sag against the counter, espresso orders forgotten.

There's a space, in the dark, a shadow of a spark
Where the wind blows, so it goes, so I know
This time—this time I fought.
And your face, it can erase, the pain in my heart
Where I stopped, and I lost, and forgot how to start.

This time, it's ours, to begin again
Please hold my hand—
Will you please hold my hand?

It's a crime, all mine, to deny that I know,
How the wind blows, where it goes—
Past someday, to never, to so long ago.
So I'm here, and I wonder, how the world didn't end
When your tears fell, and I lost you…

But I guess that depends
On if we can start again,
If you'll hold my hand—
Let me hold your hand.

Julian, focused on the music, doesn't know that the

café is resoundingly silent as he performs a final verse and chorus—lyrics I don't hear over the roaring in my ears. When the last chords fade away, he looks up with a hesitant smile.

The crowd explodes.

Rocking backward on the stool, his smile grows. "Wow, thanks," he says, laughing a little. "Not too sappy?"

"No!" yells Juliet, and many voices echo hers.

Julian chuckles. "Okay, great. I'm hoping she doesn't think so either. Should we ask her?"

The hum in my ears increases.

Julian looks straight at me. "What do you think, Rose?" Whatever expression I'm wearing makes him laugh. "She's so cute when she blushes. Uh oh, now she's glaring. I think I'm in trouble, guys. By the way, have you all heard that Rose just signed a contract with Indigo Records? Don't read the tabloids—I swear I had nothing to do with it." Over escalating cheers, he adds, "And did you also hear she's opening for Breaking Giants on tour this fall?"

My knees lock to combat sudden weakness.

"I'm pretty happy about that," Julian continues conversationally. "Rose isn't looking too happy right now, though. Think I should go talk to her?"

Tullamore gives him an affirmative answer.

He steps off the stage, handing his guitar to Owen. I

give my cousin a murderous glance—which he returns with a grin—and before Julian can corner me in front of fifty people, I lurch into motion, stalking around the counter and grabbing his arm as I go.

A wave of knowing laughter rises behind us as I haul him down the back hallway and into my office. Once inside, he kicks the door shut and comes straight for me.

Words of reproach fade with a sigh.

His hands flow around my hips, arms locking at my lower back as he lifts me. Heat envelopes me, burns through me. Our open mouths collide.

Papers scatter from my desk as he sits me on it and presses between my open legs, fingers in my hair, on my back, my neck, their movement unceasing as he claims me. Relearns me.

"I need you, Rose," he breathes, teeth on my earlobe, tongue flicking beneath, sucking on my neck until my head falls back. "Please. You're it. Everything."

YES.

But on the heels of my body's answer comes one from my heart—an immense, crippling wave of fear. Dark and searching, it sinks claws into my gut. I shudder, my body going cold and rigid.

Memories paint my eyelids in a grisly slideshow.

Julian in the hospital bed, not looking at me as he cut me out of his life. Kissing Missy at the charity benefit, laughing with her at Greta's wedding right after singing to me.

I can't leave her.

Newspaper on the table.

I made mistakes.

My fist connecting with his face.

You're it. Everything.

Empty bed.

I saw you and I wanted you.

Alone.

You've always been a symbol.

Open graves.

I wanted to drink.

Confusion. Lust. Dishonest living.

Music alone will never leave you.

Prince of Swords.

Holding a pillow over my head to dampen the sound of my parents screaming.

Love kills art.

My mother locked in the bathroom; my father pounding on the door, yelling at her to take the needle out of her arm and raise her child.

You're just like me.

Easily overwhelmed by sorrow and conflict.

Justlikeme justlikeme.

Princess of Cups.

"No," I whisper.

Julian, who stilled when I went rigid, lifts his head. Anguish in his eyes, he takes a swift step back. His chest rises and falls rapidly, hands clenching at his sides.

"I'm moving too fast. I'm sorry. You need more time."

I'm not sure where my voice comes from, but it's a freezing, barren place. "I can't do this. I can't be with you."

He jerks, reaching for me. I tense, and he lets his arm fall.

"You don't mean that," he whispers.

"Right now, I mean it more than anything."

Fighting to keep the pieces of myself together, I sink fingers into my hair, clenching until my scalp burns. My gaze roams the office wildly; my vision brightens around the edges.

"I... I can't think around you. I can't—"

"Breathe, Rose." His voice is calm and steady. "You're having a panic attack. I'd touch you, but I think that might make it worse."

"Panic attack," I echo.

Reason filters through me. Gripping the edges of the desk, I drop my chin to my chest and start breathing. Five seconds in, pause, five seconds out.

After the third cycle, the prickling of cold sweat fades, leaving me shaking in the aftermath. Swallowing hard, I look up at Julian.

His eyes scan mine, bright with compassion and no small measure of dismay.

"I did this," he says, shaking his head. "I did this to you."

I laugh shortly. "No, you didn't. My mother did."

I stare at the wall beside his head. I'm burned out. Empty and numb. Memories spill onto my tongue, building until they overflow.

"One time when I was eleven years old, my dad left on a business trip, which was really code for him taking a break from the insanity at home. I was supposed to stay with Aunt Katherine, but she was working and couldn't pick me up until late that night. Mom invited her drug dealer to the house. I think she forgot I was in the room—she shot up in front of me. When she realized I was there, she started crying and tried to explain why she had to do it."

Julian sucks in a breath but doesn't speak.

I shrug. "She told me that love killed her art, and heroin was the only thing that softened that pain." I take a slow, trembling breath and meet Julian's eyes. "It took me a long time to understand that she was talking about more than my father. Me, Julian. I killed her music. And she couldn't live without music more than she couldn't live without me."

He shakes his head. "She was sick, Rose. So sick."

I nod, but the words don't really register. "I've never

told anyone that. I honestly don't know why I just told you."

"I'm glad you told me," he says softly. "It helps me understand why you're afraid of this. Us. How the chaos last year affected you. And I'm sorry, a thousand times over, for hurting you. I want so badly to tell you that we're different—and I truly think we are—but right now, I can see that won't matter."

"I'm sorry," I say weakly.

"Don't be sorry, Rose. Ever." He pauses, voice lowering with urgency. "I'm going to show you I'm different. However long it takes. I'm not giving up."

Blinking back tears, I shake my head helplessly. "Why?"

"Because I love you, so fucking much."

Before I can even *begin* to absorb that statement, he crosses the space, grips my head to give me a kiss on my brow, then turns and leaves. The door swings closed behind him.

Stumbling around my desk, I collapse into the chair. A few seconds later, my butt vibrates. I lift up to retrieve my phone.

Aunt Katherine.

"Honestly, Aunt K, I don't want to know."

"Rose," she says softly. "Grace lied to you. Love didn't kill her. Addiction did."

My heart burns as it awakens. "And what if something kills him, too?" I demand. "What then? What the fuck do I do *then?*"

"And the alternative? What will you do if he continues in his recovery for the rest of his life and never drinks again? Will you let yourself accept the potential for happiness? Will you accept the risks along with the rewards?"

Dimly, I realize I never told her about Julian's sobriety. But at this point in my life, I'm past the point of skepticism and a few miles beyond goosebumps. She's just Katherine.

"I had a dream…" I say haltingly.

She hums. "Prince of Swords actualized. You want to know if it's true."

"Yes," I whisper.

I hear her smile through the words, "Advantageous spread. Resolved past. Clear purpose. Self-acceptance and creative power. The timing is opportune."

The timing is opportune.

"He's ready for you, child," murmurs Katherine, "but I'm afraid you're not ready for him. Be patient. Cultivate your own happiness. Only then will you find what you're looking for."

There's a knock on the office door, and it opens on Owen. He glances around, frowning. "Did Julian leave?"

My head jerks in a nod. Owen studies me a long moment, his brow clearing and compassion in his eyes.

"You're wearing your *don't ask* face, so I'm not going to ask. Can you cover me so I can eat some dinner? Greta just showed up with pizza."

"Sure," I say, and he disappears. I tell Aunt Katherine, "I gotta go. Thanks. Love you."

"I love you, too, Rosie," she says, then hangs up.

Standing, I quickly redo my frazzled ponytail and prepare to throw myself mind and body into work.

And maybe later I'll think about cultivating happiness, or eating some pizza, or *I love you, so fucking much.* And maybe, just maybe, I'll consider that I'm not her. That it wasn't love for me that killed my mother's music and then her.

Because I'm tired of being overwhelmed by sorrow.

30

THERMODYNAMICS (DECAY)

Spread over my kitchen table are the finalized details of the upcoming tour. And *holy shit*, it's finally sinking in. Between sixteen and twenty shows a month, the first leg lasting September through mid-December, then a two-week break before the second leg.

In January, the tour picks up in the UK, then Australia, New Zealand… Scanning down the column, I see Germany, France, Belgium, Norway, South America, then Canada, another break, and the final leg in the Eastern U.S.

"Good God," I whisper, rubbing my temples. "How the hell do you do it?"

Julian, leaning against the counter beside my percolating coffee maker, smiles and shrugs.

"It's what I do. The life I chose. Trust me, you're going to love it." He turns toward the cabinets. "Coffee?"

"Um, yes."

As he pulls down two mugs and starts pouring, I stare at his back, wondering if I'm still dreaming. When my doorbell woke me up twenty minutes ago, I thought it was someone who really wanted a black eye, like a vacuum salesman.

Instead, it was a grinning rockstar. The same rockstar whose calls I've been ignoring for over a week. In one of his hands was the folder currently spilling its guts all over my kitchen table, and in the other was a bag of fresh pastries.

"You know it's nine o'clock in the morning, right?" I ask as he sets a mug in front of me.

He settles opposite me, blowing on the surface of his coffee before taking a sip.

"Mmm, so good. And yes, I know what time it is. And that you're a night owl. But I missed you and wanted to see you."

I swallow coffee down the wrong pipe and cough loudly.

Julian's smile widens. "You okay?"

"Fine."

Sitting back, he crosses his arms over his chest. I try not to stare—I really do.

His smile edges toward smug. "Guess what today is."

I give my coffee another try and successfully take a

reviving gulp. "Sunday. The day of rest, when I should be sleeping until noon."

"Guess again."

"The day Breaking Giants' lead singer gets kneed in the balls."

"Stop thinking about my balls, Cunningham," he admonishes, then cocks his head. "Although, if you really want to see—"

"Just tell me!" I say quickly, but neither of us misses the fact that my cheeks are doing a tomato impression.

"I'm fourteen years sober today."

My brows shoot up, and my wide smile is unfeigned. "That's awesome, Julian. Congratulations. Or happy birthday? They say that, right?"

He nods, excitement making him adorably boyish. "Yep. Happy birthday to me. I only want one present."

My eyes narrow suspiciously. "What?"

"Oh, Rose." He laughs, the sinful sound tumbling against my skin. "I'm not going to ask you for anything sexual. Who do you think I am?"

"Julian Ashburn," I grumble.

Another laugh, tightening my stomach and nipples. *Gah.*

He adds mildly, "Just to be clear, when something does happen between us, it's not going to be me that instigates it."

"I'm sorry, what?" I ask incredulously.

Elbows on the kitchen table, he leans toward me. Sunlight teases gold flares from his eyes. "You're going to be the one to seduce me."

I force a laugh. "Is that so?"

His gaze drops suggestively to my mouth. "I give you maybe another month. Probably less."

My laugh this time is genuine. "My God, you really think you're irresistible, don't you? You're worse than Matt."

Julian shudders. "No one is worse than Matt. But back to business—I do want something from you for my birthday."

"What?"

"I want you to spend the day with me."

I blink. "Huh? How is that a present for you?"

"Trust me, it is." Julian drains his coffee and stands, pulling his jacket from the back of the chair. "I'm going to run a few errands, then I'll be back to pick you up. How's eleven sound? Does that give you enough time to wake up and get dressed? Casual is fine."

"Yes, but—"

"Great! See you then." Veering around the table, he kisses the top of my head, then leaves the room. I hear the front door open and close.

Staring at the printout of tour dates, I ask, "What just happened?"

No answers come unless Copenhagen is another word for *screwed*.

♪

A FEW HOURS LATER, Julian drives us into the parking lot of an elegant building complex in Madison Park, right on the border of Lake Washington. The name of the complex is *Shoreline Retirement*. To say I'm confused would be an understatement. He pulls to a stop under an overhang, and a liveried valet speedily approaches.

At my questioning look, he says, "Just a quick stop." He looks nervous, not maintaining eye contact.

Who are we visiting?

But I don't ask—because I have a rising suspicion. I'm not sure how I feel about it, but telling him to take me home doesn't feel right, either.

As I exit the car, Julian veers toward me and grabs my hand. His fingers are cold. I look up at him, easily perceiving his distress.

"Are you sure you want to do this?" I ask softly.

He nods with a brief, tight smile, and we walk into the building, crossing a ritzy lobby toward a concierge. At the sight of Julian, one of the two women behind the long counter stands. Smiling brightly, she comes around to shake his hand. His left hand stays clenched around mine.

"How are you, Mr. Ashburn?"

"Well, thank you, Anne. How is she feeling today?"

The woman—a nurse, I realize—smiles. "It's a good day."

Some of the tension leaks out of his fingers. "Great. Okay. This is my friend, Rose."

Julian doesn't let go of my fingers when I wiggle them, so I give her an awkward left-handed shake. "Nice to meet you," I say, wiping all uncertainty from my voice.

Internally, I'm about a minute from a freakout. *Julian's mother is here. And she's having a good day.*

"Are you ready?" asks Anne kindly.

Julian nods, and we follow her through double doors, down a hallway that could easily belong in a four-star hotel, and into a small, bright room. There are several elderly residents within, all but one of whom have attendants.

The final woman is sitting in an armchair near the windows, facing a glittering view of the lake. I can't see her face, but she's petite and white-haired, the strands smoothed back into a small bun.

Anne approaches first. "Madeline, your son is here to see you."

Julian takes a deep, unsteady breath. Oddly, my anxiety melts away in the face of his—I squeeze his fingers hard, and when he looks at me, I tell him, "I'm here."

Emotion floods his eyes, gratitude foremost among them. Sighing, he lifts his free hand to my face, a thumb sliding along my temple.

"Thank you," he whispers.

Biting my lip against my own flood of emotion, I nod.

From the chair, a small voice asks, "My son? Where?"

Julian finally relinquishes my fingers, moving toward the chair and crouching beside it.

"Hi, mom."

A wrinkled hand lifts, touching his face in a surreal echo of where he just touched me.

"Julian, my son. So handsome. Just like your father."

Anne moves to my side. Leaning closer, she murmurs, "It's been a few years since she's recognized him. What a beautiful moment."

I bite harder on my lip, which won't stop quivering. "Yes," I say lamely.

As Julian gently takes his mother's hand, Anne continues, "Early-onset Alzheimer's. She was only fifty-nine. She's been with us ten years."

Son says to Mother, "I haven't had a drink in fourteen years, mom."

Madeline replies, "Always so sensitive, my beautiful child. I couldn't protect you."

"You did everything you could. I'm healthy and safe." The catch in his voice reverberates in my chest, where my heart breaks a little for him. "Are you happy, mom? Is there anything you need?"

"Happy…" Madeline trails off, and I see her head shake. "Where's Henry? He's late for dinner."

Beside me, Anne makes a small, sad noise.

"Dad will be here soon, mom," says Julian softly.

Madeline murmurs, "You have his eyes," then suddenly stiffens. "Where am I? Where's Henry? Who are you?"

Anne hurries forward. Julian stands, taking several long steps back. He turns away and stares out the window as Anne tries to calm an increasingly agitated Madeline. Another staff member moves across the room to assist, and together they guide her from the room. As they leave, Anne gives Julian a sympathetic glance, then offers me a brief wave.

I watch them go, my heart aching, then give in to the overwhelming need to offer comfort. Julian's back is rock hard under my hesitant touch. When he doesn't respond, I simply wrap my arms around him and hold tight.

I don't know how long we stand there, but eventually he turns, his own arms rising to embrace me. Into my hair, he says, "I used to come a lot more, but eventually we realized my presence is a trigger for her. My eyes…"

I nod, squeezing him, because I don't know what to say.

"For the last few years, I've only visited on this day, to tell her I'm another year sober. She hasn't recognized me for a while. So that's something, I guess."

"Oh, Julian," I sigh into his chest, "I'm so sorry."

"I had four years with her before she started showing symptoms, and I'm eternally grateful for that. Four years to make living amends for the shit I put her through. Disappearing from rehab, never calling to tell her I was alive. Once the symptoms began, it happened so fast. It was pretty rough for a while. We'd just formed the band and weren't making any money. But she's okay now. I've done right by her."

"Yes, you have," I say, leaning back to look into his clear eyes. "This facility is beautiful. She seems very well cared for."

He nods, eyes scanning mine a moment before his lips quirk into a soft smile. "Are those tears for me, sweetheart?"

The endearment pushes heat to my face. Sniffling, I mutter, "If you hadn't noticed, I have a hair trigger for waterworks."

The pads of his thumbs wipe gently beneath my eyes.

"You do, don't you?" he murmurs. "I bet you cry when you see puppy commercials."

"Yep," I admit.

He hums, the vibration tingling against my chest, and his eyes go a familiar, dangerous darkness. "Remember when you cried after I—"

"Julian," I hiss, glancing around the room. "Of all the places…"

He just laughs, kissing my forehead before releasing me. "I know, I'm a degenerate." Grabbing my hand, he tugs me toward the exit. "Time to go, Cunningham."

"Where are we going?"

"We're playing paintball." When I sputter, he grins back at me. "We're going to wipe the field with Matt and Melody."

With a farewell wave to the concierge, he guides us outside to wait for the car. A cool breeze teases our faces and clothes, and I can almost feel the sadness releasing from us both.

"Who says I want to be on your team?" I ask.

His brow cocks. "There's no way I'm giving you an excuse to shoot me where it hurts."

I glance significantly below his belt. "Are you that afraid of me, Ashburn?"

He grins. "Nice try. Besides, I'm merely protecting the assets you love so well. Someday soon you'll thank me."

I groan. "Will you *please* get your mind out of the gutter?"

His gaze pings down my body, zeroing in on my breasts. "No can do." Wicked smile. "Especially not when I'm so, so grateful you left your coat in the car."

I frown.

Then I glance down.

Yanking my hand from his, I quickly cross my arms over my chest. Julian laughs at my reproachful scowl, and eventually, I give in and laugh with him.

"You're incorrigible, Ashburn."

The car arrives, and Julian opens my door for me. Once I'm seated, he teases, "You love me," before closing the door.

Putting on my seatbelt, I privately confront the truth.

Yes, I do.

31

(IM)PULSE

The next weeks are a whirlwind of rehearsing, meetings at Indigo, and packing. Since visiting Julian's mother—and, yes, kicking Matt and Melody's asses at paintball—our schedules have been hectic, and we haven't seen too much of each other. He still calls every day, though; depending on whether I'm feeling hopeful or afraid, I either answer or don't.

When I worry he's becoming impatient or his feelings will change, instead of stuffing the emotions or acting out of impulse, I accept them.

What will be will be.

Oddly, Julian seems to have a sixth sense about when these times occur. Within hours, I'll invariably get a borderline x-rated text message or a voicemail of him singing in the shower.

He's ready for you.

Aunt Katherine's words are a balm, and as she suggested, I focus on myself. Pilates or some other physical exercise once a day. Voice coaching, songwriting (somehow, I have to write a new album while touring almost nonstop), and spending time with family.

Greta's initial dismay over the timing of her pregnancy has been replaced by effervescent joy. Aunt Katherine is beyond tickled to be a grandma, and Owen is happier than I've ever seen him. He and Greta solidify their plans to visit me, deciding on the Austin City Limits festival in October.

Slowly, slowly, my fears begin to fade.

The last weekend in August, Cory Donovan hosts a tour-kickoff party at his Mercer Island home. It's low seventies and sunny, likely the last stretch of beautiful weather before fall descends.

When my doorbell rings, I'm in the kitchen, and yell, "Come in!" Hearing soft footsteps behind me, I tell Melody, "I know, I know, I'm wearing a bathing suit and you can't believe it."

"Care to model it?" asks a sinful voice.

I jump out of my skin, knocking a mug into the sink which thankfully doesn't break. Spinning, I look up at a smug Julian, who managed to sneak up right behind me.

"Ninja, seriously," I gasp.

He chuckles and palms the back of my head, giving my forehead his quick, customary kiss, before strolling to a kitchen chair. *His* kitchen chair. Said chair turns, and he sits, legs sprawling over the floor.

"You're staring, Cunningham."

Flushing, I look up from his toned calves, over black board shorts I remember well, and past his t-shirt clad chest to his sparkling eyes. I haven't seen him in close to a week, since an impromptu movie night with Matt and Melody.

"Sorry," I squeak, and finally summon my wits. "Where's Mel?"

"I asked if I could come get you instead." He leans forward, bracing elbows on his knees, and gives me an uncertain smile. "Is that okay? I can bring you home after."

"Uhh—"

Hurt flashes in his eyes at my hesitation. I want more than anything to take it away.

"That's fine, great. Thanks."

His answering smile is radiant. "Are you ready?"

"Y-yes."

I lurch into action, leaving the room to fetch my phone, wallet, and keys. When I return, Julian's waiting by the front door, sunlight haloing his tall frame. Electric want courses down my spine, washes outward through my limbs, before settling into a thrumming ache between my legs.

"Everything okay?" he asks softly.

I realize I'm frozen, probably wearing an expression of discomfort. "Yes," I force out. "Let's go."

The drive is silent except for the radio, the tension between us almost insufferable. I keep my hands clenched firmly in my lap to thwart the impulse to touch him. When we finally reach Mercer Island, both of us blow out relieved breaths.

Julian drives past the open gate and parks behind Matt's car. Hands gripping the steering wheel, he clears his throat.

"Sorry, Rose. I'm, uh…" He swallows, falling silent and staring out the windshield.

"It's okay," I say quickly, then admit ruefully, "Me, too."

He laughs shortly. "We're a fucking pair, aren't we? Maybe I should let Melody drive you home, after all."

"No," I say, then blink in surprise at myself.

Julian's head snaps toward me. "Rose?"

Reeling from my impulsive response, I jump out of the car and begin walking toward the house, muttering, "Smooth, so smooth."

Julian catches up to me on the threshold of the open door, his hand sliding over my lower back. "No take backs," he says in a low, rough voice. Then, as my arousal escalates to near painful intensity, he continues, "God, nevermind. I'm an asshole. You can take back whatever you want."

Calm filters through me.

I'm done waiting. I'm ready.

I grab his hand from my back, but instead of dropping it, I weave my fingers through his. I hear his short, surprised inhale, but don't dare look at him as we walk through the house to the backyard. I'm not sure my ego would survive face-planting right now.

There are fifteen or so people already here, spread between the patio and the sunny lawn. In the jacuzzi, Matt leaps to his feet, waving his arms in a completely unnecessary gesture to get our attention.

"Hey, guys!" he hollers. "Bring me a beer and get in here!"

Julian laughingly waves him off, and we linger on the patio for a few minutes, greeting and chatting with Breaking Giants' manager, Phil, as well as our shared production manager and lead sound engineer.

As the men catch up and share memories from past tours, I let my gaze wander until I see Greg and Kelly looking a touch overwhelmed near the pingpong table. Giving Julian's fingers a quick squeeze, I excuse myself and head their way. Their faces light up as I approach.

"Oh man, I'm glad you're here," says Greg, giving me a quick hug.

Kelly's hug is longer, and she whispers, "Is this real life?"

Laughing, I step back. "Strangely, yes. Thanks for

letting me drag Greg on the road, Kelly. He said you're going to fly out a few times to meet up with us?"

She nods excitedly. "Houston show, I think. And probably New York next year. I have a bunch of family in the area."

"Well, you're always welcome," I say, then add teasingly, "You could always just quit your job and come on the road with us."

Kelly blinks. "Are you for real?"

I glance at Greg to see whether or not I just put my foot in my mouth, but he's grinning, so I turn back to Kelly with my own smile.

"Hell yes. It's me, Greg, Brody, and our new drummer Murphey on the bus. We have the bunk space, and it would be awesome to have another woman around."

Greg tugs on Kelly's pale blonde braid. "Told you!"

I punch his arm. "You were waiting for me to offer? Come on, you should have just asked!"

Greg's response is lost in Kelly's squeal as she throws her arms around me. "Oh my gosh, I would *love* to come on tour with you guys! I can do your hair and makeup! I'll make you food, whatever you want!" She finally releases me to give the same straightjacket treatment to Greg.

Warm fingers cup my bare arm, giving me a second's

warning before Julian presses against my back. His chin descends to my shoulder.

"Let me guess, Kelly's coming with us." I nod, and he chuckles approvingly.

With a breathless laugh, I shift subtly to bring his hips in line with my ass. He stills, fingers clenching on my arms.

"Hot tub," he grinds out. "Now. Or I'm going to be walking around with a tent in my pants."

I blink at Greg and Kelly, who are now staring at us with wide-eyed delight. "We're going to, uh, get in the jacuzzi. You guys want to come?"

Greg laughs knowingly. "Nope. And I pity whoever else is in there with you."

"Me too," says Julian, straightening and guiding me by the hand toward the pool. Halfway there, in a pocket of space with no prying ears, he gives me a searing look. "Punishment is in order."

My dormant, debauched self wakes up with a stretch and a yawn. "Whatever you dish out, I can take."

He sucks in a sharp breath. "Oh, it's on." He glances meaningfully at my mouth. "And I know you can take what I dish out."

OhmyGod.

Grinning at my shocked face, he releases my hand to pull off his shirt. I shamelessly catalog evidence of his continued, rigorous exercise routine.

From the jacuzzi, Matt yells, "Stop eye-fucking each other! Where's my beer?"

Melody, perched on one of the steps, slaps him on the shoulder while laughing. Nick and Kat just shake their heads at us in sympathy, while the final occupant, Jackson, looks like he'd rather be at the dentist.

Julian heads for the jacuzzi and lowers himself into the steaming water, releasing a deep groan of pleasure. "This feels amazing. I'm so stiff." There's a two-count silence before he sputters, "That's not—"

Matt, Nick, Melody, and Kat burst out laughing. Jackson just rolls his eyes. "He's stiff from our run this morning, idiots."

Julian shakes his head, chuckling, before looking up at me. "Quit lallygagging, Cunningham."

Everyone laughs again.

"Lallygagging?" I repeat, pulling off my tank top and stepping out my shorts. "You're living in a different century, Ashburn."

I slip into the water beside him and find a jet, giving my own groan as it pounds into my back.

His mouth grazes my ear. "You've been working out."

"Hey!" yells Jackson. "No moving hands under the water! A little respect for the single guy, please."

Julian laughs at the reprimand that I'm both grateful

and resentful for. His fingers trail down my thigh before retracting.

Turning my head, I realize he's still very close. Moisture beads on his lips, which fall open as I stare at them. My heart pounding, I risk a glance up. Burning molasses; sunset in the desert.

And I can't wait anymore.

"When can we leave?" I ask.

His eyes close, then open. "Now."

♫

WE MAKE it back to my house. Barely. The second the front door closes, our hands are tearing off clothing. Litanies of curses come from both of us as I try to maneuver out of wet shorts.

Fabric tears. My bikini top gets thrown and dangles from the foyer's ceiling light. The first touch of my bare breasts on his chest makes us both moan. My teeth find his neck and clamp.

He lifts me roughly against the wall, and my head hits the plaster.

"Sorry," he gasps.

"Don't care," I say, aiming my mouth for his.

Our teeth clash, lips bruising. I feel him, hard and hot and thick, against my inner thigh.

"Julian. Please."

"Fuck," he hisses, "I don't have any condoms. I didn't know—think—"

"I have an IUD," I gasp, angling a hand between us. He thrusts on instinct as my fingers wrap around him. "I'm clean."

"So am I, but are you sure—"

"Quit lallygagging!" I cry, jerking my hips to feed him an inch inside me. The pressure and fullness shatter the remains of my control. "Fuck me *now*, Julian, or I swear to God—"

He sinks into me, hard and deep, again and again, driving me against and up the wall. A picture frame falls, clattering on the floor. My legs clamp around his hips, ankles locking against his lower back. He drags my arms over my head, manacling my wrists with both hands.

I'm fully possessed by him. Fully at his mercy.

And blissfully free.

"Rose, Rose, you feel so good… I don't think I can—"

The friction of him against me, the strangled words of his unraveling control, trigger an orgasm so consuming I feel unmade. I scream his name, straining against his hold, bucking like the wild animal I am. He looses another series of curses, thrusting hard and finally stilling.

His knees buckle, and we hit the floor.

Hard.

"Are you okay?" he asks with strangled laughter, his face obscured by my hair.

I groan. "My ass."

He chuckles. "Don't worry, we'll get to that beautiful ass. I just… need… maybe five months for my balls to recover."

Giggling helplessly, I manage to untangle myself and sit against the wall. Julian is splayed naked on his back, heaving for air as he tries to stop laughing.

Rolling his face toward me, he gives me a brilliant smile. "So. Loud."

I shove his hip with my foot. "You heard yourself. I'm pretty sure the neighbors think a man was just murdered in here."

He grabs my leg and yanks me from the wall. I almost knee him in the face, but somehow end up sprawled on top of him. His hands flow down my back and cup my ass, but his expression is suddenly serious.

"Don't tell me you regret this, Rose."

I take his face in my hands. "I don't," I say honestly.

He sighs, then grins. "Good. Now please get off me— you're sticky."

"Asshole, it's your *stick*." I laugh and climb to my feet. My knees feel unsteady, and *what the hell is*... "Uh-oh. I'll be right back."

Julian's laughter booms out, following my flight down the hall to my bathroom.

32

WHEN THE DEAD WON'T STAY BURIED

I clean up and throw on a cotton skirt and a camisole. Julian is in the kitchen, his shorts back on and typing on his cell phone. He looks up with a smile, one that sharpens as he sees what I'm wearing.

"Oh, that camisole and I have a history."

Smirking, I remember the night when I was sick. "Yeah, sorry about that. That wasn't very nice of me."

He hums agreement, stalking toward me to trace the outline of a nipple through the thin silk.

"You're forgiven. But this is coming in my luggage on tour. I want it under my face every night."

My heart surges against my ribs. "Julian Ashburn, that was *romantic*."

He chuckles. "I've been practicing." Dropping his phone on the counter, he gives me a swift kiss. "Let me get cleaned up, then we need to talk about pancakes. I'm starving."

I watch him go, a stupidly happy grin on my face, then hunt down my cell phone. Finding it under my torn shorts, I see one new notification. A text message from Melody.

Bahahahaha!

Thinking about how we left the party not twenty minutes after arriving, I grimace and type an apology, then delete it when I realize I'm not sorry at all. Smiling to myself, I walk back into the kitchen, tossing my phone beside Julian's before opening the fridge.

I'm reaching for the milk and eggs when my phone buzzes. Figuring it's another text from Melody, I feel blindly, grabbing it and picking it up.

Are you coming over later? miss u xx

Frowning down at the message, my eyes veer to the sender's name.

Sheridan Franklin.

And I realize I'm not holding my phone, but Julian's.

"No," I whisper, a soft plea to the universe. To whatever one of Katherine's spirit guides or mine might be listening.

"Is that my phone?" asks Julian, his tone curious but unbothered. His arm slides around my shoulders, and he kisses my temple. "Did I get a text?"

"Yes," I say hoarsely, pressing the button to illuminate the screen.

Peering over my shoulder, he sees the message. Tension ripples down his frame.

"Rose, it's not what you think." Low, urgent words.

Feeling like a robot version of myself, I hand him his phone and take a step back, closing the refrigerator and leaning against it.

Don't freak out don't freak out.

"Okay," I say calmly. *Calm so calm.* "Who's Sheridan?"

He hesitates, gaze dropping. A piece of my heart shears off, slicing as it goes.

I love you, so fucking much.

Julian drags a hand through his hair, grown back to its former tousled length. "I'm going to tell you the exact truth, so there are no misunderstandings. Sheridan is the daughter of my first sponsor. She's in the program. We've fooled around off and on over the years. After the accident, we, well…" I can't smother a flinch. "I know that's not easy to hear, but I want to tell you the truth so you don't write stories in your head."

I walk across the kitchen to put distance between us. "I'm suddenly not sure I want the truth, Julian," I say weakly.

"I'm not going to lie to you," he says fiercely.

I close my eyes. "Okay, fine. So you hooked up with her after the accident. We weren't… anything, so whatever. But have you seen her in the last six weeks?"

He sighs heavily. "Yes."

I press fingertips into my eyes. "Wow, that… sucks." I can't manage anything more eloquent.

"It's not what you think. Will you look at me, Rose? Can we talk this out?"

I lower my hands and look at him, taking in his contrite expression, his sincere eyes. And my defensive numbness buckles.

"You said you'd wait for me. I was… working on myself. You said you *loved* me, Julian. How could you sleep with someone else? How many times did you go to her? All your calls, texts… did you fuck her, then text me the same night telling me how much you missed me?"

"I didn't—" He shakes his head, growling, "You know what? Believe what you want. Goddamnit, Rose, you've given me zero assurances that you'll ever change your mind about us!"

The last shreds of calm dissolve beneath searing anger and hurt. "You couldn't keep it in your pants for *six fucking weeks?* You're a grown man, not some horny twenty-five-year-old anymore!"

He moves so fast I don't have time to react, but he doesn't touch me, merely looms over me, dark and furious. "You're inside me when I sleep and when I'm awake. There was only so much I could stand before I had to drive you out!"

"How romantic!" I yell belligerently. "Were you going to see her tonight? If I didn't put out?"

Jaw set tight, he doesn't say anything.

My anger withers; my eyes burn with tears. *Don't cry. Won't cry.*

"Do you love her?" I whisper.

Laughing humorlessly, he spins away and stalks back across the kitchen. "I love *you*, which is seeming more and more like a fucking curse."

The air vacates my lungs. "Ouch."

"Rose," he breathes, "I didn't mean that."

"I can't believe I just slept with you without a condom," I say tonelessly. "At least tell me you used condoms with her."

"Yes," he snaps.

Silence falls. A car drives by outside. A dog barks. Somewhere down the street, children squeal and shout.

"I want to be with you," he says, voice soft, threading through the quiet. "Only you. Say the word, and I'm yours. One hundred percent. All-fucking-in. But only if you can give me the same. Or are you going to run away again?"

I shake my head. "I don't know. I don't *want* to." I

meet his eyes, dark with need and pain and desire. "Maybe I don't have a right to be, but I'm still hurt. I... I need some time to process this."

"Fine," he says, nodding curtly. "Take all the time you need. Weeks, months, years, whatever."

He grabs his phone from the counter and walks past me. Turning, I watch him pick up his t-shirt and pull it on.

I'm losing him.

No, please...

But the sick feeling in my gut won't go away—the knowledge that he's been sleeping with someone else all these weeks as I was tackling my fears. Breaking down the hurt of him tossing me aside after the accident. Taking care of myself.

Cultivating my happiness.

To be ready for him.

He's ready for you.

I watch, silent and empty, as my happiness leaves, slamming the front door behind him. And because I don't know what else to do, I retrieve my phone from the far counter and call Aunt Katherine.

When she picks up, I try to speak, but all that comes out is a pained sound.

She says softly, "It was too soon."

I hang up on her. Staring out the kitchen window, I

wait for the vise on my chest to loosen enough for me to take a full breath.

I don't hear the front door open again until Julian speaks.

"It was only once after the accident. And three weeks ago, she kissed me. I didn't kiss her back, Rose. Sheridan and I have been friends a long time. I was really bent out of shape and went to her to talk about you. Obviously a mistake. That text message wasn't what you thought it was, either. She's ten years sober and having a birthday party tonight."

Deep breaths in. Deep breaths out. They help and so do his words. Enough to grant me a little perspective.

This isn't his fault. He's right—I didn't give him any assurances. I didn't ask him to wait for me. I've never even told him I love him.

He didn't sleep with her.

I don't turn around, afraid that if I see him, I'll throw myself at him and beg for forgiveness. Instead, I say quietly, "Thank you for telling me that. I can't ask you to wait for me, Julian. It's not fair, and I know that. But given the way I just freaked the fuck out, I'm obviously not ready."

"I know," he says gently. "I'm still not going anywhere."

"The tour…" I trail off.

"Like you said, I'm not a horny twenty-five-year-old.

But I am human. I'm not going to wait forever." I nod helplessly, my tongue frozen. "Will you let me touch you?"

I know what he's asking; I can feel his need. And mine.

I nod.

Footsteps on the floor. Strong, elegant fingers turning my face. Calloused fingertips stroking my neck, sinking into my hair. He draws my chin up, brushing his lips across my jaw, dragging them slowly over my cheekbone and down to my mouth. My lips part and I breathe him in, savoring his nearness and scent. Citrus and sandalwood.

We breathe each other in, then let each other go. My eyes are still closed when the front door swings softly shut.

♫

LATE WEDNESDAY EVENING, the night before we leave for tour, Melody and Greta sit on my bed eating pizza while I finish packing. They both know all the dirty details of what happened on Sunday, and while Greta's quiet sympathy isn't surprising, I'm a little unnerved by Melody's lack of response.

Finally, I ask her the question that's been stinging my tongue for an hour.

"Have you met her?"

She looks up, a slice of pizza stalled halfway to her mouth. Beside her, Greta slowly lowers the silk scarf she's been toying with.

"Uh, yeah," Melody answers. At pointed looks from both Greta and myself, she tosses the slice back into the box. "What do you want me to say? I'm on team Rose-Julian, and I really fucking hoped Sheridan would finally get the memo. But she's a cockroach. A sweet, charming little cockroach who's been following him around for a decade."

"Why did they never date?" I make myself ask.

Melody sighs. "Keep in mind most of what I know is secondhand from Matt, but what I've heard is that Julian feels very protective of her. He's known her a long time, was around when she was a newcomer in AA or whatever. She was his sponsor's daughter, though, so apparently off limits."

I think of the worn newspaper—all it meant, and still means, to him. "Julian does have a weakness for women he thinks need protecting."

"He's nuts about you, Rose," says Greta. "Anyone with eyes can see it. If he'd ever felt for Sheridan one ounce of what he feels for you, don't you think he'd be with her?"

I snort. "You're forgetting he almost married Missy."

Melody shudders. "Dark days, those. But listen to me —if you love him, you have to tell him. Missy-disaster aside, I've known Julian a long time. He's fiercely loyal. He'll treat you like a fucking goddess."

"I know," I whisper.

"This shit with the two of you…" She sighs in frustration. "It's been hard on all of us. I love you both, and I'm telling you this as your friend—you're making him really unhappy. He doesn't know if you're ever going to say yes to a relationship with him. It's wearing him down. He's been mopey all week, snapping at the guys, spending most of his time alone in his room with a guitar. It's horrible to watch."

Standing, she rounds the bed and gives me a tight hug. "Don't torture him anymore, Rose. Take the leap, or let someone like Sheridan have him. At least she loves him, and right now I'm not sure you do. I'll see you in the morning."

Leaving her words to ring in my ears, Melody grabs her purse and goes. We hear the front door open and close.

Greta clears her throat. "She doesn't know the extent of what happened in your childhood, does she?"

I shake my head, unable to voice that she doesn't know the extent of it, either. No one does.

"She's still right."

"What are you going to do?"

I stare at her blindly for a moment, then grab my keys from the top of my dresser. "I need… I need to go."

"To see Julian? I think that's a great—"

"To see my mother."

♪

THE CEMETERY GATES ARE CLOSED, so I walk along the wall and find a foothold, then climb to the top and jump over. A part of my mind—the rational part—reminds me that there are security guards around, but the majority of me doesn't care about being arrested for trespassing.

The sky is an inky black, but the moon is huge and bright, offering more than enough illumination. Though I get turned around a few times, making an unintentional loop, I eventually locate the familiar headstone. Walking straight over their graves, I sit cross-legged on the damp grass.

For a long time, I stare at the dark monument. Stars

spin overhead. The moon sinks toward the horizon. And finally, words rise up and spill into the night.

"You abandoned me. You left me to chase a high. You shot up in front of me. Once, you almost OD'd. You wouldn't open your eyes, and your lips were turning blue. I did CPR. You thought it was stupid when dad and I took that course to learn how. But I saved your life. When you came to, your junkie friends just laughed and patted me on the head.

"You brought your boyfriends home when dad was gone. My bedroom was next to yours. I *heard* you—" My throat chokes closed for a moment and my fingers dig into the grass. "You told me I stole your music. You blamed me for your addiction. You made me believe I was going to be just like you. That I would destroy everything good in my life, just like you did. And you took my dad away from me. *You killed him*. You sick, selfish bitch."

I fall silent, my chest heaving, my eyes burning and dry.

From behind me, Aunt Katherine says softly, "Tell her the rest, Rosie."

A scream of rage builds in my throat. I bite it back, pounding my fists into the ground. "I needed you, mom! I *loved* you, and you left me." The wave crashes, and I fall, sobbing, to the ground. "I hate you. I hate you. *I hate you*."

Katherine's gentle hand comes down on my head. "Now you can finally heal. Are you ready?"

I think of Julian. His smile, his strength, his voice and music. Fingers in my hair. Hand in mine. Laughing, frowning, singing. Prince of Swords. Passion and power. Everything.

He's everything—and I'm not willing to let him go.

I'm ready to fight.

"Yes."

33

WRECKAGE

On our way down the I-5 from San Fransisco to Los Angeles, one of the crew buses gets a flat tire. All four massive coaches pull off at a rest stop somewhere between nowhere and nowhere else.

The rumble and shudder of the bus jerks me from a restless sleep. For a few minutes I chase a return to oblivion, which grows more and more elusive as outside my bunk, there's rustling, thunks, footsteps, and hushed voices. By the time the automatic door opens and closes and quiet returns, I'm fully and regrettably awake.

Yanking back the curtain, I peer blearily toward the front of the bus.

"What time is it?" I croak at Murphey, who's sitting alone on a couch, looking exactly how I feel. Worn out and hungover. A chunk of brown hair hangs limply over his forehead; his eyes are bloodshot, sporting dark shadows.

Riding the energy of our three sold-out shows in San Fransisco over Labor Day Weekend, like idiots the two of us had joined Matt and Nick on a barhopping tour of Berkeley last night. I might have also been motivated by the repeated sight of Julian being swarmed by scantily clad superfans. My attempt to drown the memories failed spectacularly, of course.

I refocus on Murphey, who's staring blankly at his watch. "More importantly, Murph, why are you awake?"

He scratches the stubble on his chin. "I think I'm still drunk. It's, um, ten-fifteen."

I flop back down with a groan. "Where did everyone else go?"

"There's a diner down the road."

On cue, my stomach growls.

Murphey laughs. "I'm hungry, too. Wanna head over there?"

"Yeah, just give me a second to situate my head. Situate my life? Shit, I'm a mess."

It takes more than a second—roughly fifteen minutes, in fact—for my brain to kick on after less than five hours of sleep. Finding and changing into clean clothes requires effort severely out of proportion to the task.

I don't have the energy to tackle my hair or face,

opting for sunglasses and a hoodie before joining Murphey outside. He gives even less shits than me, remaining in his clothes from last night.

As we walk along the buses toward the road, I trade waves with a handful of crew members either smoking in the shade of the vehicles or rummaging in the luggage compartments.

I'm under the impression that my scanning for Julian is subtle until Murphey says, "He's probably eating breakfast." When I give him the finger, he just laughs. "Worst kept secret in history."

"Shut it," I grumble.

As we pass the first bus, our tour-manager-extraordinaire, Phil, pops his head out of the door. "Rose, do you have a sec?"

Swallowing a groan of disappointment, I glance at Murphey. "Enjoy your breakfast. Bring me a bagel or something?"

"You got it," he says, continuing toward the red-roofed diner visible down the road.

I veer toward the bus. "Hey, Phil, what's up?"

Instead of replying, he waves me onboard and disappears. I trudge up the steps, stalling at the top to pull off my sunglasses and let my eyes adjust to the darker interior.

The first thing I see is Julian's guitar case propped on

a leather seat, followed by Nick's bag of spare drumsticks.

Ah, because this is Breaking Giants' bus.

Julian's voice, tinged lightly with amusement, asks, "You feeling okay, Rose?"

My gaze moves sluggishly to where he sits adjacent to Phil at a corner table. Phil gives me a sympathetic smile. "Nick and Matt don't look much better."

My songwriter heart comes up with the winning response of, "Ugh, never again." I plop down on a nearby bench, trying to discreetly wipe the mascara from under my eyes while *not looking at Julian.* "What's going on?"

Phil smiles broadly. "First of all, congratulations on a huge opening weekend. For someone who's never performed large-scale venues before, you took to it like a fish."

"Thanks, Phil," I say, raccoon eyes and bedhead forgotten as the excitement of the last three nights floods me anew. "Rehearsals really paid off, and the production crew has been amazing."

"Yeah, they're a good team," he says with pride.

Julian adds, "And the fans love her, just like we knew they would."

Phil nods in agreement. "On that note, Rose, Julian and I were just tossing around the idea of you coming back for one of their encores to sing a duet. What do you think?"

My stomach dives in a way that has nothing to do with hangovers or hunger. "Um, sure. Sounds great. What song?"

"*So It Goes,*" answers Julian.

My song that he premiered at Tullamore.

I wonder inanely if he can see my pulse trying to pound through my neck. "Great," I wheeze. "The crowd last night loved it."

Phil claps his hands in approval, the sound making me wince. "Excellent. Tire should be fixed by the time everyone gets back from breakfast." He stands with a burst of energy I can't fathom at the moment. "I'm going to head over for some coffee. You two coming?"

"Nah," says Julian, throwing his arms over the back of the bench seating. "Rose, you want to hang for a bit and chat about the song?"

"Sure. Okay. Good idea."

Phil's gaze bounces knowingly between us. "Be good to each other, kids," he says, then retreats into the sunny portal marking the doorway.

I once again attempt to subtly wipe my eyes, but at Julian's low chuckle I give up. "How bad is it?"

"You stink like a barroom floor, and I'm worried there might be an animal hiding in your hair."

Laughing in spite of myself, I gather my curls and wind them into a bun, sticking ends into the center until it holds.

"I'm not sure I have the mental capacity to work on a song right now," I tell him honestly.

Especially not that song.

"No worries," he says, shrugging. His gaze falls to the table. "If you don't want to do that song, I totally respect—"

"I do," I say quickly, and his gaze leaps up. *Now or never—just tell him.* "Um, it's been pretty crazy since we left Seattle. Obviously. And I've wanted to talk to you about… things."

His brows lift. "Yeah?"

Tellhimtellhim.

"I'm talking to a therapist," I say in a rush. "On the phone once a day. It's only been three days, but it's been good so far. She specializes in… people like me. She's super expensive, but I've never spent a dime of my mother's royalty money, and I figured she might as well pay for all the therapy I need." I suck in a breath. "So… that's what I wanted to tell you."

His surprised expression softens, dark eyes melting with emotion and locked on mine. "That's great, Rose. Huge."

I can't hold his gaze, so I clasp my hands on the table and stare at them. "Thanks. We've, uh, been talking a lot about why it's hard for me to take risks. Basically, I associate risky behavior with my mother, which links to all the fear and lack of safety I felt when I was a kid."

Julian leans forward to squeeze my fingers. "I'm so proud of you. You have no idea."

Love for him surges through me in a heady rush. The words I so long to speak gather on the tip of my tongue and tumble out.

"Julian, I—"

Footsteps pound up the stairs behind me, and Matt and Jackson's voices shatter my moment of almost-confession. I swallow and look back down, but not before catching Julian's chagrined expression.

Holy shit I almost told him.

I stand on shaky legs. "I'll see you later, okay?"

I don't wait for a response, darting past a surprised Matt and almost colliding with Jackson before running down the stairs into the light.

♪

WE PLAY another three shows in Los Angeles, then move on to San Diego, followed by Phoenix, Albuquerque,

Denver, and Salt Lake City before heading south again to Vegas on our way to Texas.

It takes a couple weeks but eventually the initial shock of touring wears off, and I acclimate to life on the road. It helps that Greg, Kelly, Brody, and Murphey are mellow traveling companions; we're all more interested in resting than partying with fans or the crew.

Greg and Kelly are the epitome of a low-drama couple. They make sure to carve out time to disappear together and explore every city, even if only for an hour or two. Murphey sleeps *a lot*, and when he's not sleeping, he's either on the phone with his wife and kids or hanging with Brody, who plays video games like it's his vocation.

I spend most of my free time in the back of the bus, curled up on a plush bench with a guitar and new journal, working on songs for my next album.

Since my near-confession on the Breaking Giants' bus, Julian and I haven't had much time to talk. When our paths do intersect, we're never alone, and our conversations are an awkward rush of *hi* and *how are you* and *how did you sleep?*

He doesn't mention the camisole I bribed Greg to smuggle into his bunk. Or the small black journal filled cover to cover with every lyric I've written over the last three years. Unable to offer him the words he wants to hear, the journal is the closest thing to my heart I could give. The thought of him reading it—*ohmygod is he reading it?*—makes me alternately want to throw up and jump off the moving bus.

Although when we pass each other I still see need in his eyes, I worry daily that it's fading as he grows used to being without me. Not helping my fear are the endless streams of contest winners, select fans (why the fuck are they all attractive women?), and press who flock around him before and after each show.

By the time breakdown is finished and groups are dispersing to find parties or bars, Julian has usually disappeared into his bus to wind down and sleep.

I haven't found the courage to follow.

My therapist, Dr. Johnston—who prefers to go by Alice—is little by little helping me unravel the layers of conditioning from my mother. What once seemed so daunting turns out to be pretty anticlimactic—in a good way.

With the exception of the first several, emotionally exhausting sessions, we don't spend much time rehashing traumatic events from my childhood. They do come up occasionally, but mostly we talk about what's going on now.

As in, I just found out via 911 text from Melody that Sheridan Franklin is flying to Las Vegas to surprise Julian at our sold-out MGM Grand show.

"Sounds like you'd better get a move on," says my shrink.

"What does that even mean?" I hiss.

Since she's used to me by now, Alice just laughs. "Remember, Rose—when something triggers fear for you, it helps to define the worst case scenario."

"Worst case scenario is Julian sees her and realizes she's the freaking *one*, and they get married and have babies. And trust me, I hear how foolish that sounds but I can't help thinking it."

"It's not foolish," she says patiently. "In that scenario, what would happen to you?"

I suck in a breath. "I can't even say it out loud."

"Rose, my point—as you well know—is that a broken heart can't kill you. And if Julian decides to be with Sheridan, then he's not the one for you."

I rub my chest over my aching heart. "I can't…"

I don't know what I'm trying to say, so I fall silent. I understand that I'm supposed to learn that if the worst case scenario happens, it won't kill me, the world won't end, etc…

But *fuck,* it sure feels like it would.

"There's only one way to find out for sure," Alice continues gently. "You need to tell him you love him."

My phone beeps with an incoming text. "Hold on, doc," I say, peering at the message.

It's from Aunt Katherine.

The words blur, then sharpen.

You're ready

A chill cascades down my spine; I bring the phone back to my ear. "Okay."

"Okay, what?" asks Alice.

"I'm going to tell him."

34

WHISKEY & WHISPERS

Standing offstage in the arena packed with sixteen thousand screaming fans, I watch as Breaking Giants closes their set. When the final drumbeat sounds, the roar is deafening.

"Thank you Las Vegas!" yells Julian. The stage lights flare a final time before dimming.

The noise from the crowd remains at a fever pitch as the four men abandon their instruments and walk offstage. They know as well as anyone that their goodbye is superficial—the band will take a short break and be back for encores. From the level of demand, I'm guessing they'll do at least two more songs.

Nick, Jackson, and Matt file past me, offering grins and nods. Julian is last. When he notices me, he comes to a stop. There's limited light, but enough for me to see the sheen of sweat on his face and the steady rise and fall of his chest.

"Hey," he says with surprise. "I usually don't see you here."

Because I'm usually hiding.

Not ready to own up to my cowardice, I tell him part of the truth. "I always watch your set, but, uh, try to keep out of the way. You were great out there tonight."

He grins. "Thanks. Las Vegas crowds are fucking nuts." Slowly, his smile fades. "I'm going to sit down for a minute. Catch my breath. Will I see you after the encores?"

I nod. "Definitely."

He pauses, focus sharpening. "Maybe later, we can—"

A shrieking female form hurtles past me, leaping into Julian's arms. He catches her reflexively, stumbling back a few steps.

Giggling, she leans back in his arms. "Surprise!"

"Sheridan?" He laughs. "Where did you come from?"

Ten miles past hell and six feet deep
A divide between us wide and steep

At a touch on my arm, I look at Matt. He's frowning angrily at the redheaded monkey currently bouncing in Julian's arms.

"I fucking told her to wait in the green room. He hates interruptions during the show."

"It doesn't look that way from where I'm standing," I say, but my words are soft, swallowed by the crowd's unwavering roar.

Julian finally untangles himself from Sheridan, setting her beside him. His eyes meet mine for a moment—I can't read the expression on his face—before he says to Matt, "I'm gonna grab some water. Back in five."

Sheridan doesn't bother looking at me as she strolls toward us, her arm firmly around Julian's waist. *Message received, bitch.* What I can see of her is minimal, but I gather that she's slim and pretty, her fiery red hair in a short bob.

Anxiety ratchets up my spine, helplessness making my knees weak. I tell myself to move, to do something, say something, but my body is completely offline.

Then, as Julian passes me, his fingers trail across my palm and briefly clasp my wrist. My breath shudders from my chest, hope filling the vacuum.

"It's like Missy 2.0," Matt says tensely. "I tried to stop her, but she wouldn't take no for an answer."

"It's okay," I say, squeezing his shoulder.

His eyes find mine. "Are you sure you want to do this?"

Fuck no.

My stomach is a hard ball of nerves. My armpits are

prickling with sweat. I wipe damp palms on my hips, grateful for black pants. We've rehearsed the song several times, but Julian doesn't know I added it to the setlist tonight.

I jerk my chin in a nod. "Yes, I'm sure."

Matt smiles, grabbing me in a hug. "I'm so proud of you, Rosie Posie. You've got bigger balls than me, and mine are—"

Shoving him away from me, I let laughter ease my tension. Matt just grins, unrepentant, and hands me his half-empty bottle of water. We share the remainder, each of us contained in our quiet, preparatory headspace.

A few minutes later, the stage lights begin to rise, flirting with the berserker crowd. A backstage door opens nearby. Nick and Jackson come through, heading toward us at a fast clip. Greg appears beside me with my guitar, which I take in cold fingers.

Ten feet away, I see Phil pointing at me, mouthing, "Go, go, go!"

I look at Matt, drawing strength from the wicked smile on his face. "Kill it, Rosie. We'll be right there with you."

Breathe in.

Breathe out.

"Here we go," I whisper, and walk onto the shadowed stage toward the central mic.

Though the lights are still low, at the sight of my

silhouette the noise of the crowd shifts in breadth and tone, becoming a living force that hums against my skin and lifts fine hairs all over my body.

Angling my mouth toward the mic, I laugh. "Holy shit you guys are loud."

The general cacophony evolves again, screaming fading into applause. Soft blue illumination fills the space around me. The applause spikes again as Matt, Jackson, and Nick come back onstage.

From the front rows, I hear a growing chant. *"Julian! Julian!"*

"Don't worry, he's coming," I tell them, strumming the opening notes of *So It Goes*. Glancing over at Matt, I ask conversationally, "Is he lost?"

Matt makes a show of glancing offstage. "Hey Julian, get your ass out here!"

I see him then, standing frozen in the wings.

My heart jumps.

I throw my full attention to the music. Nick, sensing the change, comes in with a slow tempo, just brushes and soft taps on the snare. The song builds, guitar and drums, and with one last breath, I sing.

"There's a space, in the dark, a shadow of a spark, where the wind blows, so it goes, so I know this time, this time I fought..."

I sense Julian and shift my body to allow him space.

His hand on my lower back almost wrecks me, but then his voice meets mine on the chorus.

"This time, it's ours, to begin again. Please hold my hand —Will you please hold my hand?"

Somehow, I make it through the next verse, though it's a little iffy when I sing, *"And I wonder how the world didn't end when your tears fell, and I lost you… But I guess that depends…"*

Another chorus, our voices blending, then the final verse. Taking a silent cue from Julian, I lean back and let him have it.

"So will you tell me, how the wind blows—Does it go to your heart? Do you wonder, do you want, to go back to the start—Where the years stop, where we stay still, where I hold your hand… And watch the wind blow… so it goes."

The drums fade.

A final series of chords, then silence.

The crowd roars approval, and the stage lights adjust higher for the next song. Julian swings his guitar to the front of his body. With five seconds to get offstage, I say, "Goodnight Las Vegas!" and make for the wings.

Greg meets me and takes my guitar. Beside him, Kelly grins and bounces on the balls of her feet. "Yes! First phase complete!"

I nod, releasing laughter fueled by adrenaline and success. The place on my back where Julian's hand rested still feels hot. Branded.

His voice fills the arena, "The incredible Rose Cunningham, ladies and gentlemen." The nonstop cheering crests again. "This next song is dedicated to women who take risks."

As Breaking Giants launch into their well-loved single, aptly titled *Plunge,* I hurry toward the backstage door. Kelly comes with me, and we walk together down the hallway toward the dressing rooms. People mill around us, crew and press and VIPs, all waiting for the end of the show. I don't see Sheridan.

"How do you feel?" Kelly asks excitedly. "The song was perfect. I totally cried. He was so surprised!"

Still catching my breath, I smile at her. "I'm good. Still nervous, though."

We walk into my dressing room, which is blessedly empty and quiet, though the vibration from the arena can still be felt. Collapsing into a chair, I blow out a noisy breath. Kelly retrieves something from a bag on the floor and hands it to me.

My stomach jumps at the sight of the plastic keycard. I jerk to standing, tucking it safely in my back pocket.

"Room 804," she says, grinning. "I'll give him the other one."

I force out, "Great, thanks."

"Don't worry, Rose. He'll come."

I nod in response because *what if he doesn't come* is a worst case scenario I'm not willing to face.

Kelly hands me a face wipe. "Phase two. Fixing hair and makeup."

Touching up my makeup is a brief ordeal, but my disastrous hair takes twenty minutes to repair. Kelly painstakingly combs through the knotted curls, then uses a light serum to give them new life. Finally, she braids two small sections at my temples and draws them back, securing them with a clip.

"All done," she says proudly. "You look beautiful."

I grab her hand. "Thank you so much."

She winks. "Are you hungry? I can grab us some stuff from the green room if you want."

Needing to take action, I stand. "I'll go with you. I can't tell if I'm hungry, but I should probably eat something."

As we head out the door, she points at a compact overnight bag resting near my backup guitar. "Everything you need is in there. You remember how to get to the walkway leading to the hotel? I can draw a map for you..."

She, Greg, and I walked it earlier in the day, so I nod, then laugh. "I look like a mental patient right now, don't I?"

She giggles. "Kind of. Let's go get some food."

When we leave the dressing room, the hallway is empty save for security personnel and a few rushing crew members. The greenroom doors stand slightly open; the noise from inside floats to our ears. I stop, realizing the band must have come backstage already.

"Why don't you go ahead," I say breathlessly. "I think I'll just order room service when I get to the room."

Kelly frowns. "Are you sure? It's going to be a madhouse out there right now."

"I'll wait a bit," I say, then meet her gaze. "I think if I see him with Sheridan, I might lose my nerve."

She studies me a moment, then nods, reaching for and gripping my hand tightly. "It's going to work out."

"I hope so," I whisper. With a final smile, she heads toward the distant doors.

I turn back in the direction of my dressing room, but suddenly the thought of confinement makes my skin crawl. I walk further down the hallway, intending to pace until my stomach stops doing somersaults.

As I pass Breaking Giants' dressing room, voices filter to my ears from the partially open door. Familiar voices.

I freeze.

Julian: "Sheridan, I'm not kidding. Give it back."

She laughs. "Don't be that way. I'm just trying to understand what you see in her. I mean seriously, 'a voice like honey over tumbling rocks'? And this one—'his eyes are aged whiskey and tobacco'?" Her voice lowers, all laughter gone. "Who says stuff like that? It's not real life, Julian. They're pretty, meaningless words. She can't take care of you with words."

My journal.

Why the fuck does Sheridan have my journal?

I shove open the door before the thought of moving is fully formed. Sheridan gasps at the sight of me, whipping my journal behind her back.

"Rose, it fell out of my back pocket—"

Ignoring Julian, I hold out my hand toward Sheridan. My fingers and lips feel numb.

"Give it to me," I say with deadly quiet.

She flushes, either in anger or embarrassment, and extends her hand. I take the step necessary to snatch the journal from her, then spin toward the door.

My fingers are on the handle when she says, "You're just like all the others, Rose. *Passing through.* He always comes back to me."

"Sheridan," Julian snarls, "stop."

I keep walking.

35

A THOUSAND TIMES

Since I'm committed to a hotel room either way, I figure I might as well enjoy it whether or not Julian decides to show. I take a thirty-minute shower that barely dents my anxiety but still feels fucking amazing.

I order room service: a cheeseburger, fries, salad, and three desserts. When it comes forty minutes later, I'm still in the hotel robe.

He's doing press.

Greeting contest winners.

Taking pictures.

I take a few bites of everything, forcing food that tastes like ash past a wasteland throat. I text Greta to ask how she's feeling but don't respond when she asks me the same. I turn on the television, scroll through channels, then mute it because *I might miss his key in the door.*

Midnight comes and goes.

I repeatedly return to Kelly's message from an hour and a half ago.

He has the key

When one o'clock rolls around, I trade my robe for pajamas. I don't bother with the lingerie that Kelly picked up for me earlier, instead yanking on a tank top and pair of leggings. I sit on the edge of the bed and stare at the door.

Two o'clock.

I turn off the lights and crawl under the covers, then wait for tears that, despite the immense pressure under my skin, don't come.

Eventually the universe takes pity on me. I fall asleep and dream of tomorrows that never come and forever-agos.

♫

SUNLIGHT through the open curtains wakes me a few hours later. I open my eyes, blinking at the empty space beside me, then reach for my cell phone. Seeing that it's dead—Kelly forgot something, after all—I roll onto my back. A thousand tons of broken-hearted pressure sit on my chest, but still no tears rise.

The worst case scenario has come to pass. And *holy-fuckingshit*... I'm okay.

Still breathing, still alive.

Still me.

Oh, I know the pain will hit, and that it will be vicious. The next weeks are going to be a sadistic test of endurance. But I'll have my bandmates' support, and Kelly and Greg. Owen. Greta. Aunt Katherine. Doc Johnston.

I'll survive this, just like I survived my mother.

"I'm going to be okay," I say, just to hear the words out loud.

The universe seems to agree, offering me a burst of energy that I use to take another shower, tug on a sundress and light jacket, and wind my hair into a loose braid. I put on just enough makeup to cover the dark circles under my eyes and give color to otherwise pale cheeks.

As I barely took anything out of the overnight bag, packing takes five minutes. I use the TV for fast check-out, and I'm out the door less than an hour after waking.

Not surprisingly for eight o'clock in the morning on a Saturday, the hotel hallway is empty. So is the elevator that takes me down to the lobby.

When the doors open, though, I'm assaulted by sound and chaos. All across the ornate marble floors are crowds of people. Most are women, young and looking worse for wear—dressed in last night's clothing and makeup, with limp hair and tired, frantic eyes. More than a few carry high heels in their hands as they whisper excitedly with each other or squeal into their phones.

Striking out toward the distant sunlight marking the street, I muse that early mornings have a different definition in Las Vegas.

As I near the front doors, I notice the crowd seems to be converging on the right side of the lobby around an unseen focus.

A strident voice yells, "Get back! Back!"

Frowning, I watch a few hotel security guards jog across the lobby, and see yet more moving through the thickest part of the crowd.

Catching the eyes of the nearest woman, I ask, "What's happening?"

Her bloodshot eyes meet mine, then widen to comic proportions. *"Rose Cunningham?"* she screeches.

Oh, fuck.

As the collective awareness shifts in my direction, I feel sudden camaraderie with a mouse in a snake pit.

Blood in the water;

> *beware, they're coming*
> *into your veins and*
> *out your mouth running*

"Excuse me," I gasp, and push past her, toward the distant doors.

"Rose! It's Rose. Somebody stop her!"

Appeals turn to yells turn to screams.

A hand grabs my arm. I wrench free, losing my bag in the process. I couldn't care less about my meager belongings, shoving through people as panic takes hold of my body.

The doors are nearby, maybe fifteen feet away, when I collide with a massive man. Hands curl around my shoulders. A helpless shriek claws its way into my throat.

"Rose, it's Randy. I've got you."

I whip my head up. The sight of Randy's broad, gentle face brings tears of relief to my eyes.

"What—" I shake my head. "Please get me out of here."

"Rose, wait! Please!"

At the familiar voice, I frown, looking questioningly at Randy before scanning the crowd.

"Was that—" I don't finish, because Julian appears suddenly to my right, flanked by six hotel security guards.

"Rose," he breathes, and slides to his knees before me, arms locking around my hips. He buries his face in my stomach.

I blink down at his dark head, then look up at Randy, whose stoic features offer no answers. Laying my hand tentatively on Julian's crown, I whisper, "There's a lot of people around... Maybe, uh—"

"I don't care," he says, lifting his head. His eyes are tired but lucid, and track my features like he never thought he'd see me again. "I had the key. I put it down, turned around for *one second* and it was gone. Sheridan..." His lips thin and he shakes his head roughly. "She took it and threw it onto the floor of the arena. Have you *seen* the floor of an arena after a show? I was so fucking angry, Rose. I've never been so angry in my life."

He lost the key...

I glance around, seeing Randy, two more members of Breaking Giants' security, and the hotel guards struggling to hold the crowd back.

"Julian," I say stiffly. "We can talk about this later. We need to get out of here."

He releases me long enough to rise, then frames my face with his hands. Expression desperate, he snaps, "No, no! You have to listen to me. Please. I couldn't remember the fucking room number. Kelly and Greg disappeared, and Matt and the guys had already left for the afterparty. My phone was dead, but I finally found

Phil and called you from his phone. God—I must have called you a hundred times before he made me give it back to him. Your phone was off! *Off!*

"I panicked. I came here and asked the concierge, figuring what the hell, maybe fame will finally pay off, only to find out you used a pseudonym. A motherfucking pseudonym, Rose! You have to believe me, please, I'm not making this up. I told them every name I could think of that you might use, showed them your picture, demanded to see the people working yesterday—"

"Kelly booked the room," I whisper, then bite hard on my lips.

He sucks in a breath, the wildness in his eyes fading a little. "You think this is funny," he murmurs. "Tell me you're laughing."

The final shackles of misery fall away from my heart. Struggling to keep a straight face, I ask, "Did you really sit all night in the lobby of one of the busiest hotels in Vegas?"

He nods. "Since two a.m., yes. I couldn't leave. Not without finding you." His thumbs wipe gently beneath my eyes. "Don't cry, please. Tell me how to fix this."

I swallow hard. "You just did," I whisper, covering his hands with mine.

His frame shudders, head dropping with the force of his relief, a night of sleeplessness and worry finally catching up. I take the necessary step to bring us together, wrapping my arms around his torso. He trembles again, arms locking around my shoulders, his face buried in my hair. I hear a smattering of applause, then more, until the entire lobby is cheering.

A nebulous thought passes through my bright open mind—somewhere, there are spirit guides laughing.

"You forgive me?" he murmurs.

"There's nothing to forgive," I say, then look at Randy, who's grinning at us like a proud papa. "What are the chances of getting back to the elevator?"

"One hundred percent," he replies.

Escorted by security, we make it to the bay of elevators and into an empty one. Julian lets go of me only long enough for me to press the button for the eighth floor, then wraps me tightly in his arms again.

His hands slide down my back, over my dress to my bare upper thighs. His fingers clench, then move confidently upward to sneak beneath my panties.

"Is this elevator ever going to stop?" he growls.

It does.

As soon as we step into the empty hallway, Julian lifts me into his arms. I lock my legs around him and attack his neck, ear, and jaw with my mouth.

"What room?" he demands.

"804," I say, pointing to the right, then gasp and jerk

upright. "Oh God, I'm such an idiot—I did fast checkout!"

Julian stops, expression a play of consternation and amusement. "Tell me you're joking."

A door opens down the hallway. I turn in his arms, and we watch a room service cart being wheeled out. I can hardly believe my eyes when I see the barely eaten remains of a piece chocolate cake.

"Julian…" I gasp, strangled.

"That's the room, isn't it?" But he doesn't wait for a response, yelling, "Don't close that door!" and running toward it.

The poor hotel staff member doesn't know what hits him as Julian jerks the cart into the hallway, pushes past him with a, "So sorry, we'll leave you a big tip," and then we're in the room, the door swinging shut behind us.

Seconds later I'm dropped in the center of the bed. Expression tortured by need, eyes melting dark on mine, Julian pulls off my dress in a quick sweep and yanks his shirt over his head.

He devours me with his eyes, fingers sweeping down my ribs, stomach, and clenching on the flimsy straps of my underwear. The lace tears with surprising ease.

"Those were my favorite," I protest, but I'm smiling as his lips find mine.

Our mouths stay sealed together as we fumble to divest him of his shoes and jeans. My bra sails across the room and lands on a lamp. We laugh together, stealing the sounds from each other's mouths.

When the full length of him rests hard and hot atop me, I dig fingernails into his back and writhe in need. Julian wastes no time obeying my silent command. With a groan of hunger, his head drops, teeth and tongue claiming my breasts. I gasp, arching, my legs falling open for him. A hand delves confidently, one long finger sinking into me, then a second.

The pressure is perfect. The rhythm perfect. My body is his song—he knows every note. As the barest beginnings of a climax tingle in my toes, he bites a nipple, squeezing the other between two fingers.

That's all it takes.

I cry out in electric, wanton release, throbbing and bucking against his hand. Humming approval, he tastes my lingering moans with lazy strokes of his tongue.

"Fucking perfect," he murmurs.

My reply is to angle a hand between us and curl my fingers around him. I stroke until his breathing turns ragged and his hips thrust helplessly.

"I wanted to take it slow," he pants.

I smile. "Not today."

He exhales a pained sound and with a brief shift of his hips, sinks into me, stretching my sensitive flesh in delicious invasion. I grip him to me, my head thrown back, every inch of my mind and body alive beneath him.

Julian draws back and thrusts, slow and sure, angled to find over and over again that secret, sensitive place inside me. My cries fill the room. His teeth drag up my throat, nipping my chin, before his tongue dips into my mouth.

"Julian," I gasp, digging fingers into his arms, back, hips, anywhere I can reach. "Oh God, I think I'm going to—"

He knows. He wrote this song. Pace increasing to a merciless rhythm, he lifts above me to watch me come undone. His cheeks are flushed, sweat beading on his brow and chest. He's so beautiful, so *loved*, that the sight of him pushes me over the edge. My second orgasm is a slow, transforming cataclysm—a seafloor-shifting current instead of a surface wave. My scream is silent as I arch rigidly beneath him, heels tight on his ass to keep him seated inside me.

I finally collapse back to the bed, panting and twitching with aftershocks, and stare up at his gentle, triumphant smile.

Tears fill my eyes. "I love you, Julian. So much."

The smile vanishes, his features relaxing with relief and joy. Gathering me in his arms, he rises, then turns to sit against the padded headboard. I can feel him hard as steel inside me and know he's seconds from his own release. I roll my hips, testing his control, and he sucks in a breath through his teeth.

"Tell me again, sweetheart. Tell me a thousand times."

His hands settle on my waist, supporting my continued movements. I watch his jaw clenching, feel him grow even harder, and tell him. I say it over and over, until his fingers clamp on my hips and he groans, emptying himself inside me.

"I love you," I say again, brushing my mouth against his, then leaning back to see his beautiful eyes. "You're it. Everything. I'm yours. Tomorrow, today, and yesterday."

His arms wrap around me, head falling to my damp chest. "I really hope you mean that because I'm never letting you go. I'm going to marry you, Rose Cunningham, and we're going to have at least four kids."

Startled laughter escapes me. I lift his face so I can see his fierce grin. The determined gleam in his eyes.

Prince of Swords.

Everything.

So I say, "Well, we are in Vegas…"

His mouth drops open.

EPILOGUE

JULIAN

I know, you were really hoping Rose and I got married in Vegas by an Elvis impersonator. But it didn't happen, so you can stop believing the fucking tabloids. I made her wait another eight months and do things the right way. At home, with friends and family. Not a reporter or paparazzo in sight.

The sight of her walking down a flower-strewn aisle escorted by Owen and Katherine is still one of my favorite memories. The simple wreath in her long, dark hair. The clear summer sky overhead, wind rustling in the leaves, birds chirping like happy maniacs. It was goddamn poetry. As was the soft smile on her face, the tears in her eyes.

I wrote a horribly sappy song about that day, but you'll never hear it. It belongs to Rose. Sometimes, when I've done something stupid or she's pissed at me, I'll sing it to her. Usually in my underwear. Occasionally off-key.

Works every time.

My second favorite memory of our early years together is one that Rose herself would probably rather forget. It was a difficult labor. But nothing on this earth has ever compared to our child's first wail, or the look on my wife's face as the nurse placed our daughter on her chest.

I won't lie, life hasn't been all dancing unicorns and rainbows. But as her crazy Aunt Katherine told us on our wedding day, *'The darkest storm of your lives has passed.'* Don't tell Rose, but I actually believe all that mystical shit.

And so far, Katherine's been right. Yes, we're still passionate people, and yes, we argue—who doesn't?— but the trials we faced in the beginning have never been repeated.

I don't pick up a drink no matter fucking what. And when I'm gone for long stretches touring, Rose fights her own battle and makes a choice to trust me. She still sees her therapist once a month, and every year on the anniversary of her parents' death, we visit them.

And she finally, after two years, realized why the pocket watch tattooed on my chest is stuck on the time 2:12.

February 12th.

The day she lost her parents, the day that led to that photograph being taken, the day my heart flew unknowingly into her hands.

You're probably wondering about other things, too. Like whether Rose became a star in her own right. She did, but not in the way you might expect. She fulfilled her contract with Indigo, writing and releasing an album. It went gold, and though she didn't win any awards, many years later her name continues to show up on top-ten lists of underrated female songwriters.

Her lack of celebrity doesn't bother her one bit. Like she told me in the beginning (I really thought she was lying), the life of a career musician isn't for her. After her first big tour with Breaking Giants, she never went on the road again.

It was partly my fault, I'll admit. I knocked her up. Then I did it again. Four times total, just like I said I would.

Not apologizing for it.

For any of it.

Because it's been—all of it—*perfect*.

~

Thank you for reading Breaking Giants. *I hope you enjoyed the rollercoaster ride of Rose and Julian's love story!*

What to Read Next:

Breaking Silence (Matt's story)

ACKNOWLEDGMENTS

This book would not have been possible without the monumental support of my person, my partner in life, Donnie. Thank you for humoring (if not quite understanding) my tendency to unplug from the world when my muse sits hard on my shoulders. And for whisking the little one on countless daddy-daughter dates to give me time for aforementioned unplugging.

To Kim, Lacee, Amanda, V, and my parents. Your belief in me has carried me through the times when my own has lagged. To my incredible beta readers, for their honesty and excitement. And to Stella, my sweet bright star, for napping a little longer on a few key days when *please don't wake up this chapter is almost finished.*

To you, the reader—the life of an indie author isn't glamorous. We need you. *I need you.* So thank you, thank you, thank you, for taking a risk and giving me a chance. I wrote a book I wanted to read, and I hope you enjoyed reading it as much as I enjoyed writing it!

Of course, I'd be remiss not to acknowledge the incredible influence of music in my life and on this book. In particular, thank you to the following artists, whose music flowed in the background of my mind while telling the story of Rose and Julian: Belle and Sebastian, Elliot Smith, Deathcab for Cutie, The Editors, Yo La Tengo, The Strokes, Mr. Little Jeans, Imogen Heap, Bastille, Jenny Lewis, Nick Cave, Neko Case, and The National.

Finally, I'd like to acknowledge one of the themes in *Breaking Giants*, that of alcoholism and drug addiction. My prayers go out to the children and families affected by this terrible disease. And to those of you who have lived in that pit of despair and fought your way into the light of recovery, my hat is off to you all.

L.M.

March 2017

ALSO BY L.M. HALLORAN

FORBIDDEN ROMANCE

The Dark Before Light

The Fall Before Flight

The Muse

ROCKSTAR ROMANCE

Breaking Giants

Breaking Silence

Loving Wild (2025)

SMALL TOWN

Room for Us

Time for Us

DARK ROMANTIC SUSPENSE

Double Vision

Perfect Vision

The Golden Hour

Art of Sin *(Illusions Duet #1)*

Sin of Love *(Illusions Duet #2)*

ABOUT THE AUTHOR

When not writing or reading, the author can be found chasing her daughter. Some of her favorite things are puzzles, podcasts, and small dogs that resemble Ewoks. Home is Portland, Oregon.

lmhalloran.com